To Dad Xmas 84
love Donald XX.

THE

THE
CHANGING SKY

NORMAN LEWIS

Travels of a novelist

ELAND BOOKS, LONDON
&
HIPPOCRENE BOOKS, INC., NEW YORK

Published by
ELAND BOOKS
53 Eland Road London SW11 5JX
&
HIPPOCRENE BOOKS, INC.,
171 Madison Avenue, New York, NY 10016

This edition first published by
Jonathan Cape 1959

ISBN 0 907871 70 4
First issued in this paperback edition 1984
© Norman Lewis 1959

Printed and bound in Great Britain
by Redwood Burn Ltd, Trowbridge, Wiltshire

Contents

Illustrations

Publisher's Note

The photographs used in the first edition are lost. The present reissue uses imperfect reproductions in the belief that readers will prefer them to none at all.

Foreword

TRAVEL came before writing. There was a time when I felt that all I wanted from life was to be allowed to remain a perpetual spectator of changing scenes. I managed my meagre supply of money so as to be able to surrender myself as much as possible to this addiction, and charged with a wonderful ignorance I went abroad by third-class train, country bus, on foot, by canoe, by tramp steamer and by Arab dhow.

My travels started with Spain, where in the early 'thirties a *fonda* would furnish a windowless cell and an austere meal of bread, sausage and wine for the equivalent of a shilling, when Pedro Flores Atocha, last of the flamboyant bandits of Andalusia was receiving the first of the Spanish film actresses in his mountain hideout, and you sometimes saw a picture of Lenin, or of the bull-fighter Belmonte, in the places now occupied by a portrait of General Franco. In this relatively incorruptible country, where merely by leaving the main road you could, and still can, plunge immediately into Europe's prehistoric past, I spent – divided over a number of visits – a total of about three years, and I still go there to get away from the insipidity of modern times whenever I can.

After Spain it was the African *meridionale* of Italy, the Balkans, the Red Sea and Southern Arabia (in the dhow, 30 tons, undecked, crew of five, without lifeboat: a lifeboat would have been impiously calling into question God's providence), then Mexico, North Africa, three

winters in the Far East, Central America, Equatorial
Africa. At first I believed in pure travel, and that it was
necessary never to have a purpose. I arrived, watched a
little, and when my amazement began to subside, my
impressions to dull, I moved on. When I began to write
it was probably, at least in part, in an attempt to im-
prison some essence of the experiences, the images which
were always slipping, fading, dissolving, taking flight.
Later I found that the discipline of writing compelled me
to see more, to penetrate more deeply, to increase my
understanding and to discard a little of my ignorance.
Still later I began to weave the background and the
incidents of travel into my novels, and now, as I observe
the change that has taken place over the years, I wonder
if I am any longer capable of enjoying travel for its
own sake.

The test is whether or not one still wants to go on,
finally to reach those places which have always been just
out of reach: Hue on the Mandarin Road in Indo-China,
Pagan in Burma – both ringed round by insurgent armies
when I tried to go there; Tehuantepec in south Mexico –
the malaria stopped me short in Yucatan; Sana'a, capital
of the Yemen, still inaccessible through Muslim bigotry.
The fact that these places still beckon and entice gives
me hope.

Insurgents and bandits, malaria, curtains of various
kinds, whether lowered by politicians or by priest-kings
like the Imam of the Yemen – I am reminded that those
parts of the world where I have travelled most happily,
those countries which had most preserved their peculiar
style and character, always seemed to suffer from these
disadvantages, and that on the other hand those that
seemed to me hardly worth a visit and certainly not worth
writing about were those that had succumbed to a flaccid

8

and joyless prosperity which they were doing their best to export to the rest of the world. Ironically, so much that is of value has been protected by poverty, bad communications, reactionary governments, the natural barriers to progress of mountain, desert and jungle, colonial misrule, the anopheles mosquito. I think of Indo-China, exploited, neglected, and now abandoned, by the French, gloriously undeveloped, its virgin forests full of tigers, elephants, apes, and men living in happy adaptation to the Bronze Age. And then I think of Siam, which by the almost miraculous cunning of its rulers escaped enslavement by the West, only to become through liberty and prosperity hardly more than a fun-fair mirror reflection of the U.S.A. Or again I remember the dubious by-product of a relatively enlightened colonialism in French West Africa, under which negroes in the process of conversion to Frenchmen have also become week-end sportsmen and have wiped out every lion, every deer and every giraffe within easy jeep-range of all the towns.

The pieces in this collection are mostly about places to escape to when one has had a surfeit of the amenities of the modern world. Belize (colonial neglect) is a living museum, a wondrous survival of a Caribbean colony of the last century. Liberia (bad communications plus bad government) offers an extraordinary example of what can be done in the names of Freedom and Democracy when released slaves are turned loose on native Africans who until the said released slaves appeared on the scene had had the good fortune to remain free. Guatemala (colonial misrule plus reactionary governments plus endless revolution) is the last home of the uncontaminated Red Man – the Mayan Indian – living, to be sure, in much reduced circumstances, but still defending himself with fair success from all the overtures of the West. Cuba (a border-line case, this) presents a unique fusion of Spain with Africa, a chronic rebellion, and the spectacle of secret African cults gaining ground among nominal Christian whites – the majority drawn from the upper classes – who now sacrifice white cocks to Changa.

Finally Ibiza (bad communications – otherwise no comment): now at last, and alas, accessible through the provision of an air service. I wrote the piece about Ibiza in 1955, and now rereading it and making a few additions, in 1958, I am surprised to see how slight, after all, the change has been.

In the three-year interval the admiral's daughter, after taking two years off in Madrid, to think it over, came back and married the waiter, and now seems to spend her time making blouses, while the waiter continues to wait. The Turkish princess's daughter left her fisherman husband after a year of marriage, taking their baby with her.

This year an *encerrada* was organized by the women of Niu Blau with the intention of banishing an immoral woman (not a remarrying widow) from the island. It was successful. A man who had raped a girl of twelve would shortly be garrotted for his crime, although an old woman who in a frenzy of grief had thrown her daughter's illegitimate baby over a cliff had been released after a few months in prison. In Santa Eulalia, a neighbour of old, who had waited twenty-two years until he saw both daughters married off and his son in a good situation, decided that the time had come to settle an old account with a chief of the Falange. He dressed himself with the formal deliberation of a Japanese samurai, in mourning, and turned the pictures of his wife and family to face the wall, before opening fire on his enemy through his window. After that he committed suicide. (His enemy escaped with light wounds.) This year, as usual, the *curandera*, or wise woman, had arrived from Alicante, was staying at a good hotel, and paying for her holiday by giving treatment, consisting of massage with incantations, to some of the best-known citizens of the island. This year again the *guardia urbana* threatened with arrest those men who persisted in wearing shorts in Ibiza town despite all the notices about immoral dress that had been posted in the cafés. If the culprits asked what they were to do about it, the guardias told them to tie handkerchiefs round their knee-caps.

It was still a wonderful island, I decided, and would probably go on being one for just a few more years.

BIOGRAPHY

Norman Lewis has written 11 novels and 5 non-fiction works. Of the latter, his two travel books, *A Dragon Apparent*, and *Golden Earth* (travels in Burma) – both best-sellers in their day – describe his journeyings in the Far East at a time when the countries he visited were passing out of the reach of the ordinary traveller.

His novel, *The Volcanoes Above Us*, based on personal experiences in Central America in revolt, sold 6 million copies in paperback in Russia – enormously to his surprise, he says, as the book expressed no political point of view. *The Honoured Society*, a non-fiction study of the Sicilian Mafia, was serialized in 6 installments on the *New Yorker*, and his best-selling novel *The Sicilian Specialist*, incorporating at that time undisclosed facts about the Kennedy assassination, was removed from sale in some American cities following a Mafia ban. *Naples '44*, a recently published war-diary, which received high critical acclaim, describes his adventures in British Intelligence in the Italian South.

Norman Lewis regards his life's major achievement as the world reaction to an article written by him entitled *Genocide in Brazil*, published in the *Sunday Times* in 1968. This led to a change in the Brazilian law relating to the treatment of Indians, and to the formation of *Survival International*, the influential body, with branches in many countries, dedicated to the protection of aboriginal people.

Lewis relaxes by his occasional travels to off-beat parts of the world, which he prefers to be as remote as possible; otherwise he lives with his family in introspective, almost monastic calm, in the depths of Essex.

THE
CHANGING
SKY

Caelum non animum mutant, qui trans mare currunt,
Strenua nos exercet inertia: navibus atque
Quadrigis petimus bene vivere. Quod petis hic est,
Est Ulubris animus si te non deficit aequus.

They change their sky, not their soul, who run
across the sea...

...when o'er the world we range
'Tis but our climate, not our mind we change.
What active inactivity is this,
To go in ships and cars to search for bliss!
No; what you seek, at Ulubrae you'll find,
If to the quest you bring a balanced mind.

HORACE

Author's Note

Most of these pieces were originally written at the instigation of the *New Yorker*, the *Sunday Times* and *New Statesman*, to whose Editors I make grateful acknowledgment. Since the time of writing changes of political direction have taken place in one or two countries about which I wrote. I have made no attempt to bring these accounts up to date by reference to recent happenings, because what interested me was the background, and the style of life in a country, rather than the colour of the threads in the political web. Castro's revolt against Batista was, for example, a typical and recurrent Cuban situation. But Cuba with Castro in control remains Cuba. Changes in the things that have interested me are rarely effected by a mere shift of power.

N.L.

April, 1959

A Few High-Lifes in Ghana

THE important thing to bear in mind when visiting
what was once the Gold Coast and is now Ghana is
that the advice liberally proffered by old Gold Coast
hands in retirement will be designed to perpetuate a
nostalgic legend. You are warned to prepare yourself
for a scarcely tamed White Man's Grave, where you do
not omit to take Sensible Precautions, stick to sundowners,
keep your possessions in an ant-proof metal box, and wipe
the mildew off your boots at regular intervals. I fell a
victim to this propaganda to the extent of buying a pair
of mosquito boots before I left London. They were made
of soft, supple leather, fitted very tightly at the ankle,
and they reached almost to the knee, beneath which
they could be drawn tight with tapes. I put them on
once only, in the privacy of a hotel bedroom, noting that
worn with khaki drill shorts they made me look like
some grotesque Caucasian dancer. After that I packed
them away. It was a symbolic act. I had observed that in
Accra, Europeans in these days seemed to make it a
point of honour to go bareheaded in the noonday sun.
The sundowners seemed to have gone out with sola
topis. You popped into a bar and drank a pint of good
German or Danish lager whenever you felt like it. It was
hot in Accra, but not so hot as New York at its worst
and – in the dry season – not so humid either, and down
by the shore there was usually a cool breeze blowing in
from the Atlantic.

Accra turned out to be a cheerful, vociferous town with
an architectural bone-structure of old arcaded colonial

buildings – some of them vaguely Dutch or Danish in style. The streets, in the English manner, had been cut in all directions. There were corrugated-iron shack warrens right in the heart of the town, a wide belt of garden suburbs, and isolated slabs of modern architecture looking like enormous units of sectional furniture. As usual, the English had thrown away the chance – always seized by the French in their colonies – of turning the sea-front into a pleasant, tree-shaded promenade. The surf crashing on the beaches was out of sight behind the warehouses, put up at a time when trade was all and the merchants were content to put off their gracious living until they had made their pile on the Coast and could get away with it back to England before malaria or the Yellow Jack finished them off. The streets were crowded with a slow-moving mass of humanity: the men in togas, the women in the Victorian- and Edwardian-style dresses originally introduced by the missionaries but now transformed by the barbaric gaiety of the material from which they are confected. The designs with which these cottons are printed demand some comment. They are produced in Manchester, in Brussels and in Paris, from African originals, and although they recall the most striking Indian saris, there is something fevered and apocalyptic in the vision behind the drawing itself, that seems to be

By the time Ghana gained its independence many of the chiefs, already at loggerheads with the young men of Accra who in future would guide their country's destinies, saw that the end of the good old days of feudal authority could not long be postponed. A few of the most powerful chiefs such as the Assantehene, King of the Ashanti, boycotted the celebrations. Others went gloomily to the Durbar fully realizing that this would be the last opportunity they might have to display their power and treasure in this way. For the young men of Accra they were hardly more than the living museum of a past which held no interest for them.

purely African. The best results are supposed to be produced by West African artists as the result of dreams, and the artist may mix abstract symbols and careful realism in a single design, with a result that often has a drugged and demonic quality, like a descriptive passage from *The Palm Wine Drinkard*. Dark blue birds flit through an ashen forest of petrified trees; silver horses with snake-entwined legs charge furiously into a sable sky, huge metallic insects glint among the lianas of a macabre jungle; the black bowmen of Lascaux pursue griffins, fire-birds and tigers over fields of gold, with autumn leaves the size of shields tumbling about their shoulders. Why do European women rarely if ever wear these materials, although there are a few out-of-the-way shops in London and Paris where they are stocked? Perhaps because to do so would be to risk extinguishing themselves.

Amazingly an Englishman can be at home in this atmosphere, which somehow, in defiance of the genial African sun, the colour, and the seething vitality, succeeds in reproducing a little of the flavour of life in England. The African citizen of Ghana, for example, is reserved in his manner compared, say, with his counterpart in Dakar. It is hard to believe, in fact, that a century

The chiefs and their retinue came to the Durbar carrying the regalia of the tribe. Confronted with this display of massy gold, with the shining crowns, the sceptres, the staffs, the maces, the eagles, the lions and the royal dogs of ancient Egypt, one saw how it was that the Gold Coast got its name. Here power was displayed in its most crude and magnificent symbol. Besides the gold of their ancestors the chiefs brought their sacred stools (never sat upon for more than a few seconds at a time), in which the talismanic virtue of their office was believed to reside, and the trophies taken from their enemies in forgotten wars. This feathered head-dress, worn by a chief's son, was the royal standard of a defeated nation.

17

of independence will be long enough to expunge the essentially British odour of life in the Gold Coast: the cooking (Brown Windsor soup and steak-and-kidney pie), the class observances, the flannel dances, the tea-parties, and the cricketing metaphors in the speech. Even the paint on the fences in a suburb of Accra is of a kind of sour apple green never found outside Britain and her dominions. The middle-class African of Accra, too, lives in home surroundings indistinguishable from those favoured by his equivalent in the London suburbs. There is the same affection for whimsy and humorous pretence: china ducks in flight up the wallpaper, Rin-Tin-Tin book-ends, toby jugs, telephones disguised as dolls, poker-work mottoes, and jolly earthenware elves in the back garden.

It is generally believed that fraternization between whites and blacks is less complete in African territories colonized by the British than in those colonized by the French. This does not apply in West Africa. In Dakar the colour bar is officially non-existent, but it is extraordinary to see an African in a good hotel or a fashionable restaurant. The reason one is given is that they do not feel comfortable in such surroundings. The natives of Accra are not overawed in this way, and there is a fairly proportional colour representation – say ten Africans to one European – in all public places of entertainment. It was in fact quite the normal thing that my first experience of Accra night-life should be in the company of Africans.

This was in early March. Ghana was just about to receive its independence. There had been a week of celebrations, and the streets were awash with restless, slightly jaded revellers. My host was a minor political figure we will call Joseph, and he had brought with him his secretary, Corinne. We started the evening at the new Ambassadors Hotel, which is said to be one of the three best hotels in Africa. At this time there was no hope of staying there, as the Government of Ghana had filled it with foreign V.I.P.s invited for the celebrations. We sat in the bar and admired the photomontage on the wall, which included a dancing scene from *Guys and Dolls* and the towers of the Kremlin. Behind the palms a pianist in tails was striking soft, rich chords on a grand piano. Joseph and Corinne ordered Pimms No. 1, which was currently *de mode* in Accra. I noticed that the V.I.P.s present included firebrands from British Guiana and Tunisia – temporarily tamed and transformed in glistening sharkskin – and a berobed African chief who wore ropes of beautiful ancient beads, and who waved genially and said 'Ta-ta' as we came in. There was no hope of a table for dinner at the Ambassadors, so we went on to another restaurant, and there in the sombre and seedy surroundings of an English commercial hotel in a small Midland town we made the best of a highly typical meal of fried liver, tomatoes and chips.

After that we visited a night-club called A Weekend in Havana, outside which Joseph got into an altercation with a policeman over parking his car. There is often a fine Johnsonian rumble about such exchanges in Accra. 'You were attracted by the glamour of your profession. Now you must work,' was Joseph's parting shot. Later in the evening when a cabinet minister offered him an extremely stiff whisky he said, 'I am not, sir, a member of your staff, and am not, therefore, accustomed to more than singles.' Still later when an enormous Nigerian emir, gathering his robes about him, joined our table, Joseph remarked, 'I hear, sir, that your people reproduce at an alarming rate,' and the emir, who took this as a compliment, grinned hugely and replied, 'You have been correctly informed.'

A Weekend in Havana turned out to be an open-air place, with the tables placed round a thick-leaved tree that gave off an odour of jasmine. A white dove-like bird circled continually overhead as if attracted by the powerful fluorescent lighting. When we arrived the band was playing 'It's a Sin to Tell a Lie', and the dancers were gliding round in a stately Palais-de-Dance manner. About half those on the floor were in national costume and the rest in evening dress. The few European women to be seen seemed to me to be outclassed by the African girls with their splendidly becoming gowns and their majestic carriage. Corinne sat happily commenting on the private lives of those present, and closing my eyes and listening to her remarks I could hardly believe I was not sitting in a similar night-spot in London, although Corinne's voice was somewhat richer and deeper than that of any conceivable English counterpart. 'Good heavens! Isn't that Dr Kajomar with Mrs Chapman? Had *you* any idea that show was still going on, Joseph?' A girl swung past in the arms of her partner wearing one of the new slogan dresses with 'JUSTICE AND LIBERTY' printed across her ample posterior, and Corinne looking away as if pained said, 'Do you know – I do think people should draw the line somewhere!' Soon after this the band played a high-life – a dance of Gold Coast invention – which resembles a frenzied and individualistic samba. A party of British sailors from a naval vessel helped themselves to partners from the local girls and joined in this to the best of their ability, and were much applauded by the Africans. The trouble about the British – Corinne had just commented – was that they never let themselves go. Her ex-boss had been a Scotsman who had made her blood run cold by his habit of concealing his anger.

This gave me an opening to indulge in a favourite pastime, when in regions that are slipping, or have slipped, through the colonialist fingers – that of carrying out a post-mortem on the relationship between the two peoples involved, in the full prior knowledge that the findings – allowing for local variations – will be the same. Getting right down to bedrock objections, Joseph said, it amounted to the fact that the Englishman had never learned to stop complete strangers in the street, shake hands with them warmly, and ask them where they were going, and why. What was even worse, they had almost succeeded in breaking the people of the Gold Coast of such old-world African displays of good breeding, inculcated in all the bush-schools before the European came on the scene with his version of education and his insistence on the formal introduction. I knew this to be true. Only a few weeks spent in Africa – especially if not too much time is wasted in big towns where the real flavour of the country is subdued – are enough to convince one of the extreme and innate sociability of the African. Africans, as one discovers them in travelling in the villages of the interior, are never stand-offish, rude or aggressive; always ready to receive the visitor in a courteous and dignified way. This is the tradition of the country, and even in such Europeanized areas as the Gold Coast, where a boy no longer spends four years or more under the strict discipline of the bush-school learning the ideals of manhood, a stern semi-Victorian training is usually carried out in the home, with what to me are excellent results. It might even be reasonable to suggest that there are strong temperamental and emotional factors behind the façade of politics, which are

21

in reality helping to strip the Briton of his colonies. Even
in the Gold Coast, where the Englishman had learned to
become a better mixer than his French neighbour, there
remained a trace of that aloofness, that inability to get
together with the African on a footing of absolute social
equality, which makes it so difficult for him to be loved
as well as respected. Here, as in India and in Burma, the
European clubs defended their exclusiveness to the last
ditch. The Englishman was received socially by the
educated African without any reserve whatever, but the
African's civility was not fully returned, and there was
an offensive flavour of patronage in this lack of reciprocity.
The Accra Club admitted no African members or guests.
At Cape Coast only two influential chiefs had ever succeeded in joining the white man's club. The Kumasi Club
underlined its determination to hold out to the last by
posting a notice which informed the members that 'due
to the development of events' they would be permitted
on and after Independence Day to introduce guests of
'any nationality' – although the names of such proposed
guests had first to be submitted to the secretary. To
these pinpricks, to which Africans submit cheerfully and
without rancour, more serious wounds are added when
they come to England as students and find that under
some dishonest excuse – since the colour bar in England
has no admitted existence – 85 per cent of hotels and
boarding houses will refuse to admit them.

No demonstration of the virtues of imperialism – the
high-minded incorruptibility, and the like, of the white
overlords – could quite compensate the new, nationalistic
African for his being treated, whether overtly or not, as a
member of an inferior race. Thus many Africans who
have been hurt by the coolness of their reception in
England have returned to Africa carrying the germ of a

22

disease that is fairly new in that continent – anti-white racial feeling. Now the whites were on the point of surrendering their domination in the Gold Coast. The European clubs would open their doors to all. Dr Nkrumah's portrait would – despite the protests of the parliamentary opposition – replace that of Her Majesty Queen Elizabeth, on both stamps and coinage, and shortly the British Governor-General, Sir Charles Noble Arden-Clarke, would be asked to surrender his impressive apartments in Christiansborg Castle to Dr Nkrumah, and to retire to the modest accommodation previously prepared for Dr Nkrumah in the State House. But already, on the eve of independence, the newspaper editorials sounded a little less dizzy with success. There would be no colonial scapegoats about, when things went wrong in the future. The Ghanaians would have only themselves to blame if the much-publicized corruption in their public men brought about their undoing as a nation, or if the disputes with the Ashanti and Togoland minorities were allowed to deteriorate until they exploded into civil war.

Many members of the newly freed colony regarded the victory of Kwame Nkrumah and his followers as the victory of an energetic political clique which had been able – sometimes by dubious means – to impose its will upon the politically lethargic general masses. Such disgruntled opponents of the regime, who did not expect to participate in the fruits of the victory, were on the whole unhappy to see their white rulers depart, and there were refusals in several parts of the country to put out flags. That the English could pull out as they did with so little apparent reluctance, and so many protestations of good will all round, is due to the nature of their stake in the country, which does not in reality demand their physical presence. Ghana has been saved from the tragic situation of Algeria, and the almost equally unhappy situations of Kenya and South Africa, by the fact that it has never been considered suitable for European settlement. West Africa as a whole has been protected from white ownership by malarial mosquitoes, an inexorable rainy season and an absence of salubrious highlands where European farmers could have established themselves. When the demand for independence came, there was no reason not to accede to it. As things were, only British traders, technicians and colonial officials got a living from the country, and these would not be compelled to leave. The only conceivable losers might be certain African underlings with a preference for the devil they knew to the devil they didn't know and a suspicion they might be exchanging King Log for King Stork: these and the 300,000 small farmers of the Ashanti, who between them produce the cocoa that forms the country's wealth, and who in the long run – and at present with little political representation – must foot the bills run up by the politicians at Accra.

From the very beginning it has been commerce that has drawn the European to the Gold Coast, and from this commerce developed one of the gravest social cancers that have cursed the human race – the slave trade. All the maritime European nations, with the exception of the Spanish – Portuguese, Dutch, Danes, British, Swedes and Prussians – at one time or another established strongholds in the Gold Coast, and squabbled among themselves over the rich loot in captives. The English proved to possess most staying power. In recognition of their straightforward and efficient business dealings, they finally secured the much sought-after contract for the supply of slaves to the Spanish colonies, held previously by the French and then the Dutch. In the end, over one-half of the total slave trade fell into British hands. It has been estimated that between 1680 and 1786, 2,130,000 slaves were exported from the Guinea Coast, as it was then called. The wastage of life was tremendous. Livingstone believed that ten lives were lost for every slave success-fully shipped, and even at sea the carnage continued. French ships' stores, for example, included corrosive sublimate, with which slaves were poisoned when the ship was becalmed in the Middle Passage and supplies ran low (the French defended the practice as being more humane than the British and Dutch one of simply tossing the starving slaves into the sea).

From the very beginning the slave trade was carried on in a shamefaced manner, and contemporary accounts by those who took part in it are full of conscience-salving devices. Much was made of the slave's happy opportunity to be brought into contact with Christianity. Slavers piously presented themselves as the rescuers of prisoners taken in African wars who would otherwise have been slaughtered, making no mention of the fact that it was they, the slavers, who encouraged or even organized the wars. The slave merchants could be tender, too. 'I doubt not', says William Bosman in a letter written in 1700 from the castle of St George d'Elmina, 'but that this trade seems very barbaric to you, but since it is followed by mere necessity it must go on; but yet [in branding the slaves] we take all possible care that they are not burned too hard, especially the women, who are more tender than the men.' I have visited this castle and seen the rooms where the slaves were confined and where they were auctioned. What particularly struck me was the delicacy of feeling shown in the old days in the arrangement by which heads of families who had brought some dependant to be auctioned were permitted to watch the proceedings from a chamber overlooking the auction room, where they themselves would not be exposed to the reproachful gaze of their victim.

Bosman, despite his name, was a Dutchman, a man of severe morality and regular habits, who much deplored the intemperance of his English trade rivals entrenched at Cape Coast Castle some thirty miles away: ' ... The English never being better pleased than when the soldier spends his money in drink ... they take no care whether the soldier at pay-day saves gold enough to buy victuals, for it is sufficient if he have but spent it on Punch; by which excessive tippling and sorry feeding most of the Garrison look as if they were Hag-ridden.' The English, Bosman observed, were also much given to a plurality of wives, particularly the chief officers and governors of the castle, while two of the English company's agents had married about six of the local ladies apiece. This enterprise was the Royal African Company, promoted under a charter granted by Charles II. His Majesty was the principal shareholder in the venture, in which the whole of the royal family invested money. In spite of Bosman's poor opinion of the garrison a dignified protocol, as befitted a royal enterprise, was observed in all the company transactions. Slaves were branded, as a compliment to the Duke of York, the company's governor, with the letters 'D.Y.' – and the brand used was of sterling silver.

Denmark was the first European power to abolish the slave trade, by a royal order in 1792. The British followed in 1807, although a general European agreement was delayed for another twelve years by the French, who hoped in this way to gain time to be able to crush the rebellion in Haiti and restock the colony with fresh slaves. The century that followed saw the gradual adjustment of the Gold Coast to legitimate trade, based at first principally on the extraction of gold (the guinea was originally coined from the gold secured from the Gold Coast), and then the cocoa bean. The first cacao tree to be grown is supposed to have been brought from Fernando Po in the 'eighties of the last century, as the result of the enterprise of a native blacksmith, and each pod is said to have sold for £1. By 1949 the Gold Coast was producing as much cocoa as all the rest of the world put together. It is now one of the richest areas in Africa, and its total revenue from all sources is about ten times that of the neighbouring republic of Liberia, which has never been under colonial domination. It is a curious illustration of the mentality of nationalism that the politically educated citizen of Ghana now tends to play down the importance of the slave trade in the history of his country. The subject when raised is likely to be changed or to be brushed aside as historically insignificant. The memory is clearly considered derogatory to the dignity of a modern nation.

The emergence of this modern nation could never have been delayed more than a few years, but the fact that the Gold Coast became Ghana in March 1957, and not perhaps twenty years later, is largely due to the energy and the tactics of its leader, Dr Kwame Nkrumah. Dr Nkrumah was born in 1909, said by some to be the son of a market woman, and by others, of an artisan. After a few years spent in the teaching profession he went to America and gained the degree of Bachelor of Sacred Theology of Lincoln University, Pennsylvania, which a few years later granted him an honorary doctorate. When he returned to Accra, Nkrumah took over the nationalist movement, founded a new party, the Convention People's Party, with its slogans 'S.G.' (Self Government) and 'Freedom' (the two syllables are pronounced in Ghana as two separate words). Nkrumah's tactics began with a boycott on European goods, and from this, rioting and looting developed. Two short prison sentences followed, both of them invaluable to the progress and propaganda of the C.P.P., and Nkrumah was released from the second of them to become officially first 'Leader of Government Business' and then Prime Minister over a predominantly African team of ministers.

Democracy is liable to be transmuted by the old tribal tradition of government into a parody of what is understood by that word in the West. Political issues are decided not so much by party programmes – which are quite beyond the comprehension of village electors – as by the political personalities involved, and the crowds swarm to the support of the energetic and flamboyant leader. The enfranchisement of the black masses spells the end of the white man's domination – not because there is any solidarity in colour except an artificial one in the course of creation at this moment – but because the white man cannot compete with the African's knowledge of native psychology, and cannot in our time, even if he would, play on the African electors' hopes and fears with the deadly expertness of an ex-tribesman. As an illustration of what is happening all over those parts of Africa where the electoral system has been introduced, a party will often choose as its emblem an animal known for its sagacity and strength – say the elephant – while the opponents may decide on the lion. The election, in the unsophisticated countryside, now resolves itself into a contest between the merits of these two animals. The elephant followers will obviously be unsuccessful in

districts where a herd may be running wild and tram-
pling the crops, whereas lion supporters can have no hope
of gaining ground in remote pastoral areas where lions
still sometimes carry off livestock. African political parties
– and this applies not only to those of Ghana, but to the
whole of West Africa – change their programmes and
their affiliations in such a way that not even a trained
student of politics can keep up with them. Their appeal to
the mainly illiterate elector must then be simplified to
the point of absurdity. The standard of political advancement of the village masses may be judged from the fact
that when just before the election Nkrumah and his
supporters carried out a perfectly normal animistic
ceremony which consisted of formally asking the support
of the spirits of the Kpeshi lagoon near Accra, the rumour
became general that the Prime Minister had called on the
gods to kill all who voted against him. Many electors, as a
result of this, abstained from voting. Again in the Ashanti
country, where Nkrumah is not liked, his supporters had
successfully spread the report that the Duchess of Kent
when she arrived for the Ghana celebrations had actually
crowned Nkrumah king of Ghana. Many people say that
Dr Nkrumah would like to be not a mere prime minister
but a real king – and not a king over Ghana alone, at that.
French newspapers published in Dakar report that when,
several years ago, he visited a celebrated witch-doctor in
Kan-Kan, in the French Sudan, this was the prize fore-
told when the auguries were taken from the blood of a
sacrificed chicken. After the independence celebrations Dr
Nkrumah visited Kan-Kan again, but in the meanwhile
the old witch-doctor had died, and, as his successor was not
yet fully trained, no cock was sacrificed this time. A friend
of mine who saw Dr Nkrumah on this occasion noted that
he was carrying a copy of Machiavelli's *The Prince*.

The Changing Sky

The most frequent charge levelled against the C.P.P.
is that of corruption, and even to the casual observer it
would seem that many Government functionaries live in
a style remote from that made possible by their salaries.
By the time I visited Ghana it was said that no man could
expect to get on the short list for any Government appoint-
ment without a scale payment 'to the party funds', while
a British senior police official who was staying on, admitted that the length of his service probably depended
entirely on how soon it was before he received an order
to turn a blind eye on the misdoings of someone in a high
place. This general corruption in African politics is
excused, even defended, by some observers, on the ground
that it is strictly in line with the ancient tradition of the
country. Every formal human contact calls for its appro-
priate offering. When a man leaves on a journey all his
friends make him a gift, however trivial, and when he
returns he will be welcomed with another small offering.
The successful conclusion, in the old days, of an initiatory
stage in the bush-school was signalled by a shower of
congratulatory presents. A girl expected to receive
tributes of beads and cosmetics not only for her wedding,
but when she was officially recognized as marriageable.
No dispute could be brought for a chief's adjudication
without a 'mark of respect' being offered by both parties
in the case. One of the worst torments of African travel
until very recently arose out of this necessity of 'dashing'
every chief one visited on one's travels, and the problem
of disposal of the livestock one was frequently 'dashed' in
return. When I once paid a courtesy call on an important
dignitary living in a remote part of the country where the
old way of life was still followed, I was startled after we
had shaken hands to be told by the chief that he could not
receive me, 'without warning'. What he meant by this

was that I had not given him time to find a suitable 'dash', and our meeting must therefore be considered as without official existence. It also meant that the two bottles of beer I had brought for him could not be decently handed over until I had gone. These are the usages of highly complicated civilization; they are all-pervasive, and when – as at present – the old order breaks down and politicians take over from the chiefs, nothing is easier than the transition in almost imperceptible stages from the ceremonial gift to the outright bribe.

The official jollifications that took place in March 1957 in Accra, it should be stressed, celebrated in reality a situation virtually in existence since Nkrumah became Prime Minister in 1952, so that by the time I visited Ghana the country had been to all intents and purposes independent for several years. The formal take-over was accompanied by all the public junketings one would have expected, but as these were not particularly characteristic of West Africa, I took the opportunity two days before Independence Day to go on a sightseeing trip outside Accra. Hiring a taxi I drove to Ho, capital of Togoland, a hundred miles away. Although it had been feared that the Ashanti minority – many of them were opposed to union with Ghana – might cause trouble at this historic moment, it was in Togoland, in fact, where rioting was actually going on, and to which troops had been sent.

This particular day turned out to be a coolish one. We drove eastwards from Accra along a good asphalted road, shortly, as the road left the coast, entering the rain-forest belt. Here opulent woods replaced the parched scrub-lands of the coastal areas. There were frequent giant ant-hills by the roadside, pinnacled like Rhine

castles painted in the background of German old masters.
I was disappointed to see no animals, no flowers except a
few meagre daisies growing in the verges, and no birds
but turtle-doves and an occasional lean dishevelled-
looking hornbill. The African native's access to firearms
has brought about the virtual extermination of all edible
animal species in the Gold Coast. It turned out indeed to
be a great day in the driver's life, when later in the trip
a hunter offered us a large cane rat – practically the only
form of game obtainable in these days. The price asked
for this animal was 25s. The driver beat the man down
to 15s. and told me that it was a bargain at that figure. We
passed through nondescript villages plastered with
advertisements for Ovaltine, Guinness, and Andrews
Liver Salts. Africans it seems are easily persuaded to worry
about their health. There was a decrepit shack of a
restaurant called 'Ye Olde Chop Bar', and a drinking
saloon called 'Honesty and Decency'. We met a great
number of what are called 'mammy-lorries' coming down
for the Accra celebrations. These trucks, which are owned
by the world's most prosperous market-women, are

The ceremonial at the court of Byzantium could hardly have exceeded
in complexity that of the Grand Durbar of Chiefs. Each chief
sat enthroned under the critical eye of his neighbours, and defended
the dignity of his State with a keen eye for the minutiae of protocol.
Here a chief drummer awaits the signal for a change in tempo of
the music as a prominent personage comes to pay his compliments.
This was the court of Ofori Atta, the Omanhene – most powerful
of the Gold Coast chiefs, and a leading opponent at that time of
Dr Nkrumah, who has since deposed him. The Omanhene was an
African Old King Cole, complete with the merriment and the
traditional gold crown. The chief spoke English superbly, with the
slightest of Scottish accents. His predecessor's death had been
followed by what turned out to be the most sensational ritual murder
of recent years, committed in order to provide the old chief's shade
with at least one servitor in the underworld.

A Few High-Lifes in Ghana

famous for their names, which – following the principle used in the tabloid headlines – usually attempt to crowd too much information or comment into too few words. The result is sometimes unintelligible to the outsider. We saw trucks with such names as 'Still Praying For Life', 'Trust No Future', 'Still As If', 'One Pound Balance', 'Look, People Like These', and 'As If They Love You'. These trucks are driven with abandon, and their wrecked and burnt-out shells litter the roadside. The African brand of driver's fatalism is even more irremediable than most, due to the fact that the African tends not to believe in the existence of inanimate matter. Trees and rocks are capable of locomotion, so that after an accident a driver – washing his hands of something so completely outside his control – may simply say: 'A tree ran into me.'

We crossed the new bridge over the Volta and immediately entered a new country. This had been German colonial territory until 1919, when the country had come under League of Nations control and been divided rather crudely and purposelessly between the British and the French. There were few signs of jubilation in these villages. In the outskirts of Ho a shop still carried the title Buch Handlung, although it no longer sold books. At this point, we ran through the tail end of a rain

In the villages of Liberia most men hope to marry several wives. Besides the prestige the polygamous state confers, they are thereby freed from all manual labour and enabled to dedicate their lives to the arts of leisure. The women appeared to favour this arrangement on the grounds that it lessened their work, too. This one spent most of her time in languid and unproductive fishing. Half a dozen fruitless attempts with her net produced this smile but no fish. She would be content, she said, with three or four prawns to enliven the family's evening meal of inevitable cassava. Life in West Africa is easy so long as one remains content with little.

33

storm and the thick spicy odour of an old-fashioned grocer's reached us from the wet jungle.

I had a letter of introduction to Mr Mead, who had been formally known as Resident of Togoland but whose official title had now for some time been modified to Regional Officer. My arrival could not possibly have been worse timed. The situation at that moment in the surrounding villages was officially described as explosive, and Mr Mead, whose job it was to see that no explosion took place, had had no sleep for several nights. A minor upset had been caused by a tornado that had ripped through the edge of the town that afternoon, torn off some roofs, and put the town electricity supply out of action. Finally the R.O.'s wife was in the last stage of a difficult pregnancy, and a car stood by, ready, in an emergency, to rush her to Lome, the capital of French Togoland, where, Mr Mead said, the medical services were better developed than the local ones.

Mr Mead faced these difficulties with an Olympian calm. We dined splendidly on the vast polished veranda of the Residency, served by white-coated, whispering stewards who moved as stealthily as Indian stranglers. Almost certainly having first discovered through the steward in charge of the guest bungalow that I was travelling very light, Mr Mead had asked to be excused from dressing for dinner, and we ate in civilized, tieless comfort. Like all great administrators the R.O. seemed to admire and respect the customs of the people he ruled, although he thought that they were rather letting the side down in their violent and non-constitutional reaction to their integration with Ghana. My host was a master of magnificent understatement, and his only complaint arising from the vexations of the moment was that there was a shortage of bath water. About half-way through the meal a dispatch-rider arrived with an urgent message, and excusing himself hurriedly the R.O. departed for his headquarters for another sleepless night, carrying with him a copy of *À la recherche du temps perdu*.

Next day I set out to see something of Togoland. Etiquette first called for a visit to the paramount chief of Ho, but here a difficulty arose. A schism had taken place in the leadership of the Ewes of Togoland over the issue of their permanent incorporation with Ghana, and a very strong minority had asked to remain under British rule until such time as they could unite with their brothers in French Togoland to form a separate nation. When the division of Togoland had taken place in 1919 about 170,000 Ewes found themselves transferred to the British, and about 400,000 came under French control. The Ewes complained that they suffered by this change of masters. The British slice, in particular, of the ex-German colony, they said, became no more than an unimportant appendage of the Gold Coast, and from 1919 onward no Ewe had much hope of self-advancement unless he left his native country – as great numbers did – and migrated to Accra. The two political factions dividing the country – those in favour of the C.P.P. and union with Ghana, and their opponents who had lost the recent elections – now regarded each other with implacable hostility. What was perhaps the most extraordinary feature of this situation was that the original paramount chief who headed the apparently pro-British faction had come under Mr Mead's displeasure, and diplomatic relations had been broken off between him and the Residency. The British, in fact, officially supported a new pretender from the royal family – a member of the once revolutionary C.P.P. (which still talked sometimes about breaking the chains of imperialism – although in these days with no really convincing show of acrimony).

It was a problem to know which chief to visit first, as it had been hinted to me that either might feel himself slighted if it came to his knowledge that I had placed him second on the list. In the end I decided to make it the dissident chief who was notorious for his readiness to take umbrage. I found him living in a small single-storey house. From the bareness of the furnishings and the absence of comfort, I got the impression that this chief – like so many minor potentates of West Africa – was a poor man. Chiefs are elected from a number of suitable candidates drawn from the royal family and I was told later that no Ewe candidate stood much chance of election unless he was the kind of man who got up early every morning and set off, hoe over his shoulder, to work on his farm.

Chief Togbe Hodo's reception was not a genial one. I found the chief in his courtyard, wearing his working clothes and seated on a piano stool. He was a man of about sixty. According to old-fashioned local usage he affected not to notice my entry, and appeared to be absorbed in his study of the faded coronation picture which provided the room's only decoration. A 'linguist' invited me to seat myself on a worn-out sofa and whispered that the chief would answer my questions when his council of 'wing-chiefs' arrived. He then fiddled with the knobs of a radio set until he found a station broadcasting hymns, and turned this up to a fair strength. The council of wing-chiefs, who had evidently been fetched from their work, soon trooped in, and seated themselves on a miscellany of chairs that had been placed round the courtyard. There were eight of them, and one of them wore a carpenter's apron and sat clutching a plane. This was my cue, as Mr

A Few High-Lifes in Ghana

Mead had warned me, to get up and shake hands with each chief in turn, starting with the man on my right and working my way round the circle. Speaking on behalf of the paramount chief, who now appeared to have noticed my presence for the first time, the linguist now said, 'You are welcome. Pray begin your questions.' Formal palavers of this kind form a great part of African small-town life and any visitor from another country, however unimportant he may be, is expected to enter with good grace into the spirit of the thing. I don't remember what questions I asked, and these certainly only provided an excuse for the exposition by the council of their views on the burning theme of union with Ghana. Chief Togbe Hodo's Grey Eminence turned out to be a nonconformist minister, who had been hurriedly sent for. The Reverend Ametowobla had been at Edinburgh University, and he spoke with persuasion and grandiloquence in the soft accent of the Scottish capital. There had never been much hope for Togolanders, he said, since the Germans who wanted to make a show-colony of it had left. Now that they were to be delivered up to the mercies of the politicians of the Gold Coast, there would be none at all. One of the chiefs present was old enough to remember what it was like under the Germans. Herzog the German governor had wanted to outstrip the Gold Coast and had set to work with tremendous energy to develop the country. There had been compulsory schooling for all, whereas in these days there was about 85 per cent illiteracy. On the other hand the Germans had introduced forced labour. Chief Togbe Hodo made no contribution to this discussion except in his native tongue. I believe that he understood English but would have considered it undignified to dispense with his interpreter on such occasions.

37

The Changing Sky

The opposition chief, Togbe Afede Asor, turned out to be young and agreeably expansive. Once again there was the business of waiting for the assembly of wing-chiefs before he could speak, but after this he brushed ceremony aside. We shook hands. I said, 'How do you do?' and the chiefs smiled widely and said, 'Okay.' After a brief discussion of local affairs the chief asked if I had any objection to his performing a libation. This pagan custom is in wide use all over the Gold Coast, despite the most vehement protests from the Christian clergy and in particular from the Bishop of Accra, and on national occasions it is carried out by Dr Nkrumah himself in exactly the same way as his counterpart in Europe might lay a wreath on a cenotaph. Dr Nkrumah when he makes a public libation uses the traditional Hollands Gin, but Chief Togbe Asor said that Black and White Whisky would in his opinion be just as acceptable to the ancestral spirits to whom the libation would be made, and he liked it better himself. We went into the chief's living-room, which was densely furnished in Victorian style, and there the chief poured about a teaspoonful of the whisky out on to the green linoleum, at the same time praying in a loud and matter-of-fact voice for the success of any mission I happened to be on, and – as at that time he still supposed me to be a Government servant – promotion in my particular department. After that we completed the ceremony in the approved fashion by drinking a stiff whisky apiece ourselves. Chief Asor told me that he was a Catholic, and that among the Catholic flock in Togoland only chiefs were allowed to pour libations and possess more than one wife. As another chiefly privilege he had 'medicine' buried in his back-yard to protect the household from malevolent spirits. When I left he invited me to come round next

38

morning at six, when he would sacrifice a sheep in honour of the flag-raising ceremony of the new nation. He also presented me with a neatly written biographical note, reading as follows: 'Toagbe Afede Asor II was born in June 1927 by Fia Afede XII of Ho Bankoe and Abla Dam of Taviefe. He was educated at the Catholic Mission School from 1936-1946. He was Assistant Secretary to the Asogli State Council from 1947-52. He was installed on 22nd February, 1952, on the ancient Asogli Stool of Ho. Togbe Asor II was the descendant of the great grandfather Asor I of Ho who led the Ewe emancipation from Notse 360 years ago. Hobbies: Table-tennis, Walking, Gardening.' The stool referred to here is the ancient West African symbol of kingship: the counterpart of the crown in Europe. It is kept under close guard by a functionary known as the Stool Father, whose power may almost equal that of the chief. The stool is considered to be impregnated with a magical essence, which in the old days was 'fed' or revived, by the blood of human sacrifices, and although it is too small and too sacred to be sat upon, a chief may be held in contact with it in the seated position from time to time, to allow him to absorb some of its power.

After saying goodbye to Chief Togbe Asor II, I made up my mind to drive on to Kpandu, one of the principal centres of the resistance movement. In the preceding days, abandoned training camps had been found in the bush round Kpandu, and several caches of weapons and explosives had been unearthed. This was March 5th – eve of Independence Day – and it was feared that despite the precautions taken to send military units into the area, rebellion might break out at any moment. There were few signs of life in the villages we passed through. Houses and shops were shut up, and there were no decorations. The driver, who was understandably nervous at the possibility of running into a battle, took to stopping at every village to inquire about the situation along the road immediately ahead. This meant a de rigueur call on the chief and his council and a certain amount of punctilious time-wasting.

Dzolokpuita stands out in the memory. Dzolokpuita was a pretty little Italianate-looking cluster of neat stone houses built on rust-red earth and shaded by flame trees in full blossom. Here the opposing factions had withdrawn to opposite ends of the village and were waiting, so the chief told us, with their cudgels and knives, ready for the coming of night. This chief was a rare pro-Government one – that is to say, he was pro integration with Ghana, and he was in fear of his life because his party was in the minority. He was the poorest chief I had so far met. He received me on the veranda of his hut, seated in a deck-chair with a replica of his sacred stool at his side. A child's chamber-pot had been hurriedly pushed out of the way underneath the stool. The chief's linguist was literally dressed in sackcloth, although when the council of wing-chiefs came scrambling in I noted that some of them wore old French firemen's helmets – a suggestion that they had seen better times. The wing-chiefs were scared stiff – they expected to have their throats cut that night – and they fidgeted and peered nervously about while the interminable routine of formal questions and answers was being got through. It was clear to me that even in the shadow of bloody revolt the chief wasn't going to be balked of a prolonged exchange of the courtesies. After I had asked him how many children he had begotten, and he had gravely replied, 'They are numerous,' he was going on with a full recital of their names, together, so far as he could remember, with those of their mothers, until he was stopped by cries of protest from his thanes. An army truck with a soldier crouched purposefully behind a Bren gun rolled into the square, and a wing-chief went rushing out to demand its protection; but the driver hastily accelerated away again, leaving the wing-chief waving his helmet frustratedly after it. 'We shall all die, tonight,' the paramount chief said. He asked me to bring their desperate situation to the notice of Queen Elizabeth. After that a sackcloth-clad official poured a libation of locally-distilled bootleg gin, and I was allowed to get away.

I went up to Kpandu, and back through this brilliant and menaced countryside. There were soldiers drilling in little groups of threes and fours in the open spaces of small towns, with the passion and dedication that West Africans bring to their military exercises. Where there were no soldiers there were lurking groups of cudgel-armed men. The market in Kpandu was nearly deserted and dreadfully malodorous. Here they sold millions of tiny sun-dried fish, and smoke-cured cane rats that filled the air with a fierce ammoniacal stench. You could also buy lovely ancient-looking beads copied from Phoenician models, spurious amber made in Japan, short-swords used in the north for protecting oneself from hyenas, pictures of Princess Margaret and Burt Lancaster, and a clearance line of portraits of Dorothy Lamour in her sarong. While I was mooching about, a small, spruce soldier arrived with a portable gramophone, wound it up and put on a tune called 'Ghana Land of Freedom', which, while serving as a kind of unofficial national anthem, has the unusual advantage of being a high-life, and is danced to as such (the other side of the record features Lord Kitchener in 'Don't Touch Me Nylon'). While the record was played through to the ostentatiously turned backs of the few traders about, the soldier stood to attention. A moment later, what was clearly a local man of substance came up. He was dressed in Accra style in toga and sandals, and after offering me his hand in the easy genial way of unspoilt Africa he nodded at the back of the retreating soldier and we exchanged knowing smiles. 'I fear, sir, he is batting on a sticky wicket,' the new arrival said. I was inclined to agree with what was clearly an Achimota University man. And although that night, to most people's astonishment, passed off peaceably, and no one slit the throats of the chief and council of Dzolok-puita, it was a verdict that I was afraid might be applied to the nascent State of Ghana as a whole.

'Tubman Bids Us Toil'

On the whole Liberia has had a poorish press. Back in the 'thirties Graham Greene gave the impression, in his travel book *Journey Without Maps*, that he found it a sad and sinister place. John Gunther, writing in 1955, summed it up as 'odd, wacky, phenomenal, or even weird'. Lesser authorities in between have produced books with supercilious titles like *Top Hats and Tom Toms*, while some of us with tenacious memories can still recall the startled headlines in 1931 when a League of Nations committee published a report proving that slavers still hunted down their human prey in the Liberian hinterland. To me in the spring of 1947 Liberia still sounded potentially a traveller's collector's piece; so on my way home by slow stages from the Ghana independence celebrations I decided to break my journey at Robertsfield airport and see something of the country.

It happened that I was seated in the plane next to the only other passenger getting off at Robertsfield, an American rubber man who had also read John Gunther's account: he spoke of what faced us with the kind of macabre relish sometimes found in old soldiers and world travellers. 'If anything, Gunther soft-pedalled the situation,' he assured me. 'And don't, by the way, run away with the idea that this place is a kind of American colony: they push us around just like anyone else. Step out of line and you pretty soon find yourself in gaol.' I asked the rubber man if he knew Monrovia well, but he said no, they had a pretty comfortable set-up on the plantation and he'd only been down there once or twice. And that reminded him, we should be fingerprinted at the airfield. They would take our passports away, and we should have to go to the police headquarters in Monrovia to get them back. As a final warning he recommended me to keep out of arguments with Liberian officials and to submit with good grace to the going-over that awaited us in the customs.

These predictions proved to be ill-founded. It was an hour before dawn when we touched down. The immigration officer, yawning, stamped our passports wordlessly and disappeared as if dematerialized. The customs man put his mark on our bags and waved us away. A moment later my American friend, claimed by a colleague with a waiting car, was borne off to the security of his comfortable set-up, and I was left alone in the dimly lit customs shed until a boy of about fourteen appeared and offered to show me where I could get what he called 'morning chop'. There was a wait of three hours before the daily D.C.3 plane took off for Spriggs Payne airfield, Monrovia. So I went with him. We walked about a hundred yards before reaching a long building raised on piles, looking like an Indonesian long-house, which the boy said was the airport hotel. Here, he said, I should have to leave my luggage, which it was forbidden to take to the restaurant. I was suspicious of what seemed to me a possible manœuvre to dispossess me, but before I could argue a zombie came out of the hotel, took my bags from the boy, went in, and shut the door. The restaurant was a little farther on: a chink of light showing in the black shutters of the forest. The boy pointed it out and told me that he would come and fetch me when it was light. He shook hands with me and went off. At the time, this perfunctory service struck me as peculiar; but after I had been in Liberia a few days I realized that small boys preferred not to walk about by themselves in the dark.

'Tubman Bids Us Toil'

The only other occupants of the restaurant made up a conspiratorial group, muttering in Spanish at a near-by table. I was served an American-style breakfast by a taciturn waiter. While I was busy with this a young Liberian in a flowered shirt wearing a snub-nosed gangster's pistol in a shoulder holster came in and gave me a quick, power-saturated, policeman's stare. The muttering Spaniards looked up hopefully. I paid one dollar and twenty-five cents, and went outside again. Dawn was rising in total silence like grey smoke among the trees. A thick coverlet of mist lay along the low roofs of the airport buildings. There was a pharmaceutical smell coming out of the forest like the odour of dried-up gums, medicinal roots and benzoin. The air was flabby as if breathed in through a mask holding the moist warmth of one's last exhalation. I could see the boy squatting distantly by the door of the airport hotel, waiting for the daylight, to cross the no-man's-land between us.

It was a fifteen-minute flip in the D.C.3 across forty miles of swamp to reach Spriggs Payne airfield, on the outskirts of Monrovia. From the air the capital looked gay and dilapidated like a Caribbean banana port. It was crowded on to a peninsula outlined in yellow beach, with a hard white line of surf on the Atlantic side. The cheerful mossy green of the bush came unbroken right up to the neck of the peninsula. There were big ships in port, and as the plane came down you could see a few vultures drift past over the roof-tops and the tangle of traffic in the central streets.

Visitors to Monrovia have complained that it is short of public transport, that the telephone system is uncertain, that there are regular breakdowns in the basic services, that most of the streets are unpaved, and that until recently the appropriation for brass bands exceeded that for public health. On the whole they have been stolidly impervious to the city's faded charm and its colour. The ex-slaves who were the original settlers here built Monrovia in the time-improved image they carried in their minds of the American South. They built with a touching and preposterous affection for Greek columns, porticoes, pilasters and decorative staircases, and a century of Liberian sun and rain has reduced their creations to splendidly theatrical shacks. The bright, slapped-on paint no longer serves to keep up pretences, although Van Gogh would have been in his element here among all the sun-tamed reds and blues and browns. There is a carnival cheerfulness about all the sagging, multicoloured façades beneath which the citizens of Monrovia promenade with the senatorial dignity of a people whose ancestors have carried burdens on their heads in a hot country. It was Monrovia that taught me the beauty and the interest of corrugated iron as a building material, when suitably painted, with its rhythmical troughs of shade. And in Monrovia it is in lavish use.

By night, especially if there is moonlight to put back a little of the colour, the effect is strikingly romantic. The city becomes fragile, its buildings cracked and seamed with the pale internal light of Hallowe'en candles. There are visions of interiors crammed with Victoriana, and walls hung with holy pictures and framed diplomas. As the Liberians, although shy, are polite and sociable, one is continually greeted by a soft guttural 'How-do-you-do?' spoken by an invisible watcher behind a shutter. A little music is spun out thinly into the night from aged gramophones playing in barbers' shops: 'Bubbles', 'Alice Where Art Thou?' ... Cadillacs, festooned with fairground illumination and bearing their dark-skinned grandes dames and white-tied cavaliers, swish over the snow-soft laterite dust of the streets. A congregation of silent worshippers collects outside the Mosque – a yellow building with its walls edged with broken lager bottles, possessing a minaret like a fat section of drain-piping. Here, where the Faithful have cleared a space, they spread their personal prayer-rugs on a small oasis of clean white sand amid the urban debris. If it is Sunday there will be the sound of ecstatic hymn-singing from the direction of many nonconformist Houses of Worship. Every night at about ten the town's *belles de nuit* begin to lurk in the neighbourhood of the cinemas, where the last performances are coming to an end. They are dressed in the style introduced by the missionaries of the last century: blouses with leg-of-mutton sleeves, voluminous frilled skirts, honest calico underclothing – it is said – and they carry parasols.

It is by day that you notice the squalor bred from the problem of the relative indestructibility of modern waste. At Byblos and at Sidon the domestic debris of a thousand years may be compressed into a yard of dust. In Monrovia there are towering middens of imperishable rubbish; of iron, rubber and plastic that are the legacy of barely two generations. Most Monrovian houses are raised on piles, and the space under each house serves for the conceal-ment of old engine blocks, back axles, radiators and batteries. In the gardens you sometimes see one car-chassis piled upon another, their members entwined with flowering convolvulus and transfixed by the saplings of self-sown tropical fruit trees. Almost every side-street is littered with abandoned vehicles, many of them recent models which may at first have been immobilized by some small mechanical failure, but then subjected to nightly piracy for spare parts until only the bare bones have remained. The citizens of Monrovia have not yet learned to clear up their debris as they go along. Even the fragments of basic rock blasted out over a hundred years ago to level the ground for the original buildings are still left just as they fell.

Old prints of Monrovia suggest that basically the town has changed little in its appearance from the days when over a century ago the first settlers ventured to leave their tiny stronghold on Providence Island in the Mesurado River estuary and establish themselves on the mainland. These pioneers were negro freedmen returned to Africa from the United States under a scheme promoted by a philanthropic body known as the American Colonization Society. Their first decade was precarious. They suffered from disease, semi-starvation, and the attacks of slavers who probably felt that the success of this experiment in resettlement might establish a disastrous precedent for the business. The first Liberians were supported entirely by shipments of provisions from the U.S.A. and protected by the guns of American and British warships. Their numbers were strengthened by

Good manners are a preoccupation of African tribal society. Children are educated in the harsh discipline of bush-schools from which they emerge with the manners of Spanish grandees at the court of Philip II. Tribal Africans detain each other with innumerable polite inquiries and compliments whenever they meet, and are endlessly exchanging small ritual gifts. They are inclined to find Europeans brusque and boorish in their demeanour. Although the children of Accra have been spared the rigours of the bush-school, they are imbued with the charm and the courtesy of traditional Africa. Outside the industrialized areas of South Africa there are no teen-age delinquents in this continent.

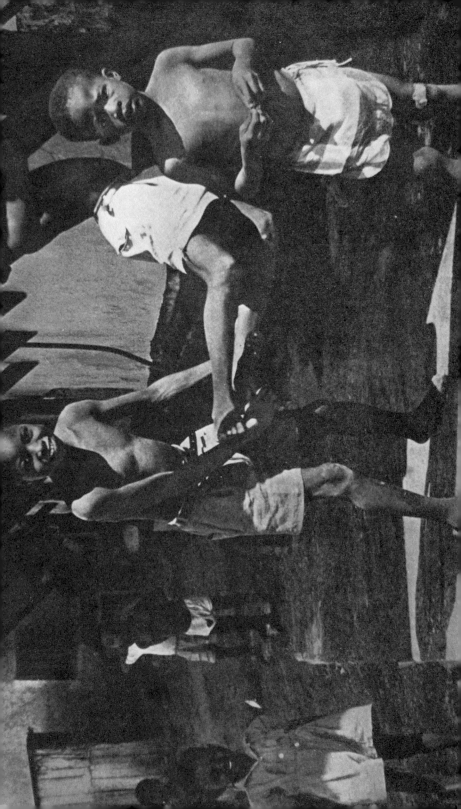

further batches of Africans released from slave-running ships, but from 1822 – the date of the first settlement – until 1840, they were ruled by white governors appointed by the American society, and the country had no official existence in international law. In 1846 the first negro president, Joseph Jenkin Roberts, prepared a constitution and Great Britain recognized Liberia as an independent republic, although the U.S.A. did not follow until 1862. The first century of Liberia's existence has been called by Liberians 'The Century of Survival'. Considerably more territory than Liberia's present extent of 43,000 square miles was originally claimed by the settlers, but this, before the days of exact surveying, and despite the frowns of the U.S.A., was constantly nibbled at by the adjacent British and French colonies.

It is said that the Liberian pioneers included many skilled tradesmen who were in fact responsible for the building of Monrovia. This spadework accomplished, later generations seem to have been content to relax. A social order recalling that of the American plantations soon developed, with the freed slaves and their descendants playing the part of pseudo-aristocratic and leisure-loving

These girls are Conyaguis from Guinea, across the north-western frontier of Liberia. Their elaborate cicatrization is not only an adornment but forms part of a disciplinary process reaching its culmination in the painful operation of female circumcision. This agonizing experience – undergone by millions of African women – is almost universally practised among the West African tribes. It has been ardently defended by many African intellectuals such as Jomo Kenyatta, more or less on the grounds of the supposed character-forming value of pain when stoically endured. Many women never recover from the infections arising from this crude surgery. Although still the prisoners of such tribal customs, the Conyaguis are in other respects emancipated. Recently they demonstrated their political evolution by voting for their country's separation from France.

49

masters, leaving all manual work to be done by such native Liberians as could be induced or compelled to do it. An elaborate social ritual was built up, from which Liberia has never fully recovered, and which sometimes seems to the foreign eye to achieve the opposite of the dignity at which it aims. All professions fell into social disrepute except those of the law, politics and diplomacy. Liberians developed into a race of astute politicians, but there were no native craftsmen, doctors, technicians, engineers – and there are few even today. In the meanwhile the hinterland, occupied by its twenty-odd tribes, remained roadless and neglected, and a concealed oppression of native Liberians by their African brothers returned from servitude gradually developed, until it was fully exposed by the League of Nations committee in 1931, with the ensuing world-wide scandal. The fact still remains that in spite of all reforms that have since been carried out, Liberia has been, and remains in practice, a species of colony in which about two million tribal Africans are governed by a minority of 150,000 English-speaking Americo-Liberians from whom they are totally separated by barriers of race, religion, language and way of life.

At the present time there is a drive towards the integration of the tribal people into what is called 'the social life of the nation'. This unification policy is a favourite enterprise of President Tubman, Liberia's eighteenth president and probably the most able and energetic figure ever to appear on the Liberian political scene. President William Vacanarat Shadrach Tubman performs the considerable feat of leading a parliamentary democracy in which no official opposition is permitted to exist. The president was elected in 1943 to serve a term of eight years, re-elected in 1951 for a second term of four years, and in 1955 once again (although he was reluctant, the *Liberian Year Book* informs us) for a further four-year term. The national jubilation at the enormous majority obtained by the president in 1955 was marred by an attempt on his life. Since this occurrence the official opposition has ceased to exist, its members having withdrawn into exile, died suddenly, or been converted with equal suddenness to the policies of the True Whig Party of which His Excellency is the leader. It is said that President Tubman, in spite of the geniality and exuberance of his character, is resentful of criticism. When the official opposition crumbled and fell, such journalistic mouthpieces of divergent public opinion as the *Friend* and the *Independent* also collapsed. The year book tells us that they were suppressed as 'irresponsible'. The two remaining newspapers, the *Listener* and the *Liberian Age*, wholeheartedly support the president's point of view. With the object of emphasizing the unanimity of the country's acclaim for the president, these papers sometimes publish eulogistic tributes from ex-opponents newly released from prison. At odd times an appreciation in poetic form may be slipped into their pages. Here is an example from a recent *Liberian Age*, which in its complete form runs to eight happy verses:

TUBMAN BIDS US TOIL

(Tune: Jesus Bids Us Shine)

By John N. George
Public Relations Officer, Sinoe County

Tubman bids us toil at the Nation's Plan,
With the Lone-starred banner building every clan
As he ever trusts us we must work,
So in your small corner don't shirk and lurk!

The Changing Sky

Tubman bids us toil in the gleeful way,
Saving every moment of the precious day;
Whether big or little we must work,
So in your small corner don't shirk and lurk!

Etc.

After a century of stagnation, in which Liberia lagged far behind the adjacent areas under white colonial domination, the country has begun to move rapidly ahead under President Tubman's firm, paternal guidance. Liberia assumed strategic importance during the last war. It could at any time provide a base in traditionally friendly territory for American armed forces defending the South Atlantic, and, along with Brazil, it is the only source of vital natural rubber bordering the Atlantic Ocean. The president's intelligent exploitation of these factors has conjured up such evidence of prosperity as the new Free Port of Monrovia, five hundred miles of new roads, a three-million-dollar bridge over the St Paul River, a sprinkling of new hospitals in the hinterland, an air-conditioned hotel with a magnificently eccentric Spanish lift, taxis, telephones, piped water and modern sewage disposal for Monrovia, and a fairly elaborate yacht for the president himself. The president's 'open door' policy has attracted foreign capital to Liberia and an assortment of American, Swiss, German and Spanish firms who now share with the Firestone Rubber Company – that great monolithic pioneer – in the considerable natural wealth of the country.

The main problem confronting these concessionaries is Liberia's acute shortage of unskilled labour. The Liberian tribesman has always been accustomed to gain the mere necessities of life with a minimum of effort. At the most he will consent to clear and burn a little virgin bush, and then leave it to the womenfolk to plant the 'dry' rice and cassava forming the basic diet. Even the women's agricultural work is very light. No hoeing, weeding or watering is done. The family simply waits for the crop to come up, and supplements its diet by harvesting a few tropical fruits. The Liberian countryman will eat anything. There are no sizeable wild animals left in the country to hunt, but the chance windfall of a serpent or a giant snail, the seasonal manna of flying ants, and palm grubs – all are joyfully accepted for the cooking-pot. The result of this catholicity of appetite is a well-balanced diet and a good physique. The amount of leisure enjoyed by a Liberian villager – especially a man of substance with a full quota of three wives to wait on him hand and foot – is quite beyond the comprehension of modern civilized man. It is natural enough that such a villager is extremely reluctant to exchange this lotus-eating existence for that of a plantation labourer working up to twelve hours a day for a wage of 30 cents, and what are called 'fringe benefits', i.e. free housing, medical supervision, and so on. When, indeed, he is driven by force of circumstances into the plantations, he will sometimes pathetically attempt to emphasize the transitory and separate nature of his life as a labourer by adopting a temporary name which often recalls the brighter side of plantation life, such as Dinner Pail, T-shirt, Pay Day, or Christmas. In these circumstances labour is simply obtained by a system of bonuses paid to local chiefs – whose word is more than law. There is nothing furtive or shamefaced about this procedure, and the amounts paid duly figure in company balance sheets submitted for stockholders' approval.

Firestone, which controls a labour force of 25,000 men to operate its million-acre concession, and which sets the pace in these matters, pays $1.50 per man, per annum, and its 1955 balance sheet discloses a total of $90,000 expended in this way. 'In addition [I quote from *Case Study of Firestone Operation in Liberia*, published in the Nation Planning Association series] a regular scale of non-monetary gifts from Firestone to the paramount, clan, and occasionally town chiefs, has also evolved.' This regular scale of non-monetary gifts for the supply of labour goes under the dignified title of the 'Paramount Chiefs Assistance Plan', and it was developed, we are assured, with the full knowledge and consent of the Liberian Government, and has also been adopted by other foreign companies.

I learned, by the way, that it was considered highly unethical to outbid one's competitors in this extremely restricted labour market. Just as a successful tradesman may consider it a good thing to contribute occasionally to the local police benevolent fund, foreign companies operating in Liberia are also notably generous in their support of charitable, educational, cultural and religious institutions in Liberia.

The minimum wage of 30 cents a day, which is between one-third and one-fifth of wages paid for equivalent labour in the adjacent colonies of the British Sierra Leone and the French Ivory Coast, is explained in the publication already quoted, as a device for keeping inflation in check. More cogently it is argued that Liberian employers of labour could not afford substantial pay increases. Liberians have been quick, in fact, to convert themselves into plantation owners, and as soon as a new road is completed it is lined on both sides with the plantations of prominent Liberians who act as small subsidiaries of Firestone. These native plantation operators obtain free seedlings from Firestone, and as long as their labour costs remain cheap, and their land can be obtained under 'advantageous' terms from tribal communities who have never heard of title deeds, they seem to be on a very good thing. Occasionally in the current scramble for land, someone oversteps the mark, and there is a rumpus in the Liberian Press. While I was in Liberia a tribe actually dared to take a foreign company to court for the illegal enclosure of its tribal land, and no one was more astounded than the tribesmen themselves when they won their case.

Considering the subservience of the Liberian Press it is extraordinary how much self-criticism can be found in its pages, combined with extreme sensibility to adverse comment from anyone outside the True Whig Party family – especially foreigners. All the private scandals of Liberian government: the corruption in the judiciary, the oppression of tribal people by district commissioners, the bribe-taking by persons in high places (with the exact amount of the bribe), are ruthlessly exposed to the foreign eye. Some of these revelations, in fact, such as the account published in the *Listener* of May 14th, 1957, of organized highway robbery on one of Liberia's two main roads – which had then been in progress for over two months, and had the backing, the paper thought, of 'top interior officials' – make almost incredible reading. Yet the same papers explode with indignation on the slightest foreign comment that might be taken as injurious to national pride. Such outbursts are sometimes lacking in a sense of proportion. Recently the *Listener* came out with banner headlines: 'Stamp Dealer Says Liberia Owns Savage Cannibal Tribes'. About one quarter of the space normally allotted to news was devoted to mulling over this slander, and there was a

55

further orgy of wound-licking in a long editorial headed 'Please Treat Us Kindly Next Time'. It turned out that an obscure stamp dealer in Boston had had the enterprising notion of printing a little geographical information on the packets he sent out. Naturally this was highly coloured stuff intended to excite the interest of the children whom one presumes would be his principal customers; but to the Liberian inflamed sensitivity it was a monstrous calumny that overshadowed any international crises, such as that of the Suez Canal, that happened to be about at the time.

There are of course no 'cannibalistic tribes' anywhere in Africa but the fact that cannibalistic practices do exist in Liberia is abundantly clear to anyone who reads the very uninhibited Liberian Press. Cases of 'medicine' murders by 'Human Elephant Men', 'Snake People', 'Water People', an organization with the macabre official title of the Negee Aquatic Cannibalistic Society, and various other criminal secret groups, are regularly reported in the newspapers. These often contain gruesome anatomical details, and are sometimes accompanied by a journalistic-reactionary demand for the reinstitution of trial by Sassywood – which in its pure form means that the suspect drinks deadly poison, brewed from the bark of the sassy tree, *Erythrophloeum guineense*, from which he is supposed to recover if innocent. Here is an example extracted from the editorial published in the *Liberian Age* of April 30th, 1956, which incidentally explains the motive behind ritual murders.

TRIAL BY ORDEAL

In the last few weeks the *Liberian Age* reported that two men and a child have been murdered to make medicine. One was to invoke the blessings of the gods so that there will be a plentiful harvest in the rice season and the others were for reasons far more dubious.

The Government might do well in the circumstances to put a check to these unwholesome and superstitious practices by reinstating trial by ordeal, commonly known as trial by Sassywood.

Admittedly, Sassywood is a pagan cult and in a Christian State pagan cults should be frowned upon and eliminated. But the fact remains that in order to check these pagan practices we must employ the one method in which practitioners of paganism have an abiding faith, namely, the Sassywood trial.

In the Revised Statutes and in the Administrative Regulations, trial by ordeal is forbidden except in minor matters and under licence of the Interior Department.

But the Constitution also provides that government should use every possible method to protect the life of the citizen and to punish the guilty of wilful murder. In such cases where life is endangered, the Government would be perfectly justified in using any legitimate method in bringing to account persons with pagan proclivities who are in the habit of so destroying life for foolish ends. The case for trial by ordeal even becomes stronger when the ordinary processes of law become powerless in finding the guilty, due to the fact that persons who normally engage in such practices belong to some society or the other which gives them protection.

The 'medicine' referred to in this article is sometimes called 'borfina'. It is manufactured from the organs of a murdered person, and as well as being employed in the

ancient magical ceremonies common to primeval humanity to promote rainfall and to influence the growth of
crops, it is in brisk demand by those who dabble in
witchcraft for their own ends. Borfina is in common use,
not only in Liberia, but in most of West Africa, and it is
reported that rich men will offer as much as 100 dollars
for a scent bottle full of the grisly stuff. In Liberia it is
obtained by professional 'heart-men' who usually work at
night and prefer women and children for their victims.
It is a sinister fact that the 'heart-men' are more active
at the period of the Christian festivals of Christmas and
Easter, when they are believed to invade even the capital
itself in search of their prey. At these times Liberian
countrymen go armed and in pairs, along the jungle
paths, and the women working in the fields keep in
touch by calling to each other at frequent intervals. It
is practically unknown for a white man to be the victim
of a medicine murder, as it is believed that medicine
obtained from a white man is of little or no value.

Trial by ordeal, I soon discovered, although not
practised in colonial regions of Africa, is an everyday
occurrence in Liberia, and I had only been in the country
about a week before I had the opportunity of seeing how
it worked. Wanting to learn as much as I could of the
interior – a little of which had become accessible in the
last few years by the completion of new roads – I hired a
taxi in Monrovia and drove across country to the frontier
of French Guinea and back, a journey taking three days.
I carried with me a letter of introduction to Mr Charles
Williams, District Commissioner of Bgarnba, where I
hoped to stay the first night, and it was at Bgarnba that
I encountered this survival of medieval justice.

Mr Williams was in court when I arrived. I sent in my
letter, and in a few minutes the commissioner came out

to welcome me. He was a tall handsome man, with a reserved, almost melancholic expression. He mentioned that he still had a large number of cases to try, and asked whether I would be interested in seeing the district court in operation. I was naturally more than interested. As we strolled back to the courthouse Mr Williams softly whistled a bar or two of 'Through the Night of Doubt and Sorrow'. I later discovered that he was a devout Episcopalian, with a great affection for *Hymns Ancient and Modern*.

The court was held in a large circular hut. About fifty members of the public were present, seated on rows of benches. The atmosphere was relaxed and informal. Most of the women had their babies with them, which they fed intermittently at the breast. The soldiers who brought in petty offenders from time to time hung about in wilting attitudes until they were dismissed. A pair of counsels, nattily dressed in sports clothes, kept up a crossfire of legal repartee. Seated behind his desk Mr Williams looked mildly judicial and perhaps a trifle sardonic. Once in a while he picked up his mallet and brought it down with a crash, sometimes to restore order, sometimes to deal with a tsetse fly that had alighted on his desk. Most of the complainants and defendants did not speak English, and as Mr Williams was a member of the Liberian ruling class and therefore spoke nothing but English, the services of an interpreter were often necessary. The interpreter translated from the tribal languages into a kind of Liberian pidgin, which I found it completely impossible to understand. Even Mr Williams was often in difficulties, and called on the interpreter to repeat a sentence.

The examination of witnesses began with the routine question put by the commissioner, 'Do you hear English?'

– followed, if the witness did in fact hear English, by a second question, 'You Christian man?' Three out of four of those appearing before the court were not Christian men, and in these cases Mr Williams ordered the administering of an oath by 'carfoo' – a liquid concoction, or medicine, prepared by a witch-doctor, which although normally innocuous, is supposed to be fatal to the pagan perjurer. Although restrained in his manner at most times, Mr Williams seemed unable sometimes to control an outburst of genial contempt when he noticed a tendency on a witness's part to hang back at this moment of the oath-taking. 'Come, drink carfoo and lie, so that you may die tonight,' was a typical invitation roared at a minor chief who showed some reluctance when the witches' brew was put into his hands. When a Christian witness avoided touching the Bible with his lips, the commissioner leapt to his feet and pushed the book into his face. 'Come on, man. Kiss the holy book, unless you are determined to lie.'

Most of the civil cases arose out of what is known in Liberia as 'woman palaver'. Mr Williams explained to me that no man of standing would have less than three wives, each having been purchased for the standard bride-price of 40 dollars, paid to the girl's father. A rich man bought wives as an investment. They worked his land for him without expecting to be paid, and they produced valuable children into the bargain. The local paramount chief, he mentioned, had a hundred wives – each one decently housed in her separate hut in his compound. Unfortunately the tendency was for a man's wives to increase in number as he himself advanced in years, and – well – you knew what it was – the women sometimes found themselves with a fair amount of time on their hands. This meant that they were inclined to get into hot water, and although most possessors of large harems took a pretty civilized view of wives forming subsidiary friendships, there were a few narrow-minded and litigious husbands who went to court, particularly to sue for the return of the 40 dollars paid, when a wife ran off with some other man. In dealing with these 'woman palaver' cases, one of Mr Williams's chief difficulties was his evident distaste for coarse language. When a man complained that his wife refused to sleep with him Mr Williams winced and put this blunt statement into the more elegant and evasive English of Monrovia. 'Your husband alleges that you refused to accord him the privilege of meeting with you,' was how he reworded this delicate circumstance, when cross-examining the wife. The only European to appear in court that day was the Italian overseer in charge of a gang of labourers working on a bridge-construction project near by. His offence was that in dismissing one of his men for malingering he had referred in a burst of anger – as Italians will – to the man's wife, using at the same time a four-letter word. This was a grave matter indeed in a country where a European can be heavily fined and deported for calling a man a 'nigger', and all work on the bridge stopped while the whole gang of workmen were brought to the court to testify. Mr Williams, after first ordering English-hearing women to leave the court, asked for the actual word complained of to be repeated. It was spoken in a stunned silence. The Italian spread his palms and smiled apologetically. One English word was like another to him. He genuinely didn't understand what the fuss was about. In the end Mr Williams read him a long lecture on vulgarity and let him off with a caution, and the Italian went away still mystified, shaking his head.

Shortly after this a woman was brought in by her

husband, who charged her with infidelity. She had confessed to five lovers – or as Mr Williams put it, to granting intimate favours to five men other than her lawful husband – and in accordance with Liberian law the husband had been awarded damages of 10 dollars against each man. The trouble was that he now claimed that the names of other lovers had been concealed. Witnesses and counter-witnesses were produced, there were charges of perjury, and it was quite clear that this had all the makings of a lengthy and endlessly complicated case, when the woman agreed to submit to trial by ordeal. With evident relief Mr Williams ordered this to take place next morning immediately after dawn.

I slept the night in the commissioner's house, and at the appointed hour next morning I went over to the local lock-up, outside which the trial was to be staged. I found the calabozo of Bgarnba to consist of a long thatched hut, on the veranda of which several female prisoners, faces plastered with white cosmetic clay, were reclining in hammocks, under the apathetic guard of a soldier of about sixteen years of age. A witch-doctor – previously referred to by Mr Williams as 'a mystical man' – had arrived, and was lighting a small fire of twigs. He was a foxy-looking old fellow dressed in a fairground mountebank's purple robe. Mr Williams was not present.

As soon as the fire was well alight the mystical man produced from the folds of his robe a metal object like a large flattened spoon, engraved with Arabic characters, and put this to heat in the heart of the fire. This was to be a version of the ordeal by the burning iron. In another variant of this type of ordeal a heated sabre is brought into contact with one of the limbs. Other ordeals in common use involve the insertion of small pebbles under the eyelids, or the thrusting of needles into the flesh.

'Tubman Bids Us Toil'

A few minutes later the wronged husband and the errant wife came on the scene. Both had dressed very carefully for the occasion – the man in a sort of yellow toga and the girl in a bright cotton frock printed with a pineapple design. They were accompanied by the clerk of the court, who wore a sports blazer with a crest on the breast pocket, and had a pencil stuck in his thick, woolly hair. A young soldier carrying a rifle trailed behind them. No one spoke or showed the slightest interest in the preparations. Liberians, other than the citizens of Monrovia, are trained by their long and rigorous years of initiation in the bush to maintain an attitude of formal unconcern in the face of all such crises. Later, I discovered that the woman had not been held in custody overnight, and may have had the opportunity to visit the head of the local women's secret society, the Sande, then in session, who might have prepared her with some 'bush-medicine' for what she had to face, or even have induced a protective hypnotic state.

Chairs were fetched, and the couple took their seats facing the fire, which was now burning briskly. They sat a few feet apart, stolidly oblivious of each other, like bored life-partners awaiting the serving of an uninspiring meal. The mystical man pulled out the iron, tested it with his spittle, and pushed it back into the fire. There was a short wait, and at a nod from the witch-doctor the girl put out her tongue. He bent over her and there was a faint sizzle. The witch-doctor went closer, peering at the girl's mouth like a conscientious dentist. He dabbed again with the iron. Nothing moved in the girl's face. Her husband looked glumly into space. The witch-doctor picked up a mug that stood ready, containing water, and handed it to the girl, who filled her mouth, rinsed the water round, spat it out, and thrust out her tongue again

63

for inspection. The witch-doctor, the clerk and the soldier then examined it closely for condemnatory traces of burning. 'Not guilty,' said the clerk in a flat voice. He took the pencil out of his hair, wrote something in a notebook, and the whole party, their boredom in no apparent way relieved, began to move off. Justice had been done.

The bush society which may well have taken a surreptitious hand in these proceedings is probably the feature of Liberian life which has most impressed – or appalled – foreigners who have visited the hinterland. African tribal life from the southern limits of the Sahara Desert to the borders of the Union of South Africa is dominated more or less by secret societies, but it is in Liberia, where European influence has been least felt, and the original fabric of tribal life therefore best preserved, that the secret societies are most strongly entrenched. There is a society for the men called the Poro, and one for the women, the Sande. These are in session alternately, each for several years. Every member of the tribe must enter the society and the prestige of the society is so great that, outside the control exercised by government officials, it is the *de facto* ruler of the country, with the grand-master

Trial by ordeal once meant the administering of a dose of poison which if vomited up meant both the suspect's survival and a verdict of not guilty. Innocence was equated with an irritable stomach. Today in Liberia, although the harsher ordeals have been abolished, the application of hot iron to various bodily parts is still practised. It is believed that those who are guilty will blister, and they are then further punished for their tender skin by a fine or imprisonment. Liberians of the interior seem very ready – particularly when the weight of evidence is against them, and they see little hope of establishing their innocence in court by other means – to try their luck at what really amounts to a final gamble.

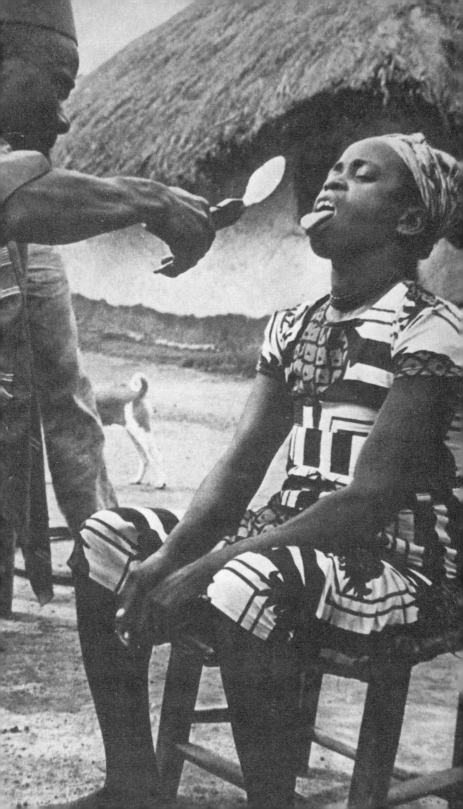

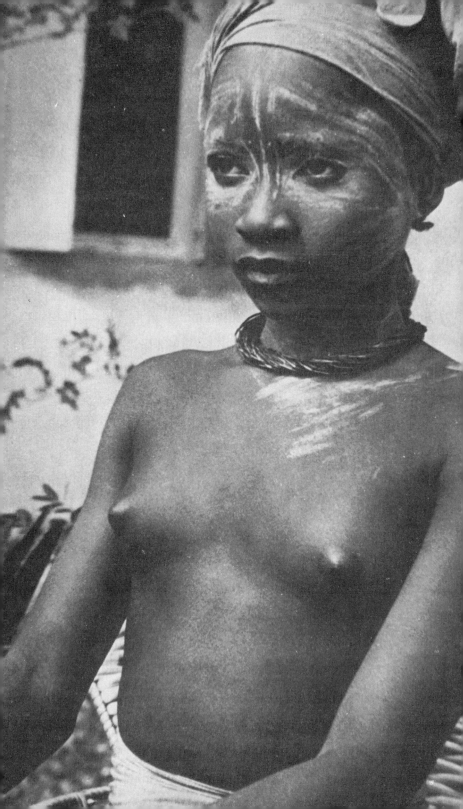

of the society as a kind of under-cover opposite number of the government-appointed district commissioner. When the women's society – the Sande – takes over from the Poro for its normal session of three years, actual power passes to the women. All major decisions relating to tribal life are decided by them, and it is customary for men to dress in symbolical homage as women, and in this guise to apply for admission to the Sande – which is of course refused.

Exact information about African secret societies is extremely difficult to obtain, even by anthropologists, but it is clear that their real purpose is to perpetuate the tribe's highly complex way of life, by the communal education of its youth, which at the same time is physically and mentally prepared for the hard life of savannah and jungle. Both societies impose a Spartan, even terrifying, discipline on their initiates. The boys must in theory – even if the practice has fallen into disuse – be transformed into warriors, must learn to defend themselves against savage animals, to take part in successful raiding parties, and to frustrate the attacks of tribal enemies. To achieve this result they are subjected to a more than military discipline; starved, flogged, made to sleep in the rain, to take part in gladiatorial combats, attacked and wounded superficially by human beings disguised as wild beasts, finally 'swallowed' by the

Young girls still enter bush-schools all over Liberia (and in many other parts of West Africa) for training in the tribal way of life. The bush-school entails education away from the parents for three or four years, and there are initiatory stages to be passed that correspond roughly to the academic examinations of the West. To celebrate the passing of such a test a girl may be allowed to visit her home, in the care of a matron who acts as a chaperone. This girl had imprudently wandered off alone, and presented herself at my host's hut to receive the small gift of money that it is usual to offer on such occasions.

totemic animal of the tribe, after which they are 'reborn'
– in theory with no memory of their past lives – as fully
initiated tribal members. The training of the girls is less
arduous, but may be even more painful since it includes
processes of beautifying by cicatrizing, tattooing, and
sometimes actually carving the flesh with knives, and
finally that scourge of nearly all African women:
clitoridectomy–performed with crude surgery, and without anaesthetics.

All the African races seem to have decided that only
supernatural sanctions can induce human beings to submit to such a course of self-improvement: so teachers in
the bush schools are masked and regarded by their pupils
as spirits. These are the celebrated 'bush-devils' of
Liberia, who vary in their importance according to their
function and who are presided over by a kind of super-
devil who is a combination of headmaster, sergeant-major
and ghost – as well sometimes as judge, and even
executioner – and who projects a power so devastating
that merely to catch sight of him as he walks in the
moonlight is death to an African. Not all this aroma of
terror is consciously a disciplinary device. The devils, who
are high-ranking members of the bush society, are
believed by adepts to be controlled at certain times by
powerful spirits, including the tribal ancestors – a belief
which may well be shared by the devils themselves.
Anthropologists in the neighbouring French Guinea,
where such aspects of tribal life are more easily observed
than in Liberia, believe that masked dancers often pass
into a kind of trance, on ceremonial occasions – or sometimes as soon as they put on their masks, which in themselves are supposed to possess a kind of separate life, and
to require 'feeding' with blood.

Remarkably enough, the life of the bush-school is

popular with Africans. After initiation – which corres-
ponds to graduation in the West – people frequently
return to the bush on a voluntary basis to take further
courses, and success in these 'post-graduate courses' is
recognized as a stepping-stone to advancement in the
hierarchy of the secret societies, and carries with it at
the same time much social prestige.

African art is seen at its best in the production of cult
objects and masks for the Poro and the Sande, and
Liberia is one of the last strongholds of vigorous, untainted African art. As the masks worn by the principal
bush-devils possess a kind of sanctity, it is not easy for a
foreigner even to inspect one, let alone purchase one. The
men who carve the sacred masks – who are usually high-
ranking adepts of the Poro – say that they do so only
when under the influence of an inspirational dream.
While I was staying in one of the villages in the bush
with an American anthropologist I shall call Warren, the
local tribe's best carver dropped in to pay one of the
formal calls which are a part of the complex social ritual
of African village life. The carver came in smiling, shook
hands, with the characteristic Liberian snap of thumb and
finger, accepted a glass of cold beer, and picked up an
illustrated book on African art that had just arrived from
the United States. 'Why you no come before, man?'
Warren asked him. 'I'm vexed with you because you no
come.' The mask-carver said he hadn't been able to
dream for weeks, and as his inspiration seemed to have
dried up, he'd gone off to look for diamonds – a popular
occupation at present in the area adjoining the Sierra
Leone frontier. Warren was relieved. He was afraid that
he had unwittingly offended the man in some way. The
elaboration of Liberian tribal etiquette makes it quite
bewildering to a white man, and although Africans will

67

make intelligent allowances for a foreigner's ignorance of good manners, it is sometimes difficult to avoid giving offence.

The mask-carver turned over the pages of the book, giggling slightly, and Warren asked him what he found funny. It was the African's turn to tread warily now. He'd probably done a six-months course in the bush-school, learning, the hard way, how to avoid hurting people's feelings, and he clearly didn't want to tell Warren that he found this collection of masterpieces chosen from the whole African continent pretty poor stuff. In the end Warren got him to express his objection – the mask-carver by the way had picked up a fair amount of English, working on the plantations. 'I no see the use for these things.' Non-Liberian African art, in fact, was as extravagant – as grotesque even – to him, as African art as a whole tends to appear to the average untutored Westerner. He just couldn't see what purpose these distorted objects could serve. The idea of art for art's sake was completely foreign to him. He flipped over the pages of the book, making a well-bred effort to disguise his contempt. None of these objects could be used in his own tribal ceremonies, so they were useless – and ugly. He was like a die-hard admirer of representational painting asked to comment on the work of, say, Bracque. The point was that his own work, which both Warren and I readily accepted as great negroid art, was as exaggerated and distorted in its own way as were all the rest in this book: except of course that all these diversions from purely representational portraiture had some quasi-sacred meaning for him. Warren had managed to buy a single mask from this man. He had made it to be worn by a woman leader of society, who for some reason had not taken delivery. The mask was kept out of sight, covered with

68

a cloth. It was dangerous because it was sacrilegious to have it in the house, and it was destined for an American museum unless the Liberian Government suddenly decided to clamp down on the export of works of art – which this certainly was.

The village of the mask-carver was the cleanest 'native' village I have ever seen in any part of the world, as well as being very much cleaner than the average village of southern Europe. Silver sand had been laid between the neatly woven huts, and there were receptacles into which litter – including even fallen leaves – had to be put. While I was there a tremendous hullabaloo arose because a stranger from another village had relieved himself in a near-by plantation instead of taking the trouble to go to the proper latrine creek in the bush. This was an exceedingly grave offence by Liberian country standards. The man was haled before the town chief, and as he had no money and therefore couldn't be fined on the spot, he was sentenced to ignominious expulsion from the village – a sentence which was carried out by a concourse of jeering children.

It was in this village too that I heard the eerie sound of the head woman bush-devil coming out of the sacred bush for a rare public appearance. We could hear the cries of her female attendants, first faint and then coming closer, as she came down the jungle path leading to the village, and a neighbour popped in to tell us that she was on her way to supervise the clearing of a creek by the women's society. Then something happened and she failed to appear. Perhaps she had been informed of the insalubrious presence of a stranger in the village, and we heard the warning cries of her attendants grow fainter again, and then stop. The men pretended to be relieved. The devil's attendants act as female lectors, and administer mild beatings to anyone who happens to cross their path.

It was while I was in Liberia that an economic use in the modern scheme of things was found for the bush-devil, and the sophisticates of Monrovia were as happy as if they had hit upon a method of extracting cash from some previously discarded industrial by-product.

Liberia possesses two predominant flourishing industries: rubber, and the mining of the extremely high-grade iron ore. Business heads on the look-out for further sources of national income recently thought of the tourist trade, which has been the economic salvation of far less viable countries than Liberia, and there was some talk even of developing tourism as a third industry. Accordingly plans were laid, and in March this year Monrovia received its first visit from a cruising liner, the *Bergensfjord*, a luxury Norwegian ship carrying 350 passengers, most of whom appeared from the passenger list to be presidents of U.S. banks and insurance companies, and their womenfolk.

Unfortunately the *Bergensfjord* docked on a Sunday, which in Monrovia is surrendered to a zealous nonconformist inactivity, the silence only disturbed by the chanting of hymns and the nostalgic quaver of harmoniums in mission halls. The town was shut up – 'like a clam' – as the *Listener* put it. Liberia's new industry was in danger of dying stillborn, when someone thought of the bush-devils, and a few fairly tame and unimportant ones were hastily sent for. Even when the tourists finally landed, the situation was in the balance. Although they had already been given handbills describing the traditional Liberian entertainment that awaited them, they found their path barred by a large and determined matron in a picture hat who was determined to protect them from such pagan spectacles as they had been promised. When asked where the devil-dancing was to take place she smiled indulgently and said, 'In Liberia we do not dance on Sunday. We remember the Sabbath day, to keep it holy.' She would then recommend various places of interest which might be visited by taxi, such as the Capitol building, the lighthouse, the near-by Spriggs Payne airfield, and the Trinity Pro-cathedral.

Most of the passengers succeeded in escaping the clutches of this well-intentioned lady, and led by an organizer of the Bureau of Folklore in a jeep, they were taken in a taxi-caravan to the vacant lot behind a garage, where the dancing was to take place. There were half a dozen assorted devils in not very good masks and all-concealing mantles of raffia, and three little bare-breasted girls who had just finished their initiation and who, despite the presence of a mob of camera-brandishing tourists, were still plainly timid of the devils. It all went off very well. The little girls did a rapid, sprightly dance, and the devils whirled and somersaulted diabolically in their manes and skirts of flying raffia. When the dancers stopped, the tourists clapped enthusiastically. They lined the girls up, took close-up portraits of them with miniature cameras, asked them their ages, shook hands, and gave them silver coins.

Next morning the Liberian Press wallowed in its usual self-criticism. Hadn't the town's lights failed and the telephone system gone dead last time a distinguished party of foreigners, headed by none other than Vice-President Nixon, had visited Monrovia? There were stories of tourists being carried off on enormous purposeless drives by taxi-drivers who didn't understand English and who charged them extortionate fares, and of others stuck in the City Hotel's Spanish lift. 'We did it again', wailed the *Listener*. ' ... Here was a chance to impress some of these big business tycoons and draw their capital here some day – but we did it again.'

In the paper's next edition, however, the situation wasn't looking quite so black. The wife of a president of a Boston safe deposit and trust company was reported to have said she loved the country and wanted to come back. Liberia's latest industry had got off to a hesitant start perhaps, but at least it was on the move.

A Letter from Belize

SOMEONE in Merida said that a good way to go to Belize was from Chetumal in south-east Mexico by a plane known in those parts as 'El Insecto', that did the twice-weekly run. My informant pointed out that this route was cheaper and more direct than going via Guatemala, as well as giving anyone the chance to get away from the insipidities of air travel with the big international lines. I agreed with him, and went down to Chetumal on a veteran D.C.3 that was the last surviving plane of a small tattered fleet once possessed by this particular company. Chetumal turned out to be a nicely painted-up little town with a wonderful prison, like a Swedish sanatorium. There were seven people at the airport seeing other people off for every one that was travelling, and going through the customs and emigration was a purely family affair. I found 'El Insecto', which was a four-seated Cessner, in a field full of yellow daisies, and helped the pilot to pull it out on to the runway. When it took off he leaned across me to make sure that the door was properly shut. There were a few cosy rattles in the cabin, of the kind that most cars develop after some years of honourable service. These added to the pleasantly casual feeling of the trip. Duplicate controls wavered a foot or two from the tip of my nose, and the pilot cautioned me against taking hold of them to steady myself in an air pocket. 'These small planes take more flying than an airliner,' he said. But apart from fiddling with the throttle lever, probably out of pure habit, and an occasional dab at the joystick, he did nothing to influence our course as we wobbled on through the air currents.

Beneath, the not very exuberant forest of the Orange Walk district of British Honduras unrolled itself. As the Cessner flew at about 2000 feet, the details were clear enough. Even birds were visible. A pair of flamingos parted company like a torn flag, and a collection of white maggots, that were egrets, were eating into the margins of a pool. We were following the coastline, a mile or two inland, with the horizons wrapped up in turbans of cumulus cloud, and a few white thorns of fishing-boats' sails sticking up through the sea's surface. Approaching Belize, swamps began to lap through the dull, dusty green of the jungle. They were gaudy with stagnation; sulphurous yellows, vitriolic greens and inky blues stirred together like badly mixed dyes in a vat. The pilot pointed out some insignificant humps, and thickenings in the forest's texture. These were Mayan remains; root-shattered pyramids and temples. Around them would lie the undisturbed tombs, the skeletons in their jade ornaments. The pilot estimated that only ten per cent of these sites had ever been interfered with.

The airport at Belize was negatively satisfying. There were no machines selling anything, playing anything, or changing money. Nor were there any curios, soft drinks or best-sellers in sight. Under a notice imparting un-interesting information about the colony's industries, a nurse waited, ready to pop a thermometer into the mouth of each incoming passenger. The atmosphere was one of somnolent rectitude. A customs officer, as severely aloof as a voodoo priest, ignored my luggage, which was taken over by a laconic taxi-driver, who opened the door of his car with a spanner and nodded to me to get in. We drove off at a startling pace down a palmetto-fringed road, by a river that was full of slowly moving, very green water. Presently the road crossed the river over an iron bridge, and the driver stopped the car. Winding down the window he put out his head and peered down with silent concentration at the water. Although he made no comment, I subsequently learned that he was probably admiring a thirty-foot-long saw-fish, which lived on the river bed at this spot, and was claimed locally to be the largest of its species recorded anywhere in the world.

From a view of its outskirts Belize promised to live up to the romantic picture I had formed of it in my imagination. There were the wraiths of old English thatched cottages (a class of structure pleasantly known in Belize as 'trash'), complete with rose gardens with half the palings missing from the fences. Some of their negro occupants were to be seen shambling about aimlessly, and others had fallen asleep in the attitudes of victims of murder plots. Pigeons and vultures huddled amicably about the roofs. Notices on gates which hung askew from single rusty hinges warned the world at large to beware of non-existent dogs.

Disillusionment came a few minutes later when we pulled up at the hotel. Here it was that I realized that what information I had succeeded in collecting about Belize before leaving England was out of date. According to an account published in the most recent book dealing with this part of the world, the single hotel had possessed all the seedy glamour one might have looked for in such a remote and reputedly neglected colonial possession. But I had arrived eighteen months too late. Newcomers are now conducted, without option, to a resplendent construction of the kind for which basic responsibility must rest with Frank Lloyd Wright – a svelte confection of pinkish ferro-concrete, artfully simple, and doubtless earthquake-resistant. As the Fort George turned out to serve good strong English tea, as the waiter didn't expect to be tipped after each meal, and as you could leave your shoes outside the bedroom door to be cleaned without their being stolen, there were – even from the first – no possible grounds for complaint. But it soon became clear that besides these considerable virtues the Fort George had many secondary attractions which peeped out shyly as the days went by. Little by little the rich, homely, slightly dotty savour of British Honduras seeped through its protective walls to reach me. I began to take a collector's pride in such small frustrations as the impossibility of getting a double whisky served in one glass. Two single whiskies always came. Also, the architectural pretensions were much relieved by such pleasing touches as the show-cases in the vestibule which displayed, along with a fine Mayan incense-burner in the form of a grotesque head, a few pink antlers of coral, odd-shaped roots, horns carved into absurd birds and a detachable pocket made of pink shells, recommended as 'a chic addition to the cocktail frock'.

Part of the Fort George's charm arose from the fact that the staff, who spoke among themselves a kind of creole dialect, sometimes had difficulty in understanding a guest's requirements. This went with a certain weakness in internal liaisons, and from the operation of these two factors arose many delightfully surrealistic incidents. At any hour of the night, for example, one might be awakened by a maid bearing a raw potato on a silver tray, or be presented with four small whiskies, a bottle of aspirins and a picture postcard of the main façade of the Belize fish market, dated 1904. The Fort George, incidentally, must be one of the very few hotels in the

A Letter from Belize

world where the manager is prepared to supply to order, and without supplementing the all-in charge, such local delicacies as roast armadillo, tapir or paca – the last-mentioned being a large edible rodent, in appearance something between a rabbit and a pig, whose flesh costs more per pound than any other variety offered for sale in the market. Of these exotic specialities I was only able to try the paca, and can report that, as usual in the case of such rare and sought-after meats, the flavour was delicate to the point of non-existence. The fascination of life at the Fort George grew steadily. It was a place where any beginner could have gone to get his basic training in watching the world go by, and many an hour I spent there, over a cold beer and the free plateful of lobster that always came with it, listening to the slap of the pelicans as they hit the water, while doves the size of sparrows fidgeted through the flowering bushes all round, and the rich Syrian – part of the human furniture of such places – drove his yellow Cadillac endlessly up and down the deserted hundred yards of the Marine Parade.

Among the many self-deprecatory reports sponsored by the citizens of Belize is one that their town was built upon a foundation of mahogany chips and rum bottles. True enough the mahogany, which is the principal source of the colony's income, is everywhere. It is a quarter of the price of the cheapest pitch-pine sold any-where else, and everything from river barges to kitchen tables is made from it. Local taste, however, which has become contemptuous of a too familiar beauty, prefers to conceal the wood, where possible, beneath a layer of fibre-glass, or patterned linoleum. As for the rum, it costs thirty-five cents a bottle, tastes of ether, and is seriously recommended by local people as an application

for dogs suffering from the mange. It is drunk strictly
within British licensing hours, which take no account of
tropical thirst, and plays its essential part in the rhythm
of sin and atonement in the lives of a people with a nonconformist tradition and too much time on their hands.

Although of almost pure negroid stock, the citizens of
Belize have succeeded in creating a pattern of society –
if due allowance is made for their economic limitations –
modelled with remarkable fidelity upon that of their
colonial overlords. From their vociferous nonconformity,
as well as the curiously Welsh accent underlying the local
creole, it is tempting to theorize that the lower-grade
colonials they come most in contact with hailed from
the Principality, and in Belize it is sometimes possible to
imagine oneself in a district of Cardiff settled by coloured
people. The evangelism of the chronically depressed area
flourishes. There is always a chapel just round the corner,
commercial enterprises give themselves such titles as The
Holy Redeemer Credit Union, and one is constantly confronted by angry notices urging repentance and the
adoption of the Good Life. Even the prophetic books are
unable to supply enough warning texts to satisfy the
Honduran appetite for admonition. An eating-house,
which advertises the excellence of its cow-heel, observes
enigmatically at the foot of its list of plats du jour, 'The
soul, like the body, lives on what it feeds.' Not, by the
way, that one Englishman in fifty thousand has ever
tasted cow-heel – a variety of soup which as far as I know
is indigenous to the neighbourhood of Liverpool, in the
country of its origin. This was only one of a number of
intriguing gastronomic survivals: 'savoury duck' – a rude
but vigorous forefather of the hamburger, once eaten in
Birmingham; 'spotted-dick' – rolled suet-pudding containing raisins; 'toad-in-the-hole' – sausages baked in

A Letter from Belize

batter: both the latter dishes once a feature of popular
eating-houses all over England, but now disregarded.

One constantly stumbles upon relics of provincial
Britain preserved in the embalming fluid of the Honduran way of life, and often what has been taken over
from the mother country is strikingly unsuitable in its
new surroundings. The minor industries, for instance,
such as boat-building, are carried on in enormous
wooden sheds, the roofs of which are supported by the
most complicated system of interlacing beams and girders
I have ever seen. One thinks immediately of hurricanes,
but on second thoughts it is clear that all this reinforce-
ment would be valueless against the lateral thrust of a
high wind. It turns out that such buildings were copied
from originals put up by Scottish immigrants, and were
designed to withstand the snow-loads imposed by the
severest northern storms.

Many of the Scotsmen themselves lie buried in the
city's cemeteries, both of which are located in the middle
of wide roads, just where in Latin America the living
would have taken their nightly promenade in formal
gardens. Many of the dead, the inscriptions tell us, were
sea-captains. They came here to die of fever, or were
sometimes murdered, and in this case the inscription
supplies the exact time of the tragedy, but no more than
this and an affirmation of the victim's hope of immortal-
ity. The tombstones serve conveniently for the drying of
the washing of the neighbours on both sides of the road.
It is not a bad place at all to lie, for those who were confident of the body's resurrection – by the white houses,
and the lemon-striped telegraph poles, with the constant
bustle and chatter of bright-eyed crows in the trees above,
and the eternal British-Sunday-afternoon strumming of
a piano in a chapel just down the road.

79

The Changing Sky

Death took these captains by surprise. It was never old age or a wasting sickness, but always the mosquito or the dagger that struck them down. No Britisher ever wanted to lay his bones anywhere but in the graveyard of his own parish church in the home country. In this lies the key to all the unsoundable differences between the Spanish and the British colonies. The Spaniard took Spain with him. The Briton was always an exile, living a provisional and makeshift existence, even creating for himself a symbol of impermanence in his ramshackle wooden house.

One of the first things that strike the newcomer to Belize who has seen anything of life in the West Indies is the mysterious absence of anything that might come under the heading of having a good time. There are no calypsos, no ash-can orchestras, no jungle drums, no half-frantic voodoo devotees gyrating round some picturesque mountebank. The Hondurans sacrifice no cocks to the old African gods, and feuds are settled by interminable lawsuits or swift machete blows, but in either case without recourse to the black magic of the obeahman. This in some ways is a pity, because by virtue of the fact that timber extraction, the main occupation, ceases with the wet season, people are left with several months to fill in, and with not the faintest idea of what to do with themselves, apart from chapel-going, playing dominoes, and suffering the afflictions of love. This highly un-African existence, with its complete ineptitude for self-entertainment, is probably the result of certain historical factors. The colony was founded by an English buccaneer called Wallace – Belize is a corruption of his name – who turned from piracy to the more dependable profits of logwood extraction. The slave-owning Wallace and his

successors were very few in number. They were exposed
to frequent attacks by the warlike Indians of southern
Yucatan, and to the constant threat of action by the
Spanish, who never recognized the legality of their settlement. The interlopers could only hope to defend themselves, and to keep their foothold, by arming their slaves,
who would certainly have taken the first opportunity of
pistolling their masters in the back, had their servitude
been unduly oppressive. In those days the English in
Jamaica produced a formidable breed of mastiff which
they trained not only to track down but to devour black
runaways, and such dogs were in great demand in the
neighbouring French and Dutch colonies. One supposes
that the atrocious treatment meted out to the blacks
whose masters felt themselves secure from outside attack
had the effect of drawing them together in their com-
pounds, conserving all that was African in their lives, and
united in their hate for all that was white. Meanwhile
the negroes of Belize, with their musketry drill, their
smallholdings and their Sunday holidays, would have
been encouraged to turn their backs on their African past
and to struggle ever onwards and upwards towards the
resplendent human ideal of the suburban Englishman.

The test of this democracy *malgré-soi* came on September 10th, 1798, when a Spanish flotilla commanded by
Field-Marshal Arthur O'Neil, Captain-General of Yucatan, appeared off Belize. The field-marshal was carrying
orders to liquidate the settlement once and for all, and
the baymen, as the English settlers called themselves,
being forewarned, mustered their meagre forces for the
defence. Reading of the remarkable disparity in the
opposing forces one realizes that here was the making
of one of those occasions that are the very lifeblood of
romantic history. The captain-general's fleet consisted of

thirty-one vessels carrying 2000 troops and 500 seamen.
The defenders numbered one naval sloop, five small trading
or fishing vessels hastily converted for warlike purposes,
plus seven rafts, each mounting one gun and manned by
slaves – a total defensive force of 350 men. The resultant
passage of arms has provoked a fair measure of armchair
blood-thirst, flag-waving, and orotund speechifying on
the annual public holiday which has commemorated it.
In 1923 a Mr Rodney A. Pitts wrote a prize-winning
poem called 'The Baymen', an ode in thirty-one verses,
which, set to music, has become a kind of local national
anthem. A sample stanza plunges us into an horrific
scene of carnage:

> Ah, Baymen, Spaniards, on that day
> Engaging in that fierce mêlée –
> Ah, never such a sight before,
> They are all dyed in human gore –
> Exhausted, wounded, some are dead,
> They're sunken to their gory bed.

The cold facts of the case, supplied by contemporary
records, paint a less murderous picture of the encounter.
There were no casualties whatever on the British side, in
an engagement which lasted two and a half hours, and
the few bodies interred later by the Spanish on one of the
cays were as likely to have been those of fever victims
as of grapeshot casualties. One thinks of the dolorous
quavering of generations of school-children through such
passages as:

> All died that this land which by blood they acquired
> Might give you that freedom their brave hearts inspired.

As usual, history turns out to be a fable agreed upon.

A Letter from Belize

Modern times have brought with them a slackening in the idyllic master-and-faithful-serving-man relationship of the past. A People's United Party has emerged, whose aim is total independence for British Honduras, and which, by way of a kind of psychological preparation for this end, urges the substitution of baseball for cricket, and the abolition of tea-drinking. The party's creator and leader is a Mr Richardson, a wealthy creole – as citizens of non-white origin are officially described. Mr Richardson's antipathy for Britannia and all her works supposedly originates in a grievance over some matter of social recognition – a familiar colonial complaint, and one that has cost Britain more territory than all her other imperial shortcomings put together. When recently the Government of Guatemala renewed its claim to Belize, the outside world speculated on the possibility of the P.U.P. operating as a fifth column in support of the Guatemalan irredentists. The answer to this, I was told, is best expressed by the local proverb, 'Wen cakroche [cockroach] mek dance 'e no invite fowl.'

The party's official organ, the *Belize Billboard*, is a journalistic collector's item, combining the raciness of a scurrilous broadsheet with the charm of a last-century shipping gazette. It is particularly strong on crime-reporting, pokes out its tongue at the British whenever it can, and carefully commemorates the anniversaries of such setbacks in the nation's story as the sinking of the Ark Royal. It is regarded with sincere affection by the white members of the colony, many of whom keep scrapbooks bulging with choice examples of its Alice-in-Wonderland prose – full of such words as 'doxy' and 'paramour'. The trade winds blow right through the advertisement section of the *Billboard*, with its bald details of goods 'newly arrived', as if they had been listed in order

83

of unloading on to the quayside: clay pipes, lamp chimneys, apricot bats (?), Exma preparations for the bay sore and ground itch, beating spoons, cinnamon sticks, bridal satin, colonial blue-mottled soap and – in the month of March – Christmas cards. Dropped like a dash of curry into this assortment from the hold of a ghost ship are the announcements of the Hindu gentleman with an accommodation address in Bombay who promises with the aid of his white pills to add six inches to your height, 'if not over eighty'.

In whatever direction the political destiny of Belize may lie, its economic future is dubious. In the past it has depended upon its forests, but ruinous over-exploitation in the half of the total land area of the colony which is privately owned has depleted this source of income and seriously mortgaged the future. The logical remedy would seem to lie in the switching over of the colony's economy to an agricultural basis. But it seems that the rhythm of seasonal, semi-nomadic work in the forest, sustained for centuries, has created what a government handbook politely describes as 'an ingrained restlessness'. In other words the Hondurans tend to become bored with a job that looks like being too steady.

The eventual solution to this problem probably lies in the tourist industry, with a glamourized and air-conditioned Belize emerging as another Caribbean playground of the industrial north – and anyone who has seen what has happened to the north coast of Jamaica in the last year or two will know what to expect. All the ingredients for a colonial Cinderella story are present. Being just beyond the reach of the Cuban and Mexican fishing fleets the Bay of Honduras is probably richer in fish – including all the spectacular and inedible ones pursued by sportsmen – than any other accessible area in the northern hemisphere. The average aficionado will lose all the tackle he can afford in a week's tussle with the enormous tarpon to be found in the river running through Belize town itself. The forests, too, abound with strange and beautiful animals, with tapir, jaguars and pygmy deer, which await extermination by the smoothly organized hunting parties of the future. The Fort George, with its deep freeze, and its swimming pool in course of construction, marks the closing of an era. I was given to understand that even this year a tourist organization calling itself The Conquistadors' Caravan was dickering with the possibility of including Belize in one of its 'Pioneer Conquistadors' itineraries, and was dissuaded only by the news that there was no night-club, no air-conditioning anywhere, no Mayan ruins within comfortable reach, absolutely no beach, and that jaguars' tracks are seen most mornings on the golf course. May other travel agents read these words and be equally dismayed.

In the meanwhile, for the collector of geographical curiosities, there is still time, although probably not much time, to taste the pleasures of a Caribbean sojourn in the manner of the last century. As a matter of fact I cannot think of any better place for someone seized with a weariness of the world to retire to in Gauguin fashion, than Belize. The intelligent recluse could even protect himself from the chagrins of the tourist era to come by renting an island, which can be had complete with bungalow and bedrock conveniences, for a few dollars a week. Here he would be in a position to knock down his own coconuts, ride on turtles, collect the eggs of boobies in season, put on a pair of diving-goggles and pick all the lobsters he could eat out of the shallow lagoon water, perhaps even note in his journal the visit of a transient alligator. Each time he crossed to the mainland to collect supplies or to see an appalling Mexican film his eye would be delighted by the prospect of Belize from the sea, resembling an aquatint from a book I possess descriptive of Jamaica published in 1830. It shows white houses with pink roofs, lying low among the thick, mossy trees; listless figures gathered at the base of an elegant, tapering lighthouse; fishing boats asprawl in the heavy water at the harbour's mouth; a few frigate birds hanging meditatively in the lemon sky that often precedes a fine sunset.

The reverse side of the medal is hardly worth mentioning. The drains *are* uncovered, but there are no mosquitoes, not much infectious disease, only an occasional plague of locusts, and for nine months of the year the heat keeps within bounds. Perhaps the hazard of the occasional hurricane should be touched upon. The last bad one blew up on September 10th, 1931, the anniversary of the naval victory of 1798; a twenty-foot-high wall of water rolled over the town, and swept the houses off the cays, and a high percentage of the death-roll of a thousand were merry-makers who were celebrating the famous victory. But taken over the years, hurricanes are a very minor risk. And while on the topic of winds, it might be considered reasonable, from an intending resident's viewpoint, to bear in mind that however hard they may blow, they do so from a remarkably consistent direction, and that this direction, that of the Atlantic Ocean wastes, is not one in which a cloud of radio-active particles is ever likely to originate.

A Quiet Evening in
Huehuetenango

IN the bleak depths of an interminable English winter
a few years ago I was suddenly seized with an almost
physical craving to write a novel having as its background
the tropical jungles and volcanoes of Central America.
Having succeeded in persuading my publishers that this
would be a good thing from both our points of view I
boarded a plane at London Airport one morose evening in
January, and two days later I was in Guatemala City. I
chose Guatemala because I had been there before and
knew something about it, but also because all that one
thinks of as typical of the Central-American scene –
primitive Indians, Mayan ruins, the wrecks of grandiose
Spanish colonial cities – is found there in the purest
concentration.

For three weeks I did my best to absorb some of the
atmosphere of life in seedy banana ports of the Caribbean
and the Pacific, where bored men in big hats still
occasionally pull guns on each other. I went hunting in
jungles said to abound with jaguars and tapir without
shooting anything more impressive than a species of
giant rat. I talked with wily politicians of the country,
survivors of half a dozen revolutions, and took tea with
exiled fellow-countrymen on isolated coffee plantations,
who had lived so long among the Indians that they sometimes stopped in mid-sentence to translate their very
proper English sentiments from the Spanish in which
they now thought into their native language.

My final trip was to the far north of the country, the

remote and mountainous area beyond Huehuetenango, which lies just south of the Mexican state of Chiapas and is reached after three hundred miles of infamous roads and stupendous scenery. Here under the Cuchumatanes, the ultimate peaks of Guatemala, even the onslaught of the Spanish Conquistadors faltered and collapsed. And here the mountain tribes were finally left in peace, to live on in the harsh but free existence of the Stone Age, touched only by the outward forms of Christianity, consoled in secret by the ancient gods, and rejecting with all their might all the overtures of Western civilization.

In the early afternoon of the fourth day, my taxi, driven by a town Indian from Guatemala City called Calmo, reached the top of the 12,000-foot pass overlooking the valley of Huehuetenango. We stopped here to let the engine cool, and noticing that the trees in this wind-swept place were covered with orchids, I astounded Calmo by suggesting we should pick some. 'Flowers?' he said. 'Where? They don't grow at this height!' I stumbled, weak and breathless from the altitude, up the hillside towards an oak, loaded with vermilion-flowered bromeliads. 'Ah,' he said, 'you mean the *parasitos*. Well, certainly, if you like, sir. When you said flowers, I didn't realize ... We call these weeds – tree-killers.' Calmo was not only an intrepid driver, but a qualified guide supplied by the State Tourist Office. He spoke a version of English which so effectively stripped the meaning from his remarks that I steered him back to Spanish whenever I could. For the rest, he was gentle, sad-looking and pious, dividing his free time between visits to churches and – although well into middle life – running after girls.

We got into Huehuetenango at four in the afternoon, and it turned out to be an earthquake town, with corrugated-iron roofs on fine churches, squat houses iced

88

over with multicoloured stuccoes, and a great number of pubs having such names as 'I Await Thee on Thy Return'. We went into one of these, each of us carrying an armful of orchids, Calmo probably hoping that no one he knew would see him bothering himself with such contemptible weeds. The woman who brought the beer had a Mayan face, flat-featured but handsome, and full of inherited tragedy. Calmo told her in his most dignified way, 'This I say with all sincerity. I want to come back to this place and marry you.' The woman said, 'Ah bueno,' shaking off the compliment as if an invisible fly had settled on her cheek. She wore a massive wedding ring, and there were several children about the floor.

After that, Calmo wanted to go into the cathedral to pray for success in that week's lottery. The cathedral had just been freshly decorated for the pre-Lenten festival with huge bouquets of imitation flowers, their stiff petals varnished, and dusted over with powdered glass. Indians were lighting candles among the little separate patches of red and white blossoms they had spread out on the flags to symbolize the living and the dead. Hundreds of candles glimmered in the obscurity of the cleared space where the Indians worship in their own way in the Christian churches, grouped in whispering semicircles round the candles, while their *shamans* pass from group to group, swinging incense-burners and muttering magical formulas. The Indians were dressed in the frozen fashions of the early sixteenth century; the striped breeches of Castillian peasants, the habits of the first few Franciscans who had scaled the heights to reach their villages, the cod-pieces of Alvarado's ferocious soldiery. They had left their babies hidden in the old people's care in the mountain caves, still remembering the days before the conquest, when at this season the rain god had taken the children for his annual sacrifice. These Indians were still surrounded by a world of magic and illusion, living characters in a Grimm's fairy-tale of our day in which the whites they see when they come down to the towns are enchanters and werwolves, who can kill with a glance, but are themselves immortal.

We went out into the sunshine again. A meteorite shower of parakeets fell screeching across the patch of sky stretched over the plaza. Soldiers, shrunken away in their American uniforms, were fishing in space with their rifles over the blood-red balustrade of the town hall, which was also their barracks. The green bell in the cathedral tower clanked five times, and the sleepers on the stone benches stirred a little in the vast shade of their sombreros. Calmo woke up an ice-cream vendor, bought a cornet, then said, 'I cannot eat it. The hot for my teeth is too great.' When speaking English he found special difficulty in distinguishing between opposites such as cold and hot.

We sat down in the car to decide what to do with the evening. The sleepiness of the place was beginning to paralyse us. Nothing stirred but the vultures waving their scarves of shadow over the flower beds. Calmo said, 'Yesterday a market-day, tomorrow a procession; so that today we have no prospect but an early night. There is really nothing to do.' As he spoke, a man came riding into the plaza on a tall, bony horse. The man looked like an Englishman on his way to a fancy-dress ball: he was lean, pink-cheeked, mildly aloof of expression, and his improbable costume of black leather with silver facings had clearly been hired out too often and was on the loose side for its present wearer. He was carrying a bundle of what looked like yard-brooms wrapped up in coloured paper. Calmo explained that these would be rockets for use in the next day's celebrations. The clip-clop of the hooves died away, and the silence came down like a drop-curtain. Huehuetenango was a place of apathetic beauty, built out of the ruin of a devastated Indian city. There was a sadness, a sense of forgotten tragedy in the air; and here it seemed that silence was a part of the natural condition. As Calmo had so often said, 'We Indians are a reserved people. Even in our fiestas. Our joys and our weepings are hidden away inside: for us only, you understand – not for the world.'

There was a notice over the hotel door that said, 'Distinction, Atmosphere and Sympathy'. The atmosphere was all-pervasive. The garden had been turned into a floral jungle encircled by borders of Pepsi-Cola bottles stuck neck-down in the earth. Quite ordinary flowers like stocks and hollyhocks were throttling each other in a savage struggle for living space, and humming-birds like monstrous bees zoomed about the agonized sea of blossom. Goldfish bowls containing roses hideously pickled in preserving fluid, stood on every table-top. The bedroom towels were embroidered with the words, 'Sleep My Beloved'.

Food in this hotel was *American Plan* – words which have now been accepted into the Spanish vocabulary of Central America and no longer refer to the system of charging for accommodation inclusive of meals, but describe a special kind of food itself – the hygienic but emasculated fare supposed to be preferred by American visitors, and now generally adopted on the strength of what are believed to be its medicinal and semi-magical properties. This time *American Plan* meant tinned soup, spaghetti, boiled beef and Californian peaches. The whole loaf of bread and a half-pound of butter of a generation ago had wasted away to two slices of toast and a pat of margarine. The milk was the product of Contented Cows, served in the original tin as a guarantee of the absence of dangerous freshness. We got through the boring ritual of dinner as soon as we could. The other guests – business men drawn from the elite ten per cent of pure white stock – were still inclined to congratulate one another on the downfall of the last government, which had not been approved of in commercial circles. 'A minimum wage. And why not? – I'd be the first. But when all's said and done, friends, what happens when you give an Indian more than 40 cents for a day's work? You know as well as I do. He doesn't show up the next day – that's all. They've got to be educated up to it.'

After dinner I resigned myself to an early evening, and went to bed under a religious picture consisting of an eye projecting rays in all directions, and beneath it the question: 'What is a moment of pleasure weighed in the scales against an eternity of punishment?' I had hardly dozed off when I was awakened by an explosion. I got up and opened the window. The street had filled up with people who were all going in the same direction and chattering excitedly. A siren wailed and a motor-cycle policeman went past deafeningly, snaking in and out of the crowd. There was another explosion, and as this was the homeland of revolutions it was natural to assume that one had started. I dressed and went out into the court-yard, where the hotel boy was throwing a bayonet at an anatomical chart given away with a Mexican journal devoted to home medicine. The boy said that so far as he knew there had been no *pronunciamento*, and the bangs were probably someone celebrating his saint's day. I then remembered the lean horseman.

A Quiet Evening in Huehuetenango

As the tumult showed no signs of abating I walked down to the plaza, which had filled up with blank-faced Indians moving slowly round in an anti-clockwise direction as if stirred up by some gigantic invisible spoon. There were frequent scuffles and outcries as young men singled out girls from the promenading groups and broke coloured eggs on their heads, rubbing the contents well into the thick black hair. The eggs were being sold by the basketful all over the plaza, and they turned out to have been emptied, refilled with some brittle, wafer-like substance, repaired and then painted. When a girl sometimes returned the compliment, the gallant thus favoured stopped to bow, and said: 'Muchas gracias.'

Calmo, whom I soon ran into, his jacket pockets bulging with eggs, said it looked as if there were going to be a fiesta after all. He couldn't think why. There was really no excuse for it. The fashionable town-Indians, most of them shopkeepers, had turned out in all their finery, headed by the 'Queen of Huehuetenango' herself – a splendidly beflounced creature with ribbon-entwined pig-tails down to her thighs, who was said to draw her revenues from a *maison de rendezvous* possessing radio-active baths. There was a sedate sprinkling of whites, hatted and begloved for the occasion.

Merchants had put up their stalls and were offering sugar skulls, holy pictures, plastic space-guns, and a remedy for heart-sickness which is a speciality of Huehue-tenango and tastes like inferior port. We found the lean horseman launching his rockets in military fashion from a wooden rack-like contraption. They were aimed so as to hiss as alarmingly low as possible over the heads of the crowds, showering them with sparks, and sometimes they cleared the building opposite and sometimes they did not. Other enthusiasts were discharging *mortaretes*, miniature

93

flying bombs, which leaped two or three hundred feet straight up into the air before exploding with an ear-stunning crack. The motor-cycle policeman on his scarlet Harley-Davidson with wide-open exhaust, and eight front and six rear lights, came weaving and bellowing round the plaza at intervals of about a minute, and a travelling movie-show was using part of the cathedral's baroque façade as the screen for a venerable Mexican film called *Ay mi Jalisco* featuring a great deal of gun-play.

A curious hollow structure looking like a cupola sliced in half had been built on the top of the town hall, and about this time powerful lights came on in its interior and nine sad-faced men in dark suits entered it by an invisible door, carrying what looked like several grand pianos. A moment later these pieces of furniture had been placed end to end to form an enormous marimba, under an illuminated sign that said 'Musica Civica'. A cosmic voice coughed electrically and then announced that in response to the esteemed public's many requests the municipal orchestra would have pleasure in rendering a selection of notable composers' works. Eighteen hammers then came down on the keys with a resounding opening flourish, and the giant marimba raced into an athletic version of 'If You Were the Only Girl in the World'.

Calmo and I took refuge from the torrent of sound in a tavern called The Little Chain of Gold. It was a place of great charm containing a shrine and a newly installed juke-box in addition to the usual accessories, and was decorated with beautiful calendars given away by Guate-malan bus companies and a couple of propaganda pictures of mutilated corpses put out by the new government after the last revolution. The Little Chain advertised the excellence of its 'hots-doogs'. Most of its customers were

A Quiet Evening in Huehuetenango

preparados Indians who had done military service and had rejected their tribal costumes in favour of brightly coloured imitations of American army uniforms. Some of them added a slightly sinister touch to their gay ensembles of reds and blues by covering the lower part of their faces with black cloths, a harmless freak of fashion which I was told had originated in a desire to breathe in as little dust as possible when foot-slogging along the country roads.

Calmo said that the main difference between a preparado and a tribal Indian was that the preparado, who had acquired a civilized taste for whisky, couldn't afford to get drunk so often as an uncivilized drinker of aguardiente.

We drank the aguardiente. It smelt of ether and had a fierce laboratory flavour. Every time the door opened the marimba music pressed on our eardrums. Calmo made an attempt to detain one of the serving girls. 'Don't go away, little treasure, and I'll bring you some flowers from the gardens in the plaza, whatever they fine me.' He received so baleful a stare for his pains that he dropped the girl's hand as if she had bitten him. At last the hour of civic music ran out. From where we sat we saw that the Mexican outlaws had ceased to gallop across the cathedral wall. The crowds had thinned into groups of stubborn drunkards. Calmo was becoming uneasy. 'In my opinion it is better to go. These people are very peace-loving, but when they become drunk they sometimes assassinate each other in places like this. Not for malicious reasons, understand me, but as the result of wagers or to demonstrate the accuracy of their aim with the various fire-arms they possess.'

We paid our bill and had just got up when the door was flung open and three of the toughest-looking desperadoes

95

The Changing Sky

I had ever seen reeled in. These were no shrinking
Indians, but hard-muscled *ladinos*, half-breeds who
carried in their faces all the Indian's capacity for resent-
ment but none of his fear. They wore machetes as big as
naval cutlasses in their belts. For a moment they blocked
the doorway eyeing the company with suspicion and
distaste, then one of them spotted the juke-box, which
was still a rarity in this part of the world. His expression
softened and he made for our table putting each foot down
carefully as if afraid of blundering into quicksands. He
bowed. 'Forgive me for addressing you, sir, but are you
familiar with the method of manipulating the machine
over there?'

I said I was.

'Perhaps then you could inform me whether the
selection of discs includes a marimba?'

I went over to the juke-box. These ladinos, I thought,
would still be living the frontier life of the last century; a
breed of tough, illiterate outcasts, picking up a livelihood
as best they could, smugglers and gunmen if pushed to it,
ready, as it seemed from the frequent newspaper reports,
to hack each other – or the lonely traveller – to pieces for
a few dollars, and yet with it a tremendous, almost deadly
punctiliousness in ordinary matters of social intercourse.
I studied the typewritten list in Spanish. There were
several marimbas. The ladino looked relieved. He con-
ferred in an undertone with the other two fugitives from
justice, came back, bowed again, and handed me a
Guatemalan ten-cent piece. 'If you could induce the
machine to play "Mortal Sin" for us, we should be much
indebted.'

I returned the ladino 5 cents change, found a U.S.
nickel – which is fairly common currency in Guatemala
– and put it in the slot, while the three ladinos edged

A Quiet Evening in Huehuetenango

forward studiously casual, but eager to watch the reptilian mechanical gropings by which their choice was singled out and manœuvred into the playing position. 'Pecado Mortal' turned out to be a rollicking *son* – a kind of paso doble – executed with the desperate energy of which the sad music-makers of Central America are so prodigal. Calmo and I were half-way through the door when I felt a tap on the shoulder. The principal bandit was insisting that we join him for a drink. 'Otherwise, my friends and I would feel hurt, gentlemen.' He laid bare his teeth in a thin, bitter smile. We went back and sat down again. While he was getting the drinks Calmo said, 'In the education of our people the most important thing taught after religion is *urbanidad* – good manners. Even those who have no schooling are taught this. I do not think that we should risk offending these men by showing a desire to leave before they do.'

A moment later our bandit was back with double aguardientes and a palmful of salt for us to lick in the proper manner, between gulps. The music stopped, and his face clouded with disappointment. Behind him a lieutenant loomed, swaying slightly, eyes narrowed like a Mongolian sage peering into the depths of a crystal, mouth tightened by the way life had gone. He was holding a coin. 'Might I trouble you to perform the same service for me, sir?' he asked politely.

It turned out that the second *mestizo* wanted to hear 'Mortal Sin' again. 'It is remarkable,' he said, 'and most inspiring. I do not think it can be bettered.' The three tough hombres moved away uncertainly towards the juke-box again, simple wonderment struggling beneath the native caution of their expressions. The needle crackled in the ruined grooves, and we heard the over-familiar overture of ear-splitting chords. Someone found the

97

volume control and turned it up fully. Every object in the room was united in a tingling vibration. The second bandit drew his machete with the smooth, practised flourish of a Japanese swordsman, and scooped the cork out of a fresh bottle of aguardiente with a twist of its point. Two more members of the band stood waiting, coins in hand.

'Mortal Sin' had been played five times, and we were still chained by the polite usage of Central America to our chairs, still gulping down aguardiente and licking the salt off our palms, when it suddenly occurred to me that it was unreasonable that an electric train should be rumbling through a subway immediately beneath us in Huehuetenango. I got up, grinning politely at our hosts, and, balancing the liquid in my glass, went to the door. The lamps in the plaza jogged about like spots in front of my eyes, and then, coming through the muffled din from The Little Chain of Gold, I heard a noise like very heavy furniture being moved about in uncarpeted rooms somewhere in space. The world shifted slightly, softened, rippled, and there was an aerial tinkling of shattered glass. I felt a brief unreasoning stab of the kind of panic that comes when in a nightmare one suddenly begins a fall into endless darkness. Aguardiente from my glass splashed on my hand, and at that moment all the lights went out and the music stopped with a defeated growl. The door of The Little Chain opened and Calmo and one of the ladinos burst through it into the sudden crisp stillness and the moonlight. Calmo had taken the ladino by the forearm and the shoulder – 'And so my friend we go now to buy candles. Patience – we shall soon return.'

'But in the absence of electricity,' the ladino grumbled sadly, 'the machine no longer functions.'

'Perhaps they will restore the light quickly,' Calmo said.

A Quiet Evening in Huehuetenango

'In that case we shall play the machine again. We will spend the whole night drinking and playing the machine.' The ladino waved in salutation and fell back through the doorway of The Little Chain.

We moved off quickly under the petrified foliage of the plaza. Nothing stirred. The world was solid under our feet again. A coyote barked several times sounding as if it were in the next street, and a distant clock chimed sweetly an incorrect hour.

'A quiet evening,' I remarked. 'With just one small earthquake thrown in.'

'A tremor, not an earthquake,' Calmo said. 'An earthquake must last at least half a minute. This was a shaking of secondary importance.'

There was a pause while he translated his next sentence into English. He then said: 'Sometimes earthquakes may endure for a minute, or even two minutes. In that case it is funny ... No, not funny, I mean very serious.'

Guatemala—The Mystery of the Murdered Dictator

THE coffee-planter I met on the plane to Guatemala
City was wracking his brains over a translation he
was making of Dylan Thomas into the Spanish. Like
many Guatemalans of the land-owning class he had
intellectual leanings. He lived for ten months of the year
in Miami and in Canada, and painted, and wrote a little
poetry. The remaining two months he spent reluctantly
on his estate. He possessed a desolate palace of a house
with one hundred and fifty rooms, of which he spoke with
a kind of horror, and two thousand Indians toiled
with increasing inefficiency in his plantations. The short-
lived Red regime of Jacobo Arbenz, which mercifully had
been squashed by the revolution of 1954, had just about
ruined them, he said. Arbenz had robbed people like him
of their land and parcelled it out to the Indians, and then
when Castillo Armas had taken over, the Indians had
naturally been driven off the land they had occupied,
leaving them surly and recalcitrant ever since. They either
simply refused to work at all, the planter said, or they
pretended to work and went in for cunning forms of
sabotage, such as chopping through the soil to sever the
coffee trees' roots, so that a week or two later the trees
sickened and withered. He had been over to Spain to
sound out the chances of importing cheap and reliable
labour from Europe, but even a Spanish labourer expected
to be paid four or five times as much as an Indian. He
paused for a moment, as we bumped over the volcanic
craters, in the weighing of possible Castillian alternatives

100

for the adjective 'sullen' as applied to art, and said, 'Of course, what we need is a strong man. I don't mean the Castillo Armas type. He was useless. Someone more like Trujillo, who'll stand no nonsense from them. The only trouble is to find one.'

So now, after four hundred years of bowing their necks under the yoke, the shrinking, silent, apathetic survivors of the grandiose Mayan civilization were beginning to fight back with what weapons they could find, and even Castillo Armas – white hope of the reactionaries – who had died so mysteriously in July 1957, had been able to do very little about it! The Indians of Guatemala are a quite extraordinary people. They have survived the slavery and the brandings, the vengeance the Inquisition visited on secret pagans, the brain-washing of their children in special institutions, the enfeeblement of the race by compulsory child-marriage, and in spite of all, they still remain a separate and self-sufficient race, defending the shrunken remnants of their ancient civilization among their mountain-tops. In many remote villages no white man is allowed to stay the night; the priest, if he remains, does so only by Indian toleration, and now they pray openly to the Mayan gods and use the Christian churches for the celebration of their ancestral rites. Where, after generations of striving and scraping, they have managed to buy back a little of their forbears' land, they often live in a kind of aristocratic communism, sharing their produce, but ruled sternly by an hereditary caste of notables and priests. But for all that, whether as peasant communities or as plantation workers, the Indians are beset by crippling poverty – and since two-thirds of the country's population are Indians, this agrarian misery is at the root of all the problems of Guatemala as a nation. There are no roads in the mountains, no doctors, and no schools. The average income of an Indian family is 28 dollars a year. Guatemala was the country of the Conquistadors, where Indians were bred like cattle for labour on huge estates, and here alone, in Central America, these estates have never been broken up. Where foreign investment has been attracted to the country it has gone not into the development of industry, but into coffee and banana plantations, thus only helping to prolong the agrarian coma, the somnolent feudalism of a banana republic. Every Guatemalan who is not a landowner would naturally like to see an end to this state of affairs, and every revolution that has taken place in the last hundred years – and they are innumerable – has basically been the struggle between the landowners, supported by the clerical party, and a frustrated, barely emergent middle class. Nearly always the landowners, strengthened in recent years by the powerful foreign interests, have come out on top. But from 1944 to 1954 there was an interlude in which almost an orgy of social innovation took place: a brief bacchanalia of long-thwarted liberalism which came to an end when the reformers, dizzy with success, but weaker than they imagined themselves to be, began a defiant flirtation with Marxism under the eye of the American Ambassador. The State Department always feels easier when the United States' flanks are covered by 'reliable' men, i.e. men like Trujillo, dictator of the Dominican Republic; and when Jacobo Arbenz, Guatemala's exceedingly unreliable president, tried to lay hands on the United Fruit Company's concession, brought communists into his government, and imported a ship-load of arms from Czechoslovakia, the State Department went into action. Arbenz's successor, Castillo Armas, who led his motley legion of mercenaries and Guatemalan exiles across the border, and then up through the southern jungles to occupy the capital, was the best man that could be found for the job. He was brave – he had survived a firing squad and, wounded as he was, tunnelled his way out of prison to escape into exile. He was supposed to be fanatically anti-Red, and yet somehow he disappointed. Castillo Armas seemed to lack the megalomania of the true dictator. He was almost too quiet and modest, and generally thought to be insufficiently ruthless in action against those designated by the men around him as enemies of the state. Guatemalans of the extreme right wing – who were now on top again – still cherished the image of Ubico, the strong-man of the old school who had reigned, rather than ruled, in Guatemala from 1931 to 1944. Ubico was proud of the fact that people trembled in his presence as he received them seated in a thronelike chair with the word 'DEMOCRACIA' lettered in gold just behind his head. Jorge Ubico ran the country like a farm, and he had a short way with dissenters. Once when his hand-picked congress were a little slow in giving their assent to a concession he was proposing to grant to the United Fruit Company, he rode down to the House at the head of a squadron of dragoons to convince them.

Poor Armas seemed the shadow of a dictator compared with this feudal bully. Not only did he fail to terrify: he was also supposed to have refused to show his gratitude in the usual way to those who had put him in power. Soon there were reports of plots on the president's life. Then one day in July 1957, while walking with his wife along a corridor of the presidential palace, Castillo Armas was shot dead. The official story put out was that the shooting had been done by a palace guard. A diary kept by this young man was produced to show that he was a communist. In this document all the assassin's thoughts and motives were set out in a florid journalistic style, well laced with familiar Marxist jargon. It was published in booklet form, accompanied by an analysis of equal literary turgidity by an eminent Guatemalan psychiatrist. Public doubts about the authenticity of this publication began to be voiced when someone who knew Romeo Vasquez, the presumed assassin, happened to mention that he was an illiterate half-Indian. A more sinister circumstance that strengthened growing disbelief was the sudden disappearance of all the other palace guards who had been on duty at the time of the murder, and who might therefore have been able to throw further light on what had really occurred. An outcry in the Press followed, for a public investigation into the circumstances of the president's death; but this was refused by the Ministry of Justice.

When I arrived in Guatemala in December, a sensational occurrence had just put the assassination of Castillo Armas back in the headlines again. A committee then sitting to investigate the activities of secret agents of the Dominican Republic in Guatemala seemed to be preparing public opinion for the shocking news that Armas had not, after all, been the victim of a Red plot, he had not been shot by Vasquez, the palace guard, and Vasquez had not committed suicide but had been killed by whoever had killed Armas. Although the committee's deliberations were being conducted in secret, a fair amount of the information it had unearthed was finding its way into the papers, and even at that stage the evidence was conclusive enough to warrant a recommendation that diplomatic relations be broken off with the Dominican Republic.

The circumstance that had set off this political explosion had come to be known as the crime of the Mirador.

Guatemala — the Murdered Dictator

The Mirador is a locally famous beauty-spot and vantage-point on the road down from the high mountains into Guatemala City. It is here that the sad, taciturn Indian porters will put down for a moment the enormous burden they have carried for a wage of perhaps 25 cents from villages sometimes days away, to look out over the city below, laid out like a scale model beneath the blue cones of the volcanoes. One night in October two grim men had brought a chauffeur called Carillo to this place, shot him, and then – ineffectually – ran over him. Such a killing, in a country where private vengeances and old political scores are fairly frequently settled by what are known as *hombres de acción*, would have received no publicity at all, but for one fact. Carillo, although terribly injured and left for dead, did not die immediately, and when a police squad-car arrived to deal with what they imagined to be a routine job, Carillo, knowing himself to be dying, whispered certain information to them, of which probably only a fraction has been divulged. Carillo, supposed until that moment to be a perfectly respectable chauffeur, sometimes employed by a tourist agency in the city to show visitors round the sights, told the police that in reality he was, to use the Latin-American euphemism, 'one of those engaged in international services', in other words a secret agent specializing in the arrangement or actual commission of political assassinations. He identified his assailants as two members of the Guatemalan secret police called Gacel and Sandoval, who, he said, were simultaneously agents of the Dominican Republic. Gacel and Sandoval, Carillo said, had received orders to silence him because he knew too much. He may even have told the policemen the exact nature of this secret, the possession of which had condemned him to death. If so, it has never been made public. A police radio-call was immediately put out for the arrest of the two men, and Gacel was picked up a little later while still driving the murder car. The interrogatory methods employed in Central-American countries are well known for their rapid eliciting of the truth, and Gacel soon admitted his guilt, and also implicated the Military Attaché of the Dominican Republic, Abbes Garcia. This diplomat, the newspapers soon noticed, had been involved in a similar crime in Mexico, and had been obliged to leave that country as a result. Gacel told the investigating officers that his particular branch of the secret police had been informed of a request made to the Government of Guatemala by that of Costa Rica to keep Carillo under observation, as he was to be employed in a plot to murder the president of that country, Señor Figueres. Gacel had reported this alarming development to Abbes, his superior in the Dominican secret service, and it was decided that now Carillo's real function had become revealed to the Guatemalan authorities, it was no longer safe to let him live. Here, perhaps, at last, a faintly illuminated pointer shows in this labyrinth of murk and murder. Figueres of Costa Rica is that almost unheard-of figure in Central America – a truly democratic leader. Costa Rica has no army and therefore no swaggering generals, it has no real poverty, and it has the highest standard of literacy as well as the highest proportion of small landowners in Latin America. The mere existence of such a regime constitutes a permanent reproach to such dictatorial regimes as those of Somoza of Nicaragua, Trujillo of the Dominican Republic, and until it suddenly exploded, that of Jimenez of Venezuela. Costa Rica is regarded by them as a plague spot and a breeding-place of political disaffection. Now recently, Castillo Armas, the 'failed' dictator, had shown disturbing signs of drifting into the

Figueres orbit, and not only had he turned his back on the Trujillo-Somoza-Jimenez strong-men's club, he had contemptuously declined to add the Guatemalan Order of the Quetzal to Trujillo's collection of seventy-odd foreign decorations.

Gacel, after producing his revelations, was held at police headquarters while it was considered how best he could be confronted with Abbes, who owing to his diplomatic status was immune from arrest. In the meanwhile life in the city was suddenly thrown violently out of gear by a very typical Central-American upheaval, and for twenty-four hours the police were kept too busy trying to control the rioting crowds to bother with Gacel. The fact was that Gacel's capture had occurred on the eve of polling day, when the caretaker government under a Señor Portillo, which had taken over after Castillo Armas's assassination, was contesting an election with two parties in the opposition. It is alleged that Señor Portillo's supporters had not been able to refrain from manipulating the ballot. They were accused of advising their adherents to cast their votes immediately the polling booths opened, and of then arranging for a shortage of ballot papers. Of the two opposing candidates, one, General Fuentes, appeared to show some promise as the future strong-man that so many Guatemalans – and, it appeared, foreign influences in Guatemala – so earnestly awaited. For several hours after the results were announced General Fuentes's men kicked in shop windows and fired off their pistols, and when things calmed down with an announcement that the elections would be annulled, and the police had time to turn their attention to Gacel again, he had gone. It turned out that while the disturbances were at their height, Colonel Oliva, chief of police of Guatemala, had appeared in person at headquarters and ordered Gacel's release. Both Gacel and the Military attaché Abbes then took off in planes for the Dominican Republic, and shortly afterwards Colonel Oliva himself disappeared.

Who is responsible for the death of Castillo Armas? So far there are only clues and pointers to a sinister possibility. Even if the Guatemalan authorities knew all the facts they might consider it impolitic, for reasons of state, ever to disclose them. The congressional investigating committee found that the Dominican Military Attaché had participated in the Mirador murder, and it seems generally assumed that this crime was linked to the murder of Castillo Armas. The committee also uncovered evidence that even before the president's assassination Dominican Embassy officials had plotted for the overthrow of the regime, and had offered arms and money to subversive persons, to be used for this purpose. Whether or not the chauffeur Carillo did the actual killing has never come out.

The True Man

AT that season the peasants burned off their maize
patches all over Yucatan, and as we drove through
the outskirts of Merida asphyxiated butterflies were
falling like coloured snow.

'Properly speaking,' said the taxi-driver, 'the title
isn't prince. We call him The True Man. His ancestor
was ruling our people when the Spanish came. Anyway,
he'll certainly appreciate your visit. The family's been
having a bit of a lean time of it lately.' The driver was a
Mayan Indian, an ex-peon with a face that watched and
listened. He had worked for some years with the foreigners
in the excavations, had picked up some of their book-
learning, and was at the moment a little dizzy from
smoking marijuana.

'As you may be aware,' he said, 'the Inquisition pro-
hibited the possession of any of the ancient books, on pain
of death. So far as I know, the prince's family had the
only one left in Yucatan. It was used for prophecy and
divination and could only be consulted by moonlight.
Their ancestor went over to the Spaniards when they
first came. They turned him into a grandee, and built
him a palace full of beds and mirrors, so it was easy
enough to hide a book. When the American archaeologist
up at Chichen-Itzá happened to hear about it, the present
prince's mother had had the bad luck to fall foul of the
cacique, who had the Government at his back; so the
matter was settled.'

We were held up in a noble street full of Indian women
dreaming their lives away behind vegetable stalls.

The Changing Sky

Night-gowned shoppers were trooping silently towards a bus shaped like a beer bottle, beside which the driver stood barking into a microphone: 'Safety, comfort and respect – and all for fifty centimos the trip. What more could any reasonable being ask for?' The taxi-driver lit up a marijuana cigarette, and a sad, anxious cartomancer approaching offered to tell us whether our wives were unfaithful. 'Understand me, friends, it isn't so much the betrayal as the constant doubt that kills in the end.' A sudden clash of bells squeezed the pigeons from a tower into the sky, and drew the sleep-walkers out of the road towards the church door. The taxi-driver stubbed out his cigarette, scrupulously offering its expiring incense to the small Virgin over the dashboard before he engaged gear.

'So naturally the cacique, who was half-seas-over as usual, sent a couple of his gunmen to collect the book. "Money!" he shouts, "money!" when the archaeologist offers to buy it. "Hold on there. Do you take me for a dealer in hens by any chance?" So the American got the book for nothing, and sold it to a museum in the States for $50,000 – or at any rate, that's the price that's usually mentioned. He was that kind of fellow, the cacique. Half a bottle of tequila and he'd been known to make his office staff dance the raspa while he took pot-shots with his pistol at their toes. As for the prince's family, you might say it was the final blow.'

Outside the town the dry-mastication of the forest had softened the road to a mule-track. We went through a string of apathetic villages, with vultures scuffling amiably among the chickens outside the huts. As the driver came to terms with the marijuana in his system the violent swerves which had enlivened the early part of the trip subsided into a regular predictable wobble.

'The loss of the book exposed us as a people to certain

inconveniences,' said the driver, 'because it dealt with things of practical value, such as how to avoid earthquakes, or the maize blight. The worst thing we had to put up with was a plague of ghosts. There were so many of them – for God's sake don't laugh – that we got to know them by name. I want to emphasize that people in all walks of life were affected. Take us taxi-drivers. We were always having some young fellow come up to the rank – you know the kind – decent watch, Borsalino, and a gold tooth or two – "Could you run us over to Uxmal?" – or somewhere like that – I mean a worthwhile fare – and then as soon as you were passing the cemetery you felt a tap on the shoulder. "Look here, friend, many apologies, and so on, but I've just thought of something. Put me down here, do you mind?" You probably got twice the proper tip, but you might as well have thrown the money away, because by the time you got back to Merida it would always have vanished into thin air.'

We found the prince in the general store he conducted for the benefit of a village, once a great town and now reduced to a hundred huts. He wore with melancholy distinction a vast hat, with a price ticket fixed to its upturned brim, and went barefoot, avoiding with mysterious unconcern the many chickens' droppings on the floor. The prince was an agent for various American products, and pretty girls in the cigarette advertisements decorating the adobe walls bared their teeth engagingly at a small sociable gathering of sombre Indians in the store. A woman carrying a parakeet on her shoulder came in for a tin of milk, and bent down to kiss his hand. The prince returned a burning glance, and said: 'Your servant to command.'

Who could have been a more promising repository than this man, of the secrets of the past's magnificence and

terror? We tried to draw out the prince to talk a little
of the splendid mysteries of his ancestor's office; of the
coming of the Conquistadors, who in these same villages
hanged any handsome girls as a precaution against their
possible effect on military discipline; of the prisoners,
baptized, then burned in batches; of slavery and the
Inquisition. The prince, anxious to oblige, seemed to
make an effort to project back his mind, to cease for an
instant to be a merchant, to awaken his soul from its bewitched sleep, to rise above this sad present of soap-
powder and torch-bulbs. His eyes were troubled and his
lips moved desperately as he groped among the shapeless
memories of his race. But the Conquest had become no
more than the smiling-sinister masque, danced inter-
minably by the villagers at their drunken celebrations: a
dream of swords and crosses, of Judas kisses, fireworks and
blood, with the savage conquerors stiffening into mild
disciples, and Cortés's swarthy Marina slowly changing
and taking form as the Mother of God. At last, as the
memory of an intolerable grievance sparked through the
oppressive shadows in his brain, the prince spoke. 'The
Spaniards forced us to buy beard-curlers,' he said. His
Indian customers slyly put up their hands to feel the

In many villages of the highlands of Guatemala the Indians have
taken over the churches, and in these they practise a combination
of Christian worship – often in a form that is almost unrecognizably
changed – with their own pre-Christian rites. Maya-Quiché Indians
of Chichecastenango, under the guidance of their own *shamans*,
are seen here worshipping the old gods on the steps of the
church (which for them recall the Mayan pyramids of old). Inside
the church a thin residue of Christianity remains – priest says
mass – but there too the shamans swing their copal incense-burners,
recite their magic formulas, and spread out their patterns of red
and white blossom – representing the souls of the living and the
dead – among the hundreds of candles alight on the floor.

occasional isolated hair on their Mongol-smooth chins, and one of them laughed – a strange and bitter sound in this country.

Before we left, The True Man kindly permitted us to photograph him, standing outside his store. He was tall for an Indian, and of an exceedingly fine presence, as he stood there hat in hand, wearing a newly laundered suit of white cotton pyjamas. He had placed himself immediately below the centre of the fascia board of his establishment, which was painted with the name of his great ancestor, preceded by his three resounding Christian names, which were those of favourite Spanish saints. Under this a notice in smaller letters said: 'QUINTANA ROO EXCLUSIVE AGENT FOR THE "SLICK" ELECTRIC RAZOR – "THE SMOOTHER SHAVE FOR MEN OF DISCRIMINATION".'

'He doesn't seem to be doing so badly after all these days,' the taxi-driver said.

The Indians of Guatemala rarely smile. They are the survivors of the ancient Maya – 'most brilliant of the aboriginal races'. What marks them as unique is their resistance to 400 years of slavery, from which they have emerged still intact as a people, race-proud, self-sufficient, confident of the superiority of their way of life to the opulent materialism that surrounds them. They are afraid of the white man and detest the Mestizo. The Inquisition taught them secrecy. Only the most sympathetic and tactful of observers, who is prepared to live among them for many years, can hope to learn a little of their practices and their beliefs.

A Letter from Cuba

ALL over Cuba one finds public buildings decorated with murals of an heroic if lugubrious kind depicting the resistance of student revolutionaries to the tyrants of their day. Often the students are shown facing a firing-squad composed either of the ferocious volunteers raised by the Spanish colonial authorities or of the no less grim-faced soldiery of one of the early indigenous dictators. None of the macabre episodes portrayed is less than thirty years old, and one supposes that at least a similar period must elapse before the young men who at the present time are carrying on this old student tradition with revolvers and with bombs, will achieve pictorial commemoration of the same kind.

The history of Cuban youth in revolt started a century ago, when the students organized the struggle against a senile and brutalized Spanish colonial regime. It was continued sporadically after the liberation from Spain, when so often the new order revealed itself as nothing more than the old order with its brand-new democratic mask fallen slightly askew. Although in many parts of Latin America the practice of parliamentary democracy is rare, exotic and incomplete, Latin-Americans, and Cubans in particular, have never ceased to carry on nostalgic courtship of the democratic ideal, seen, as it were, as an inaccessible beauty behind an ornamental grille. In periods when something which will just pass muster as democracy is achieved, when elections take place and are not too cynically manipulated, when the Press is vocal but the generals are mute, little is heard of

114

student revolutionary action. But when a dictator puts himself in power and stays there too long, the students begin to plot and soon to throw bombs, and in the end the army and the police are forced into the kind of reprisals that will one day form the subject-matter for yet more depressing murals in provincial town halls.

Nearly a quarter of a century had passed – fairly quietly by Cuban standards – since the period of chaos that followed the overthrow of the detested President Machado. Then at the end of 1956 the old periodical eruptions started again, provoked by what was beginning to look like another unshiftable dictatorship. Within the twelve months there were political assassinations, sabotage, mass demonstrations, and local uprisings. By the end of 1957 the University of Havana and most of the schools throughout Cuba had closed down, and the gaols were full of students. Many more idealistic and hot-headed young men – often barely out of their teens – had lost their lives. Nobody seemed to have any idea how the thing would end.

When I arrived in Havana in December 1957 the city was enjoying a brief respite from nightly alarms. The processional crowds of the evening were abroad again, moving in ranks down the Prado, under trees full of squawking birds, and then thinning out along the Malecon past the opulent grey baroque houses, dodging the whiplash of spray over the low sea-wall. Havana was beautiful and noisy, perfumed with cigar-smoke and oil. People lived clamorously under the flame trees in the parks, in the streets, and in a thousand bars. One remembered T. S. Eliot's 'I had not thought death had undone so many'. There were gentle-mannered philosophical pimps at all the street corners – men who, if allowed, would talk of their ancestry before describing their wares. This was

normality, but for the past year there had been incidents
on three nights out of six. There had been bomb-throwing
and sniping in the streets, and quite frequently the power
cables had been cut, blacking out the town, and thereby
exposing those taken by surprise in the darkened streets
to the incidental hazards of gun-play between snipers and
police. Even the present lull was an uneasy one, and it
was considered foolhardy to visit the cinema or theatre –
favourite locations for the planting of bombs – or even
to wander far from one's hotel at night. I found fresh
bullet-holes in the counter of my favourite bar in the
Calle Industria. A few weeks before, a regular had been
shot down by a tommy-gunner firing from across the
street. One of the barmen had lost a finger in the ragged
volley, and he held up the stump, smiling importantly,
for inspection. This occurrence had not been bad for
business. In Havana people liked to pop in for a drink in
a place where there had been a recent shooting, just as in
London they might visit an East End pub once patronized
by royalty.

My hotel window overlooked the presidential palace
and the garden-filled square in which it stands. The roads
round the square had been closed to traffic, and the
square had become a kind of no-man's-land patrolled by
police in all sorts of uniforms. There were khaki, bullet-
proof police cars ready for action at all the street corners,
and every so often one would be started up, driven rest-
lessly, with siren moaning, a few yards up the road, and
then brought back. The atmosphere in the neighbourhood
of the palace was a very trigger-happy one. Visitors to
Havana were recommended not to loiter as they passed
on the other side of the square in front of the palace, nor
to point cameras in the direction of the machine-gunners
crouching behind parapets of sandbags on the roof. These

exceptional police precautions dated from an afternoon in March 1957 when twenty-one students – who had actually brought along their own photographer – had staged an abortive attempt on the regime by driving up to the palace gates in a lorry, and then dashing out in an attempt to shoot their way up to the president's office on the second floor. A handful of the attackers almost reached their objective. But the president happened at that moment to be lunching with his wife in his residential quarters, in another part of the building, and there on the landing outside the locked office door the surviving members of the assault party died. What little hope of success this desperate venture might have had was lost from the beginning, as a result of gross lack of co-ordination. Cuban revolutionaries are weakened by much internal division. Two separate student organizations had united temporarily to plan the attack; but the larger group, who possessed a bazooka which might have made all the difference, failed to put in an appearance. The hopeless little battle was over in five minutes, but it was hours before the tanks, when they came on the scene, ceased firing with their heavy machine-guns on the surrounding buildings – in the belief that they harboured snipers. Many motorists trapped in the line of fire spent most of the afternoon lying under their cars, and a fair amount of incidental damage – some of a freakish kind – was produced by this protracted bombardment. The sculptural abstracts standing in front of the National Museum, which faces the presidential palace, were badly shot up. A friend of mine who occupied a hotel room overlooking the square came back to find a couple of suits hanging in his wardrobe full of bullet holes: the Government paid a hundred dollars in compensation for them.

★

The Changing Sky

At first I was inclined to take the view that apart from a crop of incredible new night-clubs – one of them with lawns of spurious grass and an artificial sky – nothing much had changed in Havana since I first visited the city in 1939. In those days people treated the topic of democracy with a sort of cynical resignation. In reality, they used to tell you, things weren't a great deal different from the old colonial days when the ruling Spanish bureaucracy treated the country as a kind of privately-owned farm to exploit in whatever way they thought fit. The main difference was that nowadays it was Cubans who took it out of Cubans – which was perhaps some slight consolation. Whoever was in power, he was expected to help himself to the public funds. So long as the administration contented itself with diverting say twenty per cent of the national revenue into its pockets, that was considered reasonable, if not just, and nobody grumbled much. Nor was it thought particularly scandalous when an outgoing president made it quite evident from his real-estate investments in Miami that he had become a multi-millionaire during his term of office. When a government changed it was only a change of personalities, not of principles. The old pernicious, grafting hispanic system always went on. Elections were a kind of white man's version of an African magic ritual in which nobody believed very much any more, but which was still carried on out of a kind of ancestral habit. I remembered that at the time of this first visit to Havana an unemployed man's vote cost a peso – one dollar – and I remembered too, almost being an eye-witness of a remarkable incident which occurred in the Parque Central one day when the town's loafers who congregated there decided to get together and employ a recognized trade-union practice to force up the price to one peso, twenty-five centavos.

A Letter from Cuba

A politician who had come down to the park with the intention of buying up the votes was stung, by what he considered the men's inequitable conduct, into threatening them with a tommy-gun – which somehow or other managed to go off. This was the first time I had ever heard a tommy-gun fired on a real-life occasion, although I immediately recognized the sound from my experience of films based on the Chicago scene. Passers-by who had probably experienced this kind of thing before dropped to the ground and stayed there until the distant staccato hammering stopped, and then scrambled to their feet and went racing away across the flower-beds in the direction of the sound. The siren of a police car howled briefly in the vociferous traffic, and soon policemen, pistols in hand, were herding us away from the sight of whatever had happened. Next day the newspapers came out with an account of the incident. It happened that in addition to wounding several down-and-outs, the politician had succeeded – doubtless by the purest mischance – in killing a policeman, and for this had been lynched by the police in a most gruesome fashion, described in the report with gloating attention to detail. The paper conceded ultimate victory to the loafers. From that time on, it concluded, the price of a vote would be one peso, twenty-five. At the time of the last 'election', in 1954, when the only candidate opposing President Batista thought it advisable to withdraw, the price had gone up to two pesos, fifty centavos – an accurate measure of the inflation which had taken place in the meanwhile.

This was before the days of Fidel Castro – or rather in the days when Fidel Castro was of no more importance than any other scatter-brained young revolutionary, and was several years away from being the leader of the

119

first genuine *maquis*, of the Second World War kind, to be organized in the Western hemisphere.

The Fidel Castro rebellion began with an appallingly organized attack carried out by the leader and a handful of followers in July 1953 on the miniature fortress known as the Moncada Barracks in the city of Santiago, capital of Oriente province at the east end of the island. At that time Castro, a lawyer without a practice, was twenty-nine years of age. He and a group of fellow conspirators, armed with a few pistols and rifles, assaulted the barracks in the almost insane belief that with this strong point in their hands the town of Santiago – supposed to be unfavourable to President Batista – would revolt, and that by some strange talismanic power this revolt would spread itself spontaneously through the rest of the island. Amazingly enough about half the attackers actually got into the barracks, only to find themselves trapped within a high-walled yard, their escape cut off. For a few moments they stood there, arms raised in surrender. Then the machine-guns on the wall-tops opened fire. Castro, who stayed outside the barracks, got away, gave himself up when cornered, and was delivered over to the police by the Archbishop of Santiago in person to ensure that he was not slaughtered on the spot. This was one of the many occasions when leaders of the Catholic Church in Cuba have shown themselves sympathetic to the anti-Batista revolutionaries. Castro was tried, received a sentence of fifteen years and was released nineteen months later under a general amnesty decreed by the president. That is the one and only advantage of being a Cuban revolutionary, as opposed to being a revolutionary in any other country. In Cuban revolutions the police do not take prisoners if they can help it, and they have been charged – even by judges of the high court – with the torture of suspects. But anyone who manages to survive the carnage that inevitably follows a failed revolt rarely serves more than a fraction of his prison sentence. Castro took refuge in Mexico as soon as he was released, and there began training a small band of enthusiasts in exile – all intellectuals, and sons of good middle-class families like himself – for an invasion of the home country. One of Castro's many technical errors was to issue propaganda announcements giving the approximate date decided on for this project. Cuba was to be freed from the rule of President Batista, he promised, by the end of 1956. By the middle of November therefore the island was under martial law, all garrisons were alerted, Batista's small fleet of armed launches was at sea and on the watch, and planes continually patrolled areas where a landing was most likely to take place.

Castro's 'invasion', when it finally came, was farcically mismanaged – a characteristic, evidently, of most Cuban revolutionary action. There was a good deal of support in Oriente province for Castro's movement, and on November 30th – the day when Castro should have landed – armed revolts took place in Santiago and in the four other principal towns of the province. For several hours uniformed Castro supporters were in control of the streets, and the police under siege in their barracks. Then when their chief failed to appear and army reinforcements began arriving from Havana the insurgents lost heart and began to melt away. Known opponents of the Government were subsequently arrested by the hundred, and many were shot. Castro arrived on January 2nd, 1957 – two days late – after a rough crossing, to find that the last vestige of revolt had been crushed. His total force consisted of eighty-two very sea-sick men, who were unable to find their landing beach, and finally

came ashore in a swamp. Batista's air force spotted and
strafed the boat as it came in to shore, and the men
scrambled away through water and slime, leaving most
of their arms, including two anti-tank guns, behind. As
soon as they were on hard ground the survivors, who
had only a rough idea where they were, split up. In the
distance they could see the foothills of the Sierra Maestra,
but before they could reach the shelter of its tropical
forest and its ravines most of them had been inter-
cepted and butchered out of hand by Government troops.
Only twelve men, including Castro, survived this grisly
adventure, and it was months before it became generally
known that he had in fact escaped with his life and was
hiding in the Sierra.

From this unpromising start developed the tough and
successfully-organized resistance movement that the
Castro rebels have become. The numbers of young men
now fighting in the Sierra is not known, but may
amount to a thousand, and most of the armed forces of
Cuba are kept fully employed in the effort to contain
them, while spectacular coups such as the recent kidnapping of the then world motor-racing champion, Juan
Fangio, are frequently carried out by their under-cover
groups in the cities. At such times, Castro men like to act
in the tradition of the romantic outlaw. Fangio appeared
to be charmed with their good manners during his short
period of captivity, most of which was spent in watching
on television the race in which he should have been
competing. A day or two after the Fangio incident a party
of rebels held up the National Bank of Cuba in the heart
of Havana, but instead of taking any of the cash from
the safes, contented themselves with setting fire to
thousands of cheques. In the mountains the rebels are
organized in small bands who keep constantly on the

move and avoid sleeping two nights in the same place. The rebels have with them two Catholic priests, a Protestant minister, and several doctors. Castro recently announced that for the time being he had no further use for volunteers, unless they could bring their own weapons with them.

The Sierra Maestra is the least known and most neglected area in Cuba; a seventy-miles-long range of jungled mountains with peaks rising to a maximum of 6000 feet, in which a few farmers, said to be descendants of outlaws, live in almost savage simplicity and grow a little coffee for the market. Castro, regarded locally as a kind of Robin Hood, seems to get on well with these backwoodsmen, and he and his band have repaid their good will and protection by organizing, and teaching, and medical centres, in an area where illiteracy is total and no doctor has ever been seen. The military tactics employed by the rebels are the classic methods of guerrilla warfare, in which head-on engagements with Government troops are always avoided, while ammunition and supplies are collected by surprise attacks carried out against army and police posts within striking distance of the Sierra. No one has ever discovered that Castro has any war aims other than the elimination of the present dictatorship, thus clearing the way, he says, for a new and non-Cuban kind of democracy, which has never been very clearly defined – the machinery of which is supposed to be in course of creation by members of Cuban parties in exile in the United States. He proposes to do this by disrupting if necessary the economy of the country until a point is reached when he believes that the United States, in order to protect its investments, will be compelled to apply pressure to remove Batista from power. The remarkable thing is that despite the injury to many private interests that Castro's plan of action involves, his popularity throughout the country remains high, even, it seems, with those who suffer actual damage from his acts of sabotage. It is typical of Castro that one of the first plantations to be burnt down belonged to his own family.

The man immediately at the root of the trouble, President Batista, has always loomed large behind the scenes in Cuba – even when not nominally in power – since his extraordinary coup in 1933. History offers probably no other instance of a sergeant who not only staged a successful mutiny but then went on to take over the government of the country. In 1933 Sergeant Batista was a stenographer employed in the Havana garrison. He was noted for his good looks and his persuasive charm. At that time there was a good deal of unrest among the enlisted men owing to impending pay cuts, and the country was in a state of political turmoil following the downfall of President Machado, who had just bolted in a plane to the United States. Bands of armed students who had been responsible for Machado's overthrow still roamed the streets and executed summary vengeance on supporters of Machado's tyranny. So powerful were they that before hatching his plot Batista took care first to get on good terms with the Directorio Estudiantil – the student's revolutionary committee – who in those days could actually conduct its own secret courts martial and execute by firing-squad one of its members found guilty of traitorous activities. Having won over the students, Batista proceeded to put into action a fairly simple plan of his own, which depended for its success on the fact that in those days Cuban officers were always privileged to sleep out of barracks. On this occasion, when the officers of the garrison had gone home for the night, Batista simply posted his own picked men on guard duty with orders not to admit them when they arrived for duty next day. He next phoned every garrison in the island – after the officers had of course gone home to bed – and told the duty N.C.O. that the sergeants were in command of the situation.

It seems unlikely that at this juncture Batista considered himself as the country's eventual leader, and he would probably have been quite ready to treat with a high-ranking officer for the redress of the soldiers' grievances. But the officers, led to believe that the United States would never permit a large-scale mutiny to succeed within what was accepted as its sphere of influence, broke off contact with the mutineers, retired to the Hotel Nacional, and barricaded themselves in. United States warships now appeared off Havana, and spurred on by the militant students, who threatened that they themselves would attack if he did not, and fearing that in any case he had gone too far to turn back, Batista gave the order for the assault. Batista's soldiers opened fire on the hotel with old French seventy-fives, sighting their target, it is said, through the barrels of their cannons. Considerable execution was done among the attackers by accurate rifle-fire from the hotel – many of the officers being excellent marksmen – but in the end the defenders' ammunition gave out, they were obliged to surrender, and many of them were massacred in cold blood. No marines were landed, and in a few weeks Batista was a colonel and the head of the government.

Fulgencio Batista has turned out the most capable and progressive president Cuba has ever had. His sense of humour is illustrated by his habit, in the old days when the Communist Party had not been outlawed and ran its own radio station, of giving parties for his friends at which the principal entertainment would be to listen to one of the Communist broadcaster's nightly manhandling of the president's private life. Although in recent years Batista has taken openly to a dictatorial form of rule he is surprisingly free from that brand of dictators' megalomania which makes it impossible to escape from the sight of their portraits in public places, and in the Press. Batista seems not to care greatly for publicity, and he probably does not even regard himself as an instrument wielded by divine hands for the betterment of the Cuban people. The social and labour legislation enacted since his access to power established Cuba as one of the most advanced nations in America, and he has repeatedly disappointed business and industry by his failure to abrogate the law which makes it almost impossible to dismiss an employee on any grounds, and which is regarded as one of the greatest deterrents to investment in the island. Batista is still supported by the organized workers: their wages are now at the highest point in Cuban history, and they have repaid him by refusing, so far, to respond to Castro's frequent calls for a general strike. Against this he has alienated the affection of most middle- and upper-class Cubans by his destruction of civil liberties, his Press censorship, his forthright rule through the army, and by his toleration of the many repressive excesses indulged in by his police. Although once he was believed to be unattracted by money, charges are now heard on all sides of massive corruption in his administration.

Censorship in Havana was effective – perhaps too effective. An advertisement for a make of watch, showing a bearded explorer wearing one, was banned because Fidel Castro too had a beard – though after the capture of a crate of razors the rebels were stated to be – at any rate for a time – clean-shaven. The situation in

A Letter from Cuba

Oriente province was never mentioned in the newspapers, while on the rare occasions that the Sierra Maestra was referred to in the Press it was usually called with sly irony, 'a certain mountain range'. This absence of news favoured spectacular rumour. Although the potential wealth of Cuba is based on an extreme variety of mineral resources, its present great prosperity still depends in the main on sugar, and Castro had recently promised that unless Batista went, he would burn the cane all over the island as it stood, now ready for cutting in the fields. 'A sugar harvest without Batista, or Batista without a sugar harvest', the slogan went. People up in town from Santiago said that the burning there had already started, and they had sombre tales to tell of nightly street battles in the city and a countryside given over to chaos and terror. After listening to their accounts of arson and murder I was slightly surprised to find that Cuban Airways still ran a daily service to Santiago, and as I could find no taxi that would agree to make the trip, I decided two days after my arrival in Havana to take a plane down there and see what was happening.

For the direct run to Santiago Cuban Airways used a brand new turbo-prop Viscount aircraft. This stood on the tarmac, floodlit and under heavy guard, while waiting to take off – which it did shortly after dark, following a half-hour's delay while several suspect parcels brought aboard by the five passengers were untied and found to contain no bombs. Cuba proved to be the gayest of countries to fly over at night. At 15,000 feet there were always half a dozen brilliantly lit small towns in sight below, arranged with regularity like sparkling modernistic trinkets on the black earth, each with its square-cut central jewel which was the plaza. Later, with the lights of Santiago in the distance, and where I judged the foothills of the

127

The Changing Sky

Sierra Maestra might have been, a tiny ringworm of red fire, which my fellow passengers believed to be a burning canefield, glowed in the blackness. A few minutes later we landed, were hustled into an airport bus, and driven at a rocking, tyre-screeching seventy miles per hour into the centre of the town. It was now half past nine, and a fellow passenger explained to me that if there was to be trouble, zero hour was inevitably ten o'clock, when all the town's lights might be switched off. With half an hour to go, the streets were still ablaze, with small groups of citizens clustered at their doors like gophers ready to bolt for the shelter of their burrows when the shadow of an eagle fell upon them. My hotel was on the Plaza Cespedes – a theatrical stage-setting of ancient colonial buildings. Under lamps hung like moons among blossoming trees the citizenry were still performing the decorous ritual of the evening promenade – women circling the square in one direction, and men in the other. A row of substantial burghers who sat sipping their daiquiris along

The poverty-stricken peasant of Haiti dances or makes music in his spare time. He creates musical instruments out of materials that cost nothing and are ready to hand. This is an orchestra of bamboo tubes of various sections, graded so as to produce booming, sepulchral notes of different pitch. The time is accentuated by tapping the bamboo with a stick.

In 1930 the worst hurricane ever recorded in the Caribbean area literally blew the ancient town of Santa Domingo off the face of the earth, leaving only a few of its most solid colonial buildings intact among the ruins. When the town was rebuilt it was renamed Trujillo City after the dictator who had assumed power in the interim. There are no beggars to be seen in Trujillo City, and bare-footed children are not allowed in its streets, which are quiet and clean. Pedestrians are very careful to cross the streets at the crossings, the bars close early, and the citizens go home to bed. It is very docile, and rather colourless, and sad.

128

A Letter from Cuba

the edge of the hotel veranda which overlooked the square increased the theatrical impression. As the cathedral clock struck ten the promenaders trooped out of the square as if at the completion of a scene, and on the terrace we waited in our privileged seats for the new performers to come on the empty stage. On the previous night there had been a good deal of shooting. One of the hotel guests had been caught in the suburbs in the blackout, and with the bullets flying in all directions had spent half the night under his car. But tonight all was quiet. At intervals of about half an hour an army truck bristling with guns rumbled through the plaza, but the snipers had gone from the roof-tops. One by one the guests got tired of waiting and took themselves reluctantly off to bed.

This old Ibizan peasant, left without family, has become the victim of a mysterious mental state sometimes found in the island – a sudden loss of interest in all the mild skirmishings that here replace the battle for existence. He has suddenly abandoned his land to anyone who cares to till it, ceased entirely to care about his appearance or the opinion of others. He sits with a slight smile on his lips, replying in a few words when spoken to, eating a little when his neighbours give him food. People like to have him in their houses. It is as if they recognize and respect a germ of saintliness in this good-natured rejection of life.

In Spain you have to visit the region of Las Hurdes, to the south of Salamanca, to discover a peasantry as untouched by this century as the country folk of Ibiza. Civilized inheritance customs have parcelled out the whole island between them, so that almost every man and woman has his or her patch of carefully tended earth, and there is no wealth and no real poverty. Foreign visitors who know the people of southern Europe are sometimes surprised at their reserve. They do not shout or gesticulate. Fierce regional chauvinisms existed in the island until recent years. The villagers of San Carlos, for example, did not allow people from other villages to own land there, or to court their women. This is a woman from San Carlos doing her shopping by cart in Ibiza town.

The Changing Sky

It was a relief to find that the gracious old town of Santiago hadn't changed much since I had last been there in 1939. Neglect and comparative poverty had so far defeated the cancer cells of the insipid modernism which is fast invading Havana, and had preserved the near-perfect Cespedes Square and many of the old houses with their deep balconies, enormous airy rooms, and ceilings supported, like Moorish council chambers, with numerous spare and elegant columns. Even the cracks opened by the 1939 earthquake in the towers of the Florentine-style cathedral were only now being filled in. I noted that although the hotel's vast baroque dining-room had been defaced by an American-style quick-service luncheon counter, the huge old Valencian chandeliers, with their bunches of scaly glass flowers, which had survived so many bullets and earthquakes, were still there.

By day, life went on in Santiago much as usual, although the authorities had thought it wise to remove all the police – even those normally employed on traffic duty – from the streets. With Christmas a few days ahead there was a stubborn attempt at a festive air. Whole barbecued pigs, paraded on wheel-barrows, were rapidly being reduced to sandwiches for consumption on the spot. Shops were decorated with most elaborate models in coloured paper of aeroplanes, Colt revolvers and battleships. The hairdressers were doing a fast pre-holiday trade in de-kinking the hair of the city's fashionable mulattas. There was an all-pervasive background moan of juke-boxes playing barely recognizable Christmas carols, now *de mode* in Latin America: 'The First Noël', 'God Rest You Merry, Gentlemen'. The Cuban obsession with the occult and the pseudo-occult sciences came out even more strongly here than in Havana. A departmental

130

store ran a window display of books devoted solely to the significance of numbers. Fortune-telling slot-machines abounded. A market stall was heaped with cult objects of Saint Barbara, identified by a Cuban sect known as the *Santeros* with the African god Chango. Almost as frequently as barbers' shops, one came across a *consultorio espiritual* with a peso-a-time trance-medium in attendance.

Most of the citizens of Santiago appeared to be sympathetic to Castro's cause, not only because he was out to free the whole of Cuba from the dictatorship, but because rightly or wrongly he symbolized for them the resistance of Oriente province to what they saw as its exploitation and its neglect by the central authority. I paid a visit to a local magistrate, a millionaire who was openly admitted to contribute generously to the war-chest of the Castro rebellion. He received me in an air-conditioned and book-lined study, and presented me with a new aspect of the problem. 'It's really all the fault of the English,' he said. 'I mean your pirates in the old days. We had to build the city in a low-lying position, where we hoped it wouldn't be seen from the sea. Not that that helped in the long run – your people still managed to sack it half a dozen times. If the place hadn't turned out so unhealthy, Santiago would have been the capital, not Havana. As things are, we're quite neglected. Oriente is the richest province in Cuba, but all the money goes into the pockets of those gangsters in Havana. Naturally we're for Castro to a man. What can you expect?'

Castro and his merry men lurked somewhere in the 500 square miles of almost unexplored mountain territory that began just across the bay. The Government had permitted the sugar mills to start grinding this year two weeks earlier than the usual date – December 15th – but Castro had ordered the mills to stop work, and those within striking range of the Sierra had thought it prudent to obey. At night Castro partisans all over the province were going into the canefields and planting candles there, their bases wrapped in paraffin-soaked rags. There was a great shortage of food in the mountains, and little water but the rank fluid stored in certain tropical plants, so the rebels had to renew their supplies by constant raids on the towns in the area. The most effective force in use against them on the Government side were the 'rurales', a hard-hitting body of men originally formed by one of the U.S. occupying expeditions, and steeped in the tradition of the *ley de fugas*. The rurales preferred not to take prisoners, nor did they spare anyone suspected of being associated with the rebels. Two doctors believed to have treated Castro wounded had just been slaughtered by them, producing an official protest to the Batista Government by the World Medical Association.

Despite all sensational forecasts, it soon became clear that I was going to see no action while I remained in Santiago, and when, after mooching about its peaceful streets for two days, I received a tip from a rebel sympathizer that an uprising was hourly expected in the town of Manzanillo – about sixty miles away – I hired a taxi and drove there.

All this countryside was the wonderfully unspoilt Cuba of the last century, or perhaps even of the century before. The peasants still built their huts with palm-fronds in the style of the *bohios* of the long-exterminated Siboney Indians, and surrounded them with bower bird decorations of coloured rocks. We passed through tangerine-scented tropical versions of the American frontier towns of the eighteen fifties, with swing-door saloons, and hitching posts, and gun-toting cowboys on white ponies. Two men out of three were going about with fighting cocks tucked under their arms. They fed these birds on scraps of meat and titbits of hard-boiled eggs soaked in rum, and carried them about mainly for their companionship it appeared, since fights were staged only at weekends in the structures built like miniature bull-rings on the outskirts of each village. A distraught-faced female cartomancer had planted herself at a crossroads, and told grim fortunes for twenty centavos a time. Cartomancy is regarded in Cuba as the lowest grade of prediction, and the depressed-looking cowboys who were this woman's customers flung down their coins, not even troubling to dismount to receive her austere prognostications. In this area a light haze covered the hills where the sugar-cane had been burning. Once we passed a field where a fire had just been put out, but the dry grass round its edges was still flaring with the sizzling noise of bacon frying in a pan.

The first *guardia rural* who stopped us made a memorable figure. He was dressed like an American cavalryman of the 1914-18 war, with breeches, leggings and scoutmaster's hat, and sat by the roadside under a canopy, on an elegant chair upholstered in tooled leather. He held a large automatic in one hand, a tommy-gun lay across his knees, and a bottle of beer stood by his side. It was the first of eight such encounters that day, and in one case my luggage was dragged out to be searched. This time it was a pair of consciously tough, swaggering soldiers, ne'er-do-wells of the kind that receive a week or two's training, and then, with guns in their hands and a hundred dollars a month, are let loose upon the countryside. They put on a great show of fury when they found a khaki shirt in my suitcase, the possession of which by a civilian is seemingly illegal in Cuba, and one advised the other in a rattle of slurred Spanish to 'let me have it' if I answered back. This was a moment when I remembered only too

well that civil rights had been suspended and that when
the Cienfuegos rising happened in September 1957, and
the town was battered by tanks and aviation, with the
deaths of hundreds of civilians, an N.B.C. man was flung
into gaol for thirty-six hours merely because he had had
the bad luck to be travelling in the neighbourhood at the
time. However, in the end the soldiers let me go, and we
reached Manzanillo, which is down on the coast and right
under the Sierra. Here it was only too clear by the sand-
bag parapets and the manned strongpoints, that the army
was ready for anything. A patrol of uniformed mulattoes
was searching the houses round the square when I got
there, and as soon as I took out my camera a rifle was
levelled at me. Castro's security arrangements, it looked
to me at that moment, were pretty bad.

The attack came all right, but it was not at Manzanillo,
nor at Bayamo, nor even at Santiago, as had been vari-
ously predicted, but at the small town of Veguitas on
the Santiago-Manzanillo road. This was where I had been
stopped by the guardia rural in the antique cavalryman's
outfit, and I wondered what had become of him if he
had tried to intercept the convoy of Castro men on their
descent into town. In this foray, the attackers went round
the stores after silencing opposition, and loaded four
lorries with supplies. What is characteristic of this rebellion, although remarkably out of line with tradition, is
that they actually paid for all they took, and I knew that a
proportion of the money they put down had come from
my friend the Santiago magnate. It was beginning to
look to me as though – in spite of all the early failures –
Castro's strategy was more successful than I had supposed,
and although the present Cuban dictatorship could
perhaps hold out for a long time, Castro might contrive
to hold out even longer.

The Dominican Republic

THE *New Yorker* recently published a cartoon by Whitney Darrow, in which one of his innocent and amiable American matrons was shown standing at the counter of a travel agency, clutching a trifle uncertainly a handful of brochures. 'I'm confused,' she says to the bewildered assistant. 'Tell me again which countries have dictators we like?' This joke gets over because of its awful authenticity. American innocents abroad are genuinely disturbed at the idea of dictatorships, and are inclined to wonder whether they may not in some way be condoning un-Americanisms in a system of government by their very presence as tourists in a country ruled by a dictator. They realize that Cuba and Spain are ruled by dictators, but they see little in their own Press but what is favourable to these two countries, so they feel that it is permissible as well as safe to go there. But when the shadow of U.S. official disapproval falls over a regime, and it is treated sourly by the U.S. Press, the American tourist loses interest in the country. For this reason, despite all the money that the Dominican Republic has sunk in the tourist business, Americans no longer go there to spend their winter vacations.

This sudden U.S. antipathy for a regime which until recently has always enjoyed the full and enthusiastic support of the State Department, is a direct result of the Galíndez case, described by the American Press as the most sensational mystery of its kind ever to have happened in the United States. On March 12th, 1956, Dr Jesus de Galíndez, a lecturer at Columbia University and

135

The Changing Sky

a highly respected writer on international affairs, suddenly disappeared and was never seen again. After drinking coffee with a group of his students, Dr Galíndez left them at a Manhattan subway entrance, and then vanished. Looking round for a motive for a kidnapping – if there had been one – the doctor's friends recalled that the work he had been engaged upon for his doctoral thesis at Columbia, and which was shortly to be published in book form, was to be called 'The Trujillo Era'. Dr Galíndez had worked for six years for the Dominican Government, after which he had fled the country, and it was believed that his book, when published, would prove the best-documented and most authoritative exposure of the extraordinary Trujillo dictatorship yet to appear. The case of Galíndez's disappearance received a tremendous amount of publicity in the American Press. What shocked American opinion was that this kind of thing could happen at one of the busiest hours in the day in one of the busiest parts of the City of New York. 'How *does* one vanish in New York?' the *Herald-Tribune*'s headlines demanded to know. The police found that Galíndez's mail was still being delivered, his bank account had not been touched, and the personal belongings in his flat had not been disturbed. They noted, however, that two of Generalissimo Trujillo's political opponents had recently disappeared in Cuba, and that the murder of a man called Requena, a publisher of an anti-Trujillo newspaper in New York, who had been enticed to a slum-tenement and there shot dead, had never been solved.

For months the F.B.I., fifty detectives of the Missing Persons Bureau, and various private organizations, worked on the case without uncovering a single clue. Generalissimo Trujillo, disturbed by the bad publicity that he and his regime were getting, bought whole-page

136

advertisements in American newspapers to deny charges
of his implication in Galíndez's disappearance. These
advertisements took the form of engagingly worded
letters, thought to have been composed by Trujillo himself, under a photograph of the generalissimo, in a tweed
jacket, smiling a little reproachfully at the reader. They
stopped suddenly when public interest in the case boiled
up following the disappearance in the Dominican capital,
Ciudad Trujillo, of a twenty-three-year-old American
civil pilot, called Gerald Murphy. Just before his disappearance Murphy had been talking, and even writing,
a great deal to friends about the Galíndez case, and from
what he had said and written it was possible to construct
a theory accounting for the fate of both men. In questioning Murphy's friends the police found that early in March
he had mentioned being approached by the New York
Consul-General of the Dominican Republic, with what he
had described as 'a good charter proposition' – in fact, he
was to fly a cancer patient direct to the Dominican
Republic. Following this, he hired a twin-engine Beechcroft plane, and on March 6th – six days before Galíndez
disappeared – this plane was fitted at Lindon Airport,
New Jersey, with additional fuel-tanks, increasing the
range from 800 to 1400 miles. The man who paid for this
job was John Joseph Frank, who has been convicted
by a Federal District Court for acting illegally as an agent
of Trujillo. Frank, in fact, was the man employed by the
Dominican Consul to find a suitable pilot. On March 12th –
the day of Galíndez's disappearance – Murphy took off
and flew to Amityville Airport, Long Island. By this time
he had been provided with a Dominican co-pilot, Octavio
de la Maza. This de la Maza, incidentally, had been Air
Attaché at the Dominican Embassy in London, in 1954,
and there, in the Embassy precincts, had killed a

colleague in a gun affray, since when – released by the British authorities as a result of his diplomatic status – he had been employed as a pilot on a Dominican air-line. The night-watchman at Amityville Airport, Anthony Frevele, happened to mention to a friend that he had seen an ambulance drive up, and a man who could not move a muscle taken out on a stretcher and put in the plane. Frevele's testimony would have been vital to the Department of Justice in the Frank trial, but like most of the potential witnesses in this case he did not live long enough to testify. He died of a coronary thrombosis a few weeks later. The next link in the chain of evidence – which also turned out useless to the prosecution – was the statement of a mechanic called Jackson, who re-fuelled the Beechcroft at Lantana Airport, Florida. Jackson had to enter the body of the aircraft to reach the supplementary fuel tanks that had been fitted, and he told the authorities that he had seen a figure on a stretcher, and noticed a peculiar stench, indicative he thought of a drug. Jackson, subpoenaed to give evidence at the trial, was killed a few days before it opened, when he and his father crashed in a private plane they had hired. If, as may be suspected, the intention actually existed to silence everyone who knew too much about the Galíndez case, it seems obvious that by this time Murphy's days were numbered. As an American citizen his liquidation provided unusual difficulties, but when Murphy began to talk too much there was clearly no help for it. His empty car was found at the top of a cliff over a spot where it was well known that sharks congregated, attracted by the offal thrown into the sea from a slaughterhouse. That de la Maza should have been arrested and charged with Murphy's killing seems to suggest something approaching bankruptcy of the imagination of the Dominican police. This preposterous solution was completed with de la Maza's 'suicide' by hanging in prison. He left a note saying that he had taken his life out of remorse for the killing of Murphy. This note the U.S. State Department has inspected and pronounced a forgery.

This lurid and improbable gangster-film thrown on the screen of real life has blasted for some time to come the Dominican Republic's hope of a thriving tourist traffic. When I went there in the winter of 1957 the two super-colossal hotels of Ciudad Trujillo were empty, and no enchanted lake of Celtic mythology could have looked half as forlorn as their deserted swimming pools. The management of the more fabulous of the two had just offered free facilities of all kinds, including free transport, to the local American Women's League, if only they would make use of the hotel, and go through their callisthenic exercises somewhere where they could be seen. As things were, the one or two guests who had more or less accidentally broken their journey at Ciudad Trujillo were being scared away after a day of the bewitched silences of the public rooms.

It is exceedingly difficult to get a visa to visit the Dominican Republic for a declared serious purpose, but nothing is easier than to pick up a tourist card at the airport of any of the adjacent countries, and with this, travel to Ciudad Trujillo. On arrival one encounters a long delay while baggage is minutely examined. Likely-looking passengers are frisked for arms, newspapers are taken away for inspection, and if you happen to be carrying gramophone records, as I was, there is an additional delay while these are played through. The sensation of entering a police-state is even greater than it was on a visit to Nazi Germany, and very much greater than in Fascist Italy, or in Spain. While the taciturn customs official flicks suspiciously through the pages of the Penguin he has discovered, the dictator, smiling with a kind of meticulous benevolence, looks down from three different portraits, showing him in full military tenue, in sporting clothes, and in evening dress. He is flanked by two members of his family: a brother – the nominal president – and the dictator's son Ramfis, who was created a colonel at the age of four, a brigadier-general at the age of nine, and now commands the fairly powerful Dominican Air Force.

After the completion of this slight ordeal I took a taxi to the Jaragua (this is the hotel from which Murphy was just about to check out on the day he was murdered). The Jaragua employed an American 'social manager', who greeted me with such enthusiastic familiarity that I found it hard to believe we had never met on many occasions before. While I was signing the register (still under the benevolent gaze of the members of the Trujillo family) I found him at my elbow followed by a waiter with a trolley. 'How about a cup of coffee?' he asked. 'Get some sparkle in that eye!' Other attempts had been made to simulate a homely American atmosphere. For example a row of gambling machines had been placed at the end of the open-air restaurant, and persons who had perhaps been engaged specially to do this – they were certainly not hotel guests – jerked and crashed the handles of these all through dinner, and through most of the night. In one way, however, a stay at the Jaragua fell short of expectations. I was assured before coming to the country by people who claimed to have had the experience, that my luggage – whether locked or not – would be opened and thoroughly searched while I was at dinner. This did not happen.

The Dominican Republic

Ciudad Trujillo was a little disappointing; a tidy and bloodless tropical edition of a Miami suburb. The great hurricane of 1930 is partly to blame for this. It literally blew the town off the face of the earth, leaving only the cathedral, the superb colonial churches, and a few noble houses built like massive old Aragonese inns, now incongruously surviving in featureless modern streets. The avenues were clean, well paved, well lit, and pedestrians crossed them only at definite points, sternly guarded by policemen with flashing lamps. The shop windows were full of the American goods bought with the proceeds of the sugar crop which the Dominican Republic sells almost in its entirety to England. This was December in the tropics, and as the commercial Christmas has recently been promoted in Latin America, many of the shop windows had been sprayed on the inside with artificial frost, and articles for sale such as calculating machines and refrigerators had been decorated with 'angel's hair' and plastic snow. Christmas trees stood in the public squares among the canna and the hibiscus. A roving loudspeaker van cruised up and down the main street roaring the praises of a medicine called Estomacal between verses of 'Abide with Me', which is believed in Latin countries to be a Christmas carol.

I discovered that a few minutes from the centre of Ciudad Trujillo the image of this rather flavourless prosperity soon fades. The town comes flamboyantly to life with a red-light area a mile across, and with tens of thousands of fiercely painted wooden shacks of the kind in which most Dominicans have probably always lived. In the country the picture, on the whole, is that of the resigned and decorous poverty of a civilized people. In a few small, painted towns a frivolous doll's-house architecture has weathered the hurricanes, and in the evening

141

the marriageable girls put on their lavender plastic macintoshes and sit on their door-steps all along the streets to see the world go by. The most substantial building in all these towns is the police headquarters (every car passing them must stop, for the driver to announce his name and destination) and the central feature is always a monument raised by the grateful citizens to their Benefactor. Such monuments usually take the form of an impressive obelisk, sometimes provided internally with a lift to carry visitors to the top. 'God and Trujillo' is no longer the inevitable inscription, townships in these days being expected to think up original wording for their tributes. One I saw said, 'No statesman in the history of the world has done so much for his country.'

This may be an exaggeration. In the twenty-seven years that have gone since Trujillo took over power – after an election in which, according to the U.S. Ambassador of the day, he polled more votes than there were voters – he has been responsible for considerable material progress in the Dominican Republic. He has wiped out the country's external debt, restored law and order (sometimes by employing methods considered repugnant in a democratic regime such as the *ley de fugas*), he has built roads, schools and hospitals, and dealt with all opposition in an unflinching manner, thereby putting an end to civil discord. The best known example of Trujillo's resoluteness of purpose occurred when in 1937 he decided to stop the illegal entry of Haitian sugar-cutters from across the border, and a number, estimated at a minimum as 7000, and at a maximum as 20,000, of these defenceless people were bayoneted by his troops.

Trujillo's incessantly praised benefactions have not excluded himself and his family. The extent of his personal fortune is unknown, but as the country's first merchant – as he is officially titled – it is certainly colossal. Nearly all the members of the Benefactor's enormous clan – uncles, brothers, nephews and cousins – hold, or at one time have held, important positions in the state. Even his daughter Flor de Oro's original husband, Porfirio Rubirosa (she subsequently divorced and remarried six times), still enjoys high favour. Never can there have been such a family man since Pope Alexander VI. The dictator's one weakness appears to be an excessive taste for adulation. There can be no sermon by the Archbishop, no ambassadorial speech, no editorial, without its routine and therefore meaningless injection of approbation for the regime. Trujillo smiles at the reader from almost every page of every newspaper. Portraits, busts and plaques bearing Trujillo's effigy are everywhere, and this has led to brisk rackets in the sale of unauthorized and spurious cult objects, which no shopkeeper or householder dare refuse to buy. Sometimes this adulation is unwittingly transformed into cruel irony as in the case of the sign over the lunatic asylum in the town of Nigua: 'We owe everything to Trujillo.'

Perhaps after all the last word about this astounding regime has been said by the unfortunate Galíndez himself, because, as fortune would have it, the attempt to silence him came three days too late to achieve its object; his manuscript had already been sent to the publishers. His book *The Era of Trujillo* has now been published, has reached numerous editions in Latin America, and its author has been granted a doctorate honoris causa (post mortem) of Columbia University in recognition of his work. The tone of this book is cool, passionless and scientific: a model analysis, in fact, of the phenomenon of dictatorship in general, as well as a precise and formidably documented one of that of Trujillo in particular. Galíndez abstains from expressions of opinion until the last chapter, and then he says: 'In a democratic regime the death of a chief of state does not cause any difficulty in the normal transition to the next period; but after a dictator nothing remains ... the Era [of Trujillo] leaves no foundations behind it, no political parties, no leaders with authority, no doctrine. All must be started again from the bottom.'

Caribbean Africa

IT was Sunday, and it had been raining, when I drove across the frontier from the Dominican Republic into Haiti. All the girls were on their way home from church, carrying their glittering shoes, and lifting their skirts above their knees to wade through streams that continually cut the road. Nothing much had changed here since a hundred and fifty years ago, when the French had discovered among these mountains the folly and the futility of a belief that total terror could win for them a colonial war. After the extinction of the cruellest and most successful of the colonial regimes, while at the height of its prosperity, the ex-slaves razed the plantations, and destroyed the irrigation systems that it had cost the labour of a century to construct. Then they settled themselves to a future of implacable poverty and a life that was the memory-image of the ancestral existence of the forests of Guinea. The old African faiths peopled the ruined countryside with diviners and mystics, and the spirits of children who had died in the womb, and who waited everywhere in the forest paths to clutch imploringly at the traveller's ankles. The backwoods of Haiti are full of strange survivals. Someone had just rediscovered some Poles, descendants of the defeated legion of General le Clerc – Bonaparte's brother – living as charcoal-burners on a mountain-top. In these remote parts there were no public services to speak about, practically no schools, no employment apart from pottering about in one's own vegetable patch, and no hope of any improvement in one's situation. Even government employees were several months in arrears in their salaries.

145

The Changing Sky

In spite of this the Haitians looked cheerful enough. They danced a great deal, and you could hear the drums thudding away continually inside their gaudily painted little shacks. On Saturday nights they still practised the fervid rites of Africa, and on Sunday they went to mass in the Catholic church. The air round their villages was sweet with the odour of fried bananas, on which they lived, and people who had nothing to do simply lay in hammocks and chewed cane.

We groped our way cautiously down the road, through the streams and round the landslides. Sometimes road and river-bed would be united for a hundred yards, and large greyish kingfishers went hurtling past on both sides of the car, and we could see the little fish darting away from the car's front wheels. A girl came splashing past on horseback, riding side-saddle in a great foaming of muslin skirts, a Bible clutched in her white-gloved hand. We passed through a village called Peu de Chose, full of ghostly black versions of French grandees with white Napoleon beards, panama hats, spats and Malacca canes. There were tombs in some of the gardens – little Gothic mansions of two or three storeys, with offerings of food pushed in through the windows. The village shop was a stall at which a girl sat, smoking a cob pipe, her skirts pulled half-way up her black thighs. She sold single and half cigarettes, tomato paste and olive oil by the spoonful, and small dried fishes' tails at one cent apiece. After this village came the spectre of a Norman town containing a square with a bandstand, a steepled church, a *mairie*, and a public *pissoir*. A herd of pygmy cows occupied the main boulevard, where they browsed on the fallen blossom of the flame trees.

Port au Prince filled the valley at the end of the long calamitous road; first of all the suburbs with their dwarf chateaux of painted clapboard and corrugated iron, then the business centre laid out in rows of sagging, multi-coloured wooden façades, looking like an early-nineteenth-century aquatint of Kingston, Jamaica. The town was hot and indolent and neglected. There were perilous holes everywhere in roads and pavements where drain-covers had been taken off and never put back. They still butchered their animals hideously in an open-air slaughterhouse, in full public view. A great effort to capture tourist trade had provoked the clearing of about half the pestilent water-front slums, and you could now stroll by the sea and watch the lemon-coloured boats coming in bringing bananas, charcoal, and dried fish from forgotten little ports inaccessible by road. Of tourists there were none at all to be seen. The money that had gone into building the casino and the hotels seemed to have been thrown away. Taxis drove up and down the sea-front hooting sadly at indifferent pedestrians, and forlorn *belles de nuit* lingered profitlessly under the coconut palms of the new promenade. I stayed in a vast, deserted hotel, its silence disturbed only by the rumble and whir of refrigerators. A notice advertising 'Authentic Voodoo Ceremonies in a Cool Place – Five Dollars' had the word 'Suspended' scrawled across it. At the Centre d'Art you could pick up a masterpiece of primitive art for a few dollars, because only foreigners thought it worth collecting these small apocalyptic visions of illiterate Haitian negroes. The trouble was that a few months previously there had been a street battle between two army factions in Port au Prince, in which artillery had been engaged. After that the tourist ships had stopped coming, thus depriving Haiti of its second most important source of revenue and plunging it into one of the deepest economic crises of its history.

The Changing Sky

The battle of May 25th, 1957, was a ridiculous piece of not very comic comic-opera, with badly armed, badly trained men making a botch of murdering each other in the city's principal square. Only the most practised pathfinder in the Caribbean political underbrush could trace his way back through the maze of intrigue that culminated in this bloody little farce. The final phase of the drama was the attempted seizure of power by a General Cantave at the head of a military junta. The provisional government then existing promptly declared the general an outlaw, and called upon a Colonel Armand to take over the army. So that May morning three decayed French seventy-fives were pushed and trundled into the wide, flowery square known as the Champs de Mars, and pointed roughly in the direction of the Dessalines barracks 200 yards away, which General Cantave had made his stronghold. The general was given fifteen minutes in which to surrender, and at the expiration of that time the wonderful bombardment began. One gun exploded with its first round, killing its crew outright. Shells from the others whooshed over the roof of the barracks to fall mostly in the sea, one of them missing by not more than ten yards a Dutch steamer just about to tie up in port. The only plane in the Haitian Air Force considered capable of carrying a bomb was then got into the air. This was a veteran transport machine, and an eighteen-year-old bomb carried in the cabin was kicked out of the open door when the pilot found himself roughly over the Dessalines barracks. The bomb actually fell among the tamarisks and oleanders of the Champs de Mars – and, failing to explode, broke a civilian's leg. Meanwhile the Haitian Navy's single gunboat fussed up and down just offshore, menacing the barracks with a gun which could not be induced to fire. The action came to an

148

end when the gunners in the Champs de Mars, who had omitted to bring small arms for their own protection, were massacred among the flowers by a patrol of riflemen who sallied out from the barracks. Thus ended the latest of Haiti's innumerable revolutions. Colonel Armand, seeing that his attack had failed, managed to flee the country. Even then nothing came of General Cantave's military coup. A new president who took over the government later in the day of the cannonade survived only two weeks, after which he was arrested, imprisoned, and then exiled.

The recurrent political sicknesses of Latin America, with their regular crop of revolutions both grim and farcical, are complicated in Haiti by an extra factor – the colour conflict. There is an almost complete separation between pure negroes and Haitians possessing varying admixtures of white blood. The mulattoes of Haiti are the socially elite – the descendants of French planters and the inheritors of a ruined feudalism. These men who hark back so desperately to the white side of their ancestry send their sons to school in Paris, and hedge their daughters about with the strange ceremonial detailed in etiquette books of the last century. They have a seigniorial attitude to all forms of productive and manual labour, and where the waning revenues from their estates fail to suffice for their needs, they may dabble in business – or in politics, regarded as a purely business venture. The conflict between mulatto and negro is always there, whether visible or below the surface. Ninety per cent of the population are pure negroes, a few of whom struggle to the top in the professions. The army is all negroid. This military avenue to power has always been neglected – to their cost – by the mulattoes. Whenever the army is in power in Haiti there is a negro president, who loses no time in manœuvring mulatto politicians out of any key positions they may hold, and the mulattoes in turn use all their economic power, their superior education and political experience, to keep black presidential candidates out of office. This subtle and complex war of the colours, so little of which is seen by the casual observer, is grafted on to all the other endemic political ills of the Caribbean; the insatiable corruption, the spoils system in government, the farce of democratic procedure with which dictatorial regimes are masked. All these problems too are aggravated in Haiti by the chronic economic misery of a country which is one of the poorest and most over-populated in the world. Many Haitian fishermen cannot afford boats or tackle. They use crude log-rafts and home-made harpoons, and, fishing for sharks, their average income is 25 cents a day. A peasant family may produce a dollar's worth of vegetables in a month in excess of the food needed for their own consumption. The destitute of Port au Prince camp out in one of the world's most terrific *bidonvilles,* a kind of slum Venice in which the canals are open drains. Social and economic chaos is intensified by a complete lack of political stability. The year 1957 may have set a record for this century in Haitian turbulence, as in six months there were seven changes of government.

A considerable hidden influence in Haitian politics is exercised by the *houngans,* or priests of the Vodun religion – once again, especially when a black president is in power. The houngans are the heads of the old African bush societies, minus their devil masks, and in time-sobered Caribbean form; while Vodun is a patchwork of cults brought by slaves from all over West Africa, from Senegal to the Congo. Many of the teeming gods of the Haitian pantheon, such as Damballa, the great serpent of Dahomey, and Chango, the Yoruba deity of battle and the forge, are still traceable to their African source. To these have been added several Christian saints, a former president called Nord Alexis, a brace of eighteenth-century French generals – one with a reputation for assuming material shape in order to molest young girls – and a leery, rum-swilling nobleman, Baron Samedi, who is custodian of graveyards and the dead. All these supernatural beings are more or less at the call of the houngan, through the celebration of the Vodun rites, and his power and prestige are thereby formidable. It was the houngans of old who organized and led the uprisings that put an end to French rule in Haiti, and many a presidential candidate in these days has made a surreptitious pilgrimage to a *hunfor* – the Vodun shrine – to beg a powerful houngan's support in an electoral campaign.

The most picturesque houngan of this century, whom I met just before his death, was 'Ti-Bossa, an aged and illiterate peasant, the possessor of banana plantations, a sugar mill, a wrecked Cadillac car, and – in true African tribal style – forty wives, all decently housed in separate shacks. 'Ti-Bossa was said to be the *Éminence Grise* behind a succession of governments. His magic powers were believed by most Haitians to be so formidable that by a mere effort of concentration he could shut up an enemy in an enchanted *Mapu* tree. Like most houngans, 'Ti-Bossa was benign in the practice of his singular gifts and his great speciality was saving politicians from being sacked when changes of government took place. This he did, on payment of a fee commensurate with the importance of the job, by pouring a little white powder over them and at the same time 'willing' the new president to overlook their names when the list for the revocation of posts was being prepared. The smashed-up Cadillac was the first to be imported into Haiti. Soon after it had been unpacked and was standing in the showroom of the Port au Prince agency, 'Ti-Bossa, dressed in his patched cottons, walked in followed by a barefooted boy carrying a paper parcel, which proved to contain the car's price in single dollar notes. 'Ti-Bossa paid over the money, and after a quarter of an hour's verbal driving instruction, drove off. Miraculously he reached home after a thirty-mile drive over one of Haiti's most disastrous roads. A week or two later he loaded the car with wives and set off on a tour of his spiritual satrapy, but this time almost immediately ran into a ditch and smashed his shoulder. Several hundred of his congregation man-handled the wrecked car back to 'Ti-Bossa's compound, after which a structure of the kind in which religious ceremonies are conducted was built over it and it was left to slowly moulder away.

When I saw the old man he was still as much of a power as ever. He received me kindly, robed in a sort of cabalistic dressing-gown, and apologized for not being able to shake hands, as this, he said, would involve him in a loss of magnetic power. 'Ti-Bossa showed me his favourite fighting cock, which he fed on raw meat, eggs and rum. He even favoured me with a brief glance at the interior of his shrine. This contained a certificate of membership of the Rosicrucian Order and a picture of Maitresse Erzulie, the Haitian goddess of love, shown as a dark-faced Madonna with a sword-pierced chest, beneath which numerous offerings had been placed, those in liquid form held in Coca-Cola bottles. The old houngan, although about twice my age, addressed me affectionately as 'Cher Papa'. He told me that he regarded himself as the stabilizing influence in Haitian affairs, and that as soon as he had seen Haiti properly on its feet again he hoped to apply his psychic powers to the problem of promoting world peace.

This interview took place eight years ago, and the prospects for Haiti seemed to have dimmed rather in the interim. The world outlook for coffee – Haiti's only important export – was uncertain, and there might be both falls in prices and production restrictions. A hoped-for American loan was off, since in September one Jean Talamas, a Syrian with an American passport, had been taken from the United States Embassy for a questioning at police headquarters which he had not survived. Tourism had sickened and died since the events of May 25th. A United States aid administrator expressed the view that seventy-five per cent of the country's population would shortly go hungry; and there wasn't a lot to be done about it either, he thought, because the last time American surplus food had been sent to a famine area, 1600 tons of it had never reached its destination.

'Ti-Bossa's name came up again in conversation with a man who ran a moribund tourist agency. He was a young mulatto with grand French manners who had put in a year at the Sorbonne, but who still contrived to believe in the existence of zombies, which he assured me could be distinguished by their way of speaking through the nose. 'All this couldn't have happened in 'Ti-Bossa's time,' he said. 'He would never have let things get as bad as this.' We were talking about the fateful battle in the Champs de Mars. ''Ti-Bossa would have gone down there and put a spell on them if necessary. But there it is – there aren't any men of his stature left these days.'

The Road from Hoa-Binh

ABOUT twenty miles from Hanoi the security police were waiting in a cutting. They stopped the car and pointed to a line of tanks and lorries drawn up at the roadside. 'We are now at the front,' said the captain. Somewhere far away, bombs were thumping down with the sound of prize potatoes being emptied out of a sack on to an earth floor. A few legionaries, rosy-cheeked and bearded like fierce Santa Clauses, awaited in boredom their turns to move off. When the security officer went fussily away, the captain told his driver to pull out of the line and go up to the head of the queue. Waiting until the half-track in front had a lead of a hundred and fifty yards, we started off after it. This method of moving vehicles singly through the danger zone had recently replaced the convoy system. Before reaching Hoa-Binh there were a hundred natural death-traps. Whenever the Viet-Minh felt like doing so, they could pick off an isolated car, but the new arrangement had put an end to the regular massacres that took place when a solid jam of vehicles, immobilized, say, by the blowing of a couple of bridges, was annihilated at the pleasure of the attackers.

We climbed through a landscape of Hebridean harsh-ness. Fishermen with thighs protruding from their palm-leaf coats as muscular and symmetrical as those of frogs, dipped nets the size of large handkerchiefs into muddy streams. The water's surface shivered with the explosion of heavy guns in the casemates above. The roar of our engine in a low gear muffled the sound of their

154

discharge; but we felt the blast, a gentle, recurrent concussion as if rubber-insulated chassis-members had worked loose, and were beating together under the car. Topping a low hill we saw the jungle flowing towards us through shallow valleys, and on the southern horizon arose a jagged denticulation of hills. These were the mountains of Chinese landscape painting, called '*calcaires*' by the French, who are as impressed by them as are the Chinese. The captain groped for his camera, then changed his mind as we passed an abandoned car with a sprinkling of clean holes in the body-work.

The opportunity for photography soon came. A group of men holding their guns like tired deerstalkers barred the road. We pulled up in a spattering of distant fire-crackers. A sergeant-major, grinningly invulnerable, came up saluting. 'A bit of a scrap up in the woods, sir.' 'What's that down there?' the captain asked, his eye caught by the tortoise-like shifting of something under a blanket. Following his gaze, the sergeant-major seemed a little surprised. 'A couple of chaps caught a packet.' A strange primness suddenly muted the professional insensibility of his voice. 'That one lost both legs, and his privates.' Thin rain and plum-blossom blew in our faces as the captain composed his picture: the bodies at the dramatic inter-section of the thirds, the middle-distance with its roofless pagoda, the background of fabulous mountains. A click of the shutter, and we moved off.

Under some unseen compulsion peasants were working with feverish energy to clear the jungle back from the road. 'The verb "*défricher*" is not exactly correct,' the captain said in gentle correction. 'It means, to clear for cultivation – which is hardly the case. At all events, it is a waste of time. It would take years to clear the jungle back to beyond machine-gun range of the road. Perhaps after all we are justified in using your verb, although the agricultural aspect is certainly unintentional.' He waved his hand towards a low hill-top, shaved of its vegetation and scarred with defence-works. 'Can you imagine what it is like to be up there waiting to be attacked? In this war you may sit in such a post for two years, even three, without ever seeing the enemy. Then one night your first action happens, and often it is your last. I don't mind confessing that I get an eerie sensation.

'Is it cowardice? I hope not. It is the feeling that I am at grips with something ant-like rather than human. These unemotional people in the grip of some blind instinct. I feel that my intelligence and my endurance are not enough. Take for instance those fellows they send up to dig holes close to the wire, before an attack. You'd expect them to show some human reaction when our supporting guns start dropping shells amongst them; but they don't. They go on digging until they're killed, and then some other kind of specialist fellows come crawling up and drag the bits and pieces away. Some time later that night you know the shock-troops are going to come up and get into those holes, and then you're in for it. Losses simply don't bother them. All they're concerned about is not leaving anything behind. Do you know, they actually tie a piece of cord to every machine-gun, so that as soon as the chap who's using it gets knocked out they can haul it back to safety.'

The rearing shapes of the *calcaires* took up the captain's attention. On all sides these massive limestone ruins soared up from the matted jungle, their surfaces seamed and pitted like carious teeth. Whole armies could have played hide-and-seek about their bases, protected from the air in innumerable caverns, and from the ground behind an impenetrable palisade of tree trunks. Even tank-crews might have felt themselves nakedly exposed as their road wound slowly through these sinister labyrinths. Beyond a natural gateway, where the *calcaires* closed in on the road in a miniature Khyber Pass, lay Ao-Trac, principal defence-post on what remained of Route Coloniale No. 6, and supplies base for Hoa-Binh, which was ten miles farther on. Strongpoints had been built at fifty-yard intervals in the bottleneck outside Ao-Trac, and here hundreds of Vietnamese suspects were purging their offence by forced labour, while Senegalese overseers, ebony-masked colossi, strode switch-armed amongst them.

Sun broke through the clouds lying along the rim of surrounding hills, and shone on the steel, the canvas, and the earthworks of Ao-Trac. The officers' mess was in a dug-out and every time the heavy guns fired, earth slid down like loose snow from the sloping roof. 'I echo,' said the colonel, 'General de Lattre's words, namely that we are here to stay for ever. To these I add in the humility befitting my lesser rank – if God wills it; plus a single stipulation – that they continue to send us a sufficiency of shells, and half a litre of wine per man per day.' He laughed suddenly; a full-blooded man, happily acclimatized to the proximity of death. The junior officers produced obedient guffaws.

'We try to look after ourselves here,' the colonel said, 'with particular emphasis on the rations. The men get the same food as the officers. Might as well be comfortable as long as – ' The diabolical crash of 155 mm. howitzers drowned the rest of his words, and set the unfilled Burgundy glasses chiming thinly. Shells plunged with harsh sighs into the sky and exploded six seconds later in staccato thunder. 'By the way,' the colonel said, 'I'm afraid Hoa-Binh's quite out unless you feel like being parachuted in. The Viets are shelling the Black River ferry now. Sank the ferry-boat yesterday with the second round at two thousand metres. They use those recoil-less mountain guns they make up themselves. Very easy to man-handle. Means they can keep shifting them all the time, and all we can do is to plaster the whole area and hope for the best.'

Suddenly a dull, grumbling undertone of heavy machine-gun fire had filled in the silences in the cannonading, and crashing echoes chased each other across the valley below. 'It's unusual for the tanks to be in action this time of day,' the colonel said. He pushed back his chair and got up. 'I'm afraid I must leave you. Hope you'll be staying the night. You'll find it a bit primitive – and of course noisy. We've hardly settled in yet, but I've great plans for the future. Come back and see us in a year's time, and I promise you you won't recognize the place.'

Five days later, in Hanoi, General Salan called a Press conference. Its point came towards the end of a discourse lasting forty minutes, but the correspondents, knowing what was coming, could take only a connoisseur's mild interest in the peroration. 'People put it to me this way,' said the general, his fine brooding eyes fixed rather reproachfully on his audience. ' "Having achieved your purpose in forcing the enemy to give battle – having destroyed in that battle his two best-equipped divisions – why do you retain so many men in a position where from lack of opposition they can no longer be effectively employed?" In deference to this logic, which is un-answerable,' said the general, 'I have decided to displace the centre of gravity of our forces, which will hence-forward be concentrated in the delta, and Hoa-Binh, which is now without value to us, has been evacuated. I do not wish to disclose the number of casualties we sustained in this totally successful operation (which caught the enemy completely off his guard), but I will inform you that less than ten were killed.'

Festival in Laos

THE Laotian lady disposed her silks over the spare oil can in the back of the jeep and rearranged the pearls in her hair, and as we moved off, the French major at her side leaned forward and said in my ear: 'She's an authentic Royal Highness, entitled to a parasol of five tiers.' Overhearing this, the police lieutenant, who was at the wheel, shook his head smilingly. 'Three tiers, old man.' The major waved his hands in exasperation. 'We've been friends for fifteen years,' he said. 'I can't think why we never married.' This officer was in the operations branch of the G-Staff. He was thoroughly Laos-ized, a moderate opium-smoker, gentle-mannered, and quite good at kite-fighting. As an individualist he preferred the single-handed manipulation of a small male kite, to joining one of the teams it took to handle the enormous and unwieldy females. The police lieutenant's Laotian wife, who rode in the front between her husband and myself, looked like Myrna Loy. Her beauty had been dramatized by a recent cupping, which had left a reddish disc in the centre of her forehead. Although she had climbed vigorously into her seat in the jeep, her normal walking gait was an unearthly glide. We were all off to a pagoda festival near Luang Prabang.

Glimpsed from the road above it, through the golden mohur and the bamboo fronds, Luang Prabang, on its tongue of land where the rivers met, was a tiny Manhattan – but a Manhattan with holy men in yellow in its avenues, with pariah dogs, and garlanded pedicabs carrying somnolent Frenchmen nowhere, and doves in its sky. Down at the town's tip, where Wall Street should have been, was a great congestion of monasteries. Even in 1950, although the fact went unnoticed in the Press, the Viet-Minh moved freely about the Laotian country-side, and Luang Prabang was accessible only by rare convoys and a weekly plane. But every French official dreamed of a posting to this place, thought of as one of the last earthly paradises – a kind of Aix-les-Bains of the soul.

The festival for which we were bound, the lady of the five-tiered parasol assured us, was quite extraordinary. She had sat on its organizing committee, and to make quite sure that it excelled in the friendly competition that existed between pagodas over such arrangements, a mission had been sent across the border into Siam in search of the most up-to-date attractions. As this wealthy, independent, and highly Westernized state was regarded in Indo-China as the Hellas of South-East Asia, we could expect singular entertainment.

Within the pagoda enclosure, indeed, East and West met and mingled like the turbulent currents of ocean. Monks tinkered expertly with the wiring of amplifying systems over which, that night, they would broadcast their marathon sermons on Pain, Change and Illusion. Dance hostesses from Siam, dressed as hula girls, with navy-blue panties under their grass-skirts, traipsed endlessly round a neon-illuminated platform, to the moaning of a Hawaiian orchestra. They were watched, a little doubt-fully, by a group of lean-faced young men with guitars on their backs, who, the police lieutenant assured us, were Issarak guerrillas who had joined forces with the Viet-Minh. The Issaraks, he said, had probably come down for the festival from a near-by village they had occupied some days before.

The Changing Sky

Loudspeakers howled in space, like disembodied spirits, and were silent. A few outdoor shows attracted early audiences. Thai-style boxers slogged and kicked each other – breaking off to bow politely between the showers of blows. A performance of the Manohara, the bird-woman of the Tibetan lake, had drawn a circle of country-people in gold-threaded silks; rustics whose untainted imagination still showed them the vast range of the Himalayas in a sweep of a player's hand, and a rippled lake's surface in the fluttering of his fingers. Many flower-decked stalls attended by lovely girls displayed the choice merchandise of the West: aspirins and mouth-wash, purgatives, ball-pointed pens, alarm-clocks – the spices and frankincense of our day. For those who dared to defy the abbot's ban on the traffic in intoxicants within the holy precincts, there were furtive bottles of black-market Guinness, which, mixed with Benedictine, has become a favourite aphrodisiac in Siam. Ignoring the major's horrified appeals, the princess bought a tartan skirt and a plastic shoulder-bag.

But the ultimate triumph of the festival, and chief testimony to the organizing committee's enterprise, was concealed in a gay-striped Tartar pavilion erected in the centre of the enclosure. Towards this the ladies now led the party, and having bought the candles and posies of champa flowers which served as admission tickets, we took our seats on a bench facing a low stage with foot-lights, curtained wings, and a back-cloth painted with battle scenes between humans and javelin-armed apes.

A young man in a shirt decorated with Flying For-tresses blew a trumpet, and five thin girls dressed in beach suits came tripping on to the stage. They were well-known ballet dancers, the ladies whispered. Their whitened faces, set in tranquil death-masks, obeyed the convention imposed by the performance of the Hindu epics. Their hands were tensed to create an illusion of passion and incident. While the audience sat in silent wonder, the young man blew his trumpet again, and as the eloquent fingers fumbled swiftly with zips, hooks and eyes, garments began to fall. '*Regards-moi ça!*' exploded the major. '*Un strip-tease!*'

The trumpet was heard for a third time, and the five thin girls placed their hands, palms together, and bowed to the audience. Then, gathering up their clothing, they turned and tripped daintily from our sight. Outside, night had fallen, and we walked in a fluorescent glare that leeched our cheeks, and painted on us the lips of vampires. The ladies were subdued and thoughtful from the cultural experience they had undergone, as they might have been after a visit to an exhibition of abstractionist art. The major said: 'If you wish to suggest that, in the sense of building railways and roads, France did little or nothing for Laos, then I agree. In other ways – and I say this proudly – we preserved it with our neglect. As you've observed tonight, we can't keep progress out for ever. It was a wonderful country; and if you want to see what it will be like in a few years' time, just go and have a look at Siam. Of course, the Viets may take it over. In any case, the charm we've known is a thing of the past. As for the future, you might say it's a toss-up between the strip-tease and the political lecture.'

The Manohara, as we passed it again, had reached a moment of supreme drama, when the wandering prince, having stolen up behind the unsuspecting bird-woman, is about to snatch off her wings. A gasp of intolerable suspense went up from the crowd. At that moment the steel guitars began a rumba, and the supposed Issarak guerrillas, plucking up courage at last, clambered on to the stage, and went grinning and posturing in the wake of the hula girls. There was one small member of the band who hung back, it seemed from shyness, but with the rest he had bought his ticket, and a girl came and knelt at the edge of the stage and sang to him – probably about a dream land far away.

An Individualist

EARLY in 1946, when the French forces were re-
occupying Cochin-China, the villagers of Bien Dong
heard that the troops were coming their way. To be
on the safe side they hid themselves, and the soldiers,
following the procedure laid down for such cases, burned
the village before moving on. Thereafter the people of Bien
Dong spent several months in uncomfortable dispersion,
living on shrimps and small fish they caught in irrigation
ditches. Finally a literate member of their number happened to pick up a propaganda leaflet inviting all such
homeless people to go back to the remains of their villages
and make a fresh start. A military post would be established in each village, the leaflet said, and in this way
they would be protected from future inconveniences.

Most of the peasants felt a sentimental attachment for
the locality of their ancestral tombs, so that, as soon as
the news got round, people began to stream into the
village again and to start work rebuilding their houses.
They were surprised to find themselves under the
protection not of one post but of two – built on opposite
sides of the village. One was a neat brick tower put up
by the French, and garrisoned for them by their
Vietnamese auxiliaries. The other, a primitive log-built
affair, was occupied by Caodaist militia. The Caodaists
were a militant religious sect, formed in the 'twenties in
southern Indo-China. They applied Catholic organization
to a hotch-potch of Buddhism, magic, and ancestor-
worship. They also practised spiritualism, and included
the non-fictional works of Sir Arthur Conan Doyle among

their sacred books. It is said that they aimed at nothing short of the eventual conversion of the whole of Asia, and that in support of this ambition they showed a masterly grasp of the economics of a militant faith.

The people of Bien Dong found that the Caodaist troops were under the orders of a bishop of the sect, acknowledged by the faithful as one of the multiple reincarnations of Victor Hugo. They were enchanted to find that, although the Vietnamese auxiliaries levied the usual contributions, the Caodaists piously abstained from collecting the expected toll. However, as soon as the work of rebuilding was complete, the bishop summoned the notables and informed them of the village's conversion to Caodaism. He went on to explain that vegetarianism was a tenet of the new faith, and that henceforward all fish caught in the paddy-fields and streams would be sold to enable them to assist financially in the proselytizing labours of the church. The notables, now deacons, nodded their heads in stunned agreement and went off to an evening meal of rice and vegetables.

The villagers were just getting over this shock when the new troubles began. The next village, about two miles away, practised a ferocious brand of Catholicism. Since 1840, when the last of the missionaries in those parts had been dismembered by order of the Emperor, this community had lived in a spiritual vacuum, and the canon had somewhat degenerated. In accordance with French policy of arming religious minorities against the presumably atheistic Viet-Minh, the Catholics had been given weapons and had fortified their village with a stockade and a moat. They had given up cultivating their rice-fields, and, led by a bloodthirsty old priest previously notorious for administering corporal punishment in person to the erring females in his congregation, they were accustomed to sally forth at night to prey on isolated farms. One night they raided Bien Dong, carrying off a stock of paddy and three girls. The Vietnamese defenders of the brick tower regretted, when appealed to, that they had no orders to attack anyone but the Viet-Minh. The Caodaist bishop said that he would have to refer the matter to the Caodaist Pope, but in the meanwhile would hold a seance to obtain more precise information on the affair.

Feeling that the time had come to shelve their tradition of Buddhist non-resistance, the people of Bien Dong chose a champion from among their number, a certain Tran Van Lang. Van Lang was a biological curiosity, remarkable for his sheer bulk among people of notably slender stock. Besides being dour and uncouth in manner, he was quite illiterate. He had already fallen foul of the bishop by refusing to abandon the practice of eating the semi-incubated eggs for which he had an inordinate passion. Van Lang persuaded the defenders of one of the many posts in the vicinity to sell him their rifles, after which, terrifying them with a picture of their probable fate when their superiors found out, he got them to join forces with him. Next night he attacked the Catholics, choosing for the assault the hour when vigilance was known to be relaxed owing to their habit of gathering in the church to sing canticles. The Catholics were routed, and their fortifications demolished, and Van Lang and his men returned to Bien Dong with a great store of arms. Following this the bishop was invited to remove his seat elsewhere, and the population reverted forthwith to their carnivorous habits.

Van Lang now set about rebuilding one of the brick houses that had not been completely destroyed, adding, however, a turret, in which he installed a permanent look-out with a machine-gun. When several of the ex-deacons began to follow suit, he talked them into the necessity of similar defensive arrangements. Van Lang contracted for the building, and supplied the guards from his private army. An ex-deacon who thought such precautions excessive had hand-grenades thrown through his window, supposedly by one of the Viet-Minh patrols that occasionally passed through at night. There were one or two landlords with bad records who were afraid of putting their noses outside their houses, for fear of being kidnapped by the Viet-Minh and detained in the Plaine des Joncs for a period of 're-education'. In such cases, Van Lang provided bodyguards, stipulating a minimum of four men. A new paddy de-corticating mill was obliged to invest in the most expensive defence system, plus a dozen permanent guards. Additional sources of revenue were levies on the lorries of the Chinese merchants passing through the village, a percentage on the toll charges at the local ferries, and the occasional requisition of the cargo of one of the canal junks. As this was known as 'keeping order', Van Lang was soon promoted to the headship of a canton of villages.

In keeping with his new authority, the reception room of his house is always decorated with the best artificial flowers, and has been dignified with pillars of precious wood from Tonkin, costing 3000 piastres each. The furniture is strictly functional in design, but as a concession to local taste the original plain surfaces have been encrusted with mother-of-pearl. An affair like an umbrella stand occupies the centre of the room. This was designed by Van Lang himself, and visitors hang their rifles and Sten guns on it. Van Lang receives his guests dressed in the flowered-silk gown of one of the mandarins of the old school, a slight bulge at one side denoting the

An Individualist

position of a heavy automatic. Champagne and sweet biscuits are invariably served and the new Chef de Canton, now literate, murmurs a few complimentary phrases in French.

In Indo-China the present belongs to such outstanding individualists as Van Lang – and there are many of them. They have always come up in the troublous times, and the most capable usually ended their days as provincial governors. But at this moment the future is somewhat obscure. There is no guarantee of what might be described as a stable condition of disorder. The thunder of distant artillery has recently been heard once again in Bien Dong, and Van Lang knows that a regrettable national unity will be the certain outcome of victory by the other side. He has noted uneasy stirrings among the bureaucrats in the service of the present Vietnamese Government. Sensing with their politicians' intuition that the golden age may be drawing to a close, they are showing a tendency to sell up their possessions and get the proceeds safely away to France. Unfortunately for Van Lang, he is not cut out for strategic withdrawals. In a general stampede, men of action of his type would certainly be left to face the music, which – to put it at the mildest – would mean a very long period indeed of re-education.

Golden Goa

SOON after dawn the Goa shore lifts itself out of the
sea, a horizon of purplish rocks and palms sabred by
the dark sails of dhows. The Indian trippers who came
aboard at Bombay, fashionably scarfed, in tweeds and
corduroys, have accepted a mood of southern lassitude,
and now gather in pyjama-clad groups to gaze respect-
fully shorewards. As the ship swings into a river-mouth
the shores close in, a red watch-tower on every headland,
and baroque chapels gleaming through the greenery.
Over the starboard-bow Nova Goa is painted brilliantly
on the sky, a hubbub of colour with bells chiming in the
churches built on its high places. A few minutes later
the gang-plank goes down, and as the passengers are
released into the smiling apathy of the water-front, a
flock of mynahs settle on the ship's rigging. A line of
golden omnibuses wait to bear the voyagers away to
distant parts of the territory. The town itself is served by
calashes of skeletal elegance, drawn by ponies who, even
while dozing in the shafts, are unable to relax their
straining posture. For foreigners there are taxis of
reputable old Continental make, such as De Dion Bouton.
They are decorated with brass-work and advertisements
for German beer. Although their owners are usually
Christians, Hindu gods, considered as more effective in
purely routine matters of protection than, say, St
Christopher, squat amongst the artificial flowers over the
dashboards.

The quayside, which is really the heart of the town, is
presided over by a statue, not – as one would have

expected – of the great Albuquerque, founder of the colony, but of one José Custodio Faria, who, the inscription relates, 'discovered the doctrine of hypnotic suggestion'. Faria, who is not mentioned in short textbooks on the subject, is dressed in a wicked squire's cloak of the Wuthering Heights period, and is shown strikingly in action. His subject – or victim – a young lady with a Grecian hair-style, has been caught in the moment of falling, one trim foot in the air, left hip about to strike the ground, while Faria leans over her, fingers potently extended. Her expression is rapt; his intense, perhaps demoniacal. The background to this petrified drama is a row of shops and taverns, coloured like the wings of tropical birds and decorated with white plaster scrollwork, seemingly squeezed out of a tube.

A stranger, newly landed, is whisked quickly beyond the range of Faria's ardent gaze. Ahead of him strides the porter, carrying on his shoulder the luggage which several small boys, running on either side, reach up to touch with their fingertips, as if it contained relics of extraordinary curative virtue. This attendance entitles them to claim a reward of one anna apiece. The baggage is then placed in the taxi, and the newcomer is driven to the Hotel Central, because it is a long way from the centre of the town and therefore a worthwhile taxi-fare. All this happens to be to the good. The Central is a precious repository of the atmosphere of Goa, and worthy of mention not on account of its advertised attraction – the small tiled dungeon, called a bathroom, available with every room – but of many less tangible charms unappreciated by the management. The fine old Portuguese colonial building growing naturally from the red earth of Goa is the colour of Spanish oxide, with its main façade covered in green tiles and a white make-believe balcony

moulded on one wall. Coconuts and frangipani blossoms
float down a jade-green stream at the back of the house,
and burnished, bright-eyed crows come hopping into the
front rooms and try to fly away with the guests' sun-
glasses. The beach is just across the road, and you can sit
and watch Goans prowling about it in search of the
nacreous discs with which they repair their old-fashioned
mother-of-pearl windows. A cab-driver sleeps on his seat
under a banyan tree just outside the dining-room, and
when any guest wants to go, the waiter leans out and
wakes him up by pulling the end of his whip.

Old Goa is eight miles away up the river. With the
exception of five great churches standing impressively
isolated in a jungle clearing, it is a Carthaginian ruin.
The Bom Jesus, vast and superbly baroque, houses the
principal treasure of the old Portuguese Indies in the
shape of the mortal remains of St Francis Xavier,
the great evangelist who was not quite successful in the
conversion of the Japanese. Owing to its world-wide
reputation for miracle-working the mummified body has
undergone a gradual decrease in size. Inspired by the
example of a Pope who asked for an arm to be severed
and sent to him,[1] pilgrims have succeeded, under an
osculatory pretence, in gnawing small portions off the
saintly anatomy and carrying them away in their
mouths. Sometimes these were recovered, and the
phalanx of a thumb is kept in a silver reliquary, which,
after it has been wrapped in a protective cloth, is placed
in the visitor's hand.

St Francis Xavier, although of indisputable sanctity,
was partly responsible for the bringing to Goa of the
Inquisition, which he believed to be essential for the
survival in the Indies both of the Portuguese influence

[1] It was subsequently put to use as a curative application for his haemorrhoids.

and the Christian religion. In Goa the Inquisition functioned as more of a political than a religious instrument; an efficient security service, supreme in jurisdiction and secret in procedure. Its prisoners, well fed and housed in two hundred hygienic cells, were subjected to constant psychological pressure in accordance with the most modern practice. The object was their reduction to an utter and unquestioning conformity to the discipline which the Portuguese, as a small community surrounded by vast hostile forces, believed necessary to their survival. In this the Inquisition was rarely unsuccessful, and during the century and a half of its active mission only about eight hundred and fifty of the incorrigibly independent were burned to death on the open space which has now become a football field. Even such a modest exercise of disciplinary action, however, was enough to shock the tolerant East, and render almost hopeless the task of evangelization.

As a weapon of self-defence the Inquisition was less successful than others, such as the social equality offered to all converts to the Christian religion. This was a colony with no 'Natives'. A Christian, whether of Portuguese or of Indian birth, was a Goan, and distinctions soon became unthinkable in the face of the intermarriage policy, which has bequeathed to so many admirable P. & O. stewards the purposeful faces of *Conquistadors*.

A mellowed authoritarianism still pervades the Goanese air and constitutes a provocation to the nascent democracy across the frontier. For example, everything printed in the local Marathi language – even a marriage invitation – must be submitted to the censor. Such pin-pricks set off explosions in the Indian Press. In January *Filmindia* – not the kind of journal, one would have thought, to bother itself with the problems of India's remaining pockets of colonial rule – emitted almost a Hitlerian scream of exhausted patience, under the heading 'Portuguese Pirates in India!' This article, provoked by an order under which all Indian films shown in Goa must bear Portuguese sub-titles, began by the declaration that 'a White man is always a nuisance to the rest of the human race', and went on to describe Goa as a place where a small crowd of white-skinned Portuguese rulers practised colonial imperialism over eight million coloured Indians. The truth is that one can walk about all day in Goa without seeing a white skin, and that the fifty per cent of the Goanese population which professes Christianity would exceedingly resent being described as Indians. There is in fact less colour prejudice in Goa than in India, and no Goanese paper would be allowed to publish the matrimonial advertisements for brides of fair or 'Jewish' colour which are a regular feature of the Indian Press. It is indeed unlikely that Goa would return to India in the event of a plebiscite being held. The Christian Goans would certainly vote to remain as they are, while many of the Hindus believe that they are better off economically under Portugal; for Goa shows few signs of the really appalling poverty common throughout the Indian countryside.

Certainly *Filmindia* was on firmer ground when it accused Goa of large-scale smuggling activities, although it did not add that this was done through the connivance of corrupt Indian frontier officials. Across the border flows a torrent rather than a stream of those things for which the hunger of the East is insatiable: fountain-pens, watches, and patent medicines. A more important traffic is that of gold, carried not in lorries but in the bodies of the smugglers themselves, and whole human caravans, thus strangely burdened, are regularly marshalled for the trek across the frontier. Herein lies the source of Goa's present prosperity, and on the strength of it half a street of delightful old buildings has been torn down and replaced by a miniature Karl Marxhof in grey cement, housing shops which sell nothing but American goods. Thus perishes the charm which poverty protected.

Goa's other immediate commercial advantage depends on the fact that it is an alcoholic oasis in a largely dry sub-continent – a paradise for the Indian week-ender who has been unable to wangle a doctor's certificate classifying him as an addict and therefore entitled to a ration of costly liquor. In Goa he can sit and drink all day, so long as he succeeds in concealing obvious intoxication, for at the slightest disorder a policeman will appear, to conduct the celebrant to a cell, which is likely to be less well-arranged than those provided in the Inquisition building of old.

Goa prides itself on the sobriety of its pleasures. There are no popular amusements beyond an occasional snake-charming and a well-censored cinema show. Night-clubs do not exist. If you want to listen to music, you must go down to the water-front to the Café Praia, where Arabs, pious and withdrawn – who are supposed to do a little gold-smuggling on their own account – sit pulling at their hookahs and drinking *qishr*, a decoction made to their own specification from the husk of the coffee-bean. Some-times they tell the owner of the place to switch off Radio Cairo, and begin to hum nasally and to pluck at the strings of archaic instruments. At ten o'clock a paternal authority sends all citizens home to bed by turning out the city lights. Obediently the Arabs get up from their table and grope their way down to their canoes. The dhows are anchored in mid-stream, with the silhouettes of ancient ships on decorative maps. Even if there is no moonlight you can follow the path of the canoe by a ripple of phosphorescence as the spoon-like oars stir the water, or by the declining notes of a flute.

The Moïs

THE Moïs, a handsome Malayo-Polynesian people inhabiting the central plateaux of Annam, are celebrated for their unique race-memory, which some believe is evidenced by the description in their sagas of the mammoth and the megatherium. To the casual visitor to their country, however, they are more remarkable for their amiable practice of ritual drunkenness. The consumption of rice alcohol is essential to the propitiation of numerous demons; therefore the good life is one spent in respectable intoxication, offering as its reward a happy death from disease or old age, and a comfortable after-life somewhere in the bowels of the earth. Per contra, the social outcast, who in neglect of the rites tends to lapse into a state of disreputable sobriety, will probably break his neck in an accident and spend the hereafter miserably wandering in the heavens. A Moï village is said to be one of the few places in the world where domestic animals, gorged on fermented rice-mash, are to be seen reeling about, as tipsy as their owners. The words 'Nam lu', uttered in grave welcome to the stranger, and meaning 'Let us get drunk together', have all the exhortatory fervour of an invitation to common prayer. Such a visitor, having shown himself able to stay the pace in the ensuing drinking bout, which may last twelve hours, will have won tribal respect by a demonstration of exceptional piety.

The survival of the fittest is very much a reality among the Moïs. Infant mortality before the age of five reaches seventy per cent, and only physically perfect infants are

177

reared. The sick are indifferent to treatment, since the possibility of being carried off by a decent infection eliminates the risk of the greatly-to-be-feared death by violence or accident. Pursuing this line of thought, lepers are regarded as having been born under a lucky star, as they do no work, are fed by the tribe, and are certain of an exemplary end. For all this, the Moïs appear to lead cheerful existences, completely devoid of metaphysical complexity, since life's blessings are held to depend solely upon the performance of prescribed rites; while misfortunes – from the failure of the rice crop, to the birth of twins – are the natural consequence of ritual inadequacy. As an example of the general principle involved, a crime is not attributed to the innate viciousness of its perpetrator, who is rather to be sympathized with as the involuntary instrument of a spirit offended by his victim. When brought to justice, the guilty person is likely to be condemned to provide a sacrifice in conciliation of the spirit in question, and both the parties involved participate in a ritual guzzle.

The fecklessness of Moï existence has always charmed the French – especially by contrast with the dangerous industry and sullen political consciousness of their Vietnamese neighbours – and it is with alarm that the authorities have awakened to the realization that the race is on the point of disappearing. This has provoked a belated flurry of activity in an attempt to find some method of checking the process, and I recently had the opportunity of accompanying a young official, engaged on such a project, to the village chosen for his experiments. The village had been selected for its remoteness, and therefore relative isolation from European degenerative influences, and also because the chief was a man of unusual intelligence and ability. He turned out to be an impressive figure, with the face of a Renaissance cardinal, dressed in a splendidly ornamented jacket and loincloth, and carrying under his arm a Japanese military diploma and a version in English of the Gospel of St Mark, which he greatly prized as a fetish. The chief's name was Prak, meaning 'money'. He was the only rich man within several days' march – possessing five elephants, three wives, and innumerable sacred jars and gongs. This affluence was accepted as evidence of the utter correctness of his religious observances. Under supernatural compulsion he had committed two murders, but these had been atoned for by the most lavish ceremonies.

Prak and his retinue of notables welcomed us with offerings of rice, eggs and tobacco, and ushered us into the common room of the *case*, a fine example of a Moï long-house, about sixty yards in length, elegantly made of plaited bamboo and raised from the ground on posts. Before business could be discussed there were indispensable forms to be observed. The gong orchestra began its deafening rhythm. The sacred jars were lined up, bamboo tubes thrust into their necks, and the guests invited to take up their positions on the drinking stools. The tutelary spirits' protection for the newcomers was invoked by incantations and the sacrifice of a white hen, and the drinking got under way. For the success of the ceremony it is essential for each guest to drink the measure of three cow-horns of spirit. There is no evading this obligation: one starts with a full jar and, as one draws up the liquor through the bamboo tube, the level is constantly restored by an extremely watchful attendant. As it is only after these preliminaries that the Moïs may join in, it will be seen that, in negotiating with them, outsiders are placed at a disadvantage.

After about an hour of this, the administrator, having

made no more than the barest concession to the usages, asked for the palaver to begin. On previous visits, after lecturing the tribe on their precarious position (since their submission twenty years previously the number of adult males had declined from eighty-four to forty), he had got them to agree to starting a kitchen garden, in the hope of a marketable surplus of produce, from the sale of which medicine and mosquito nets could be bought. The scheme was well under way, and on this occasion he proposed to explain the necessity for a sick-bay. Once again he rubbed in the familiar argument. 'The spirits are angry with you. You are unworthy of your ancestors. If you go on in this way you will be gone in twenty years and the Annamites will be living in your land, as they live in the land once occupied by your people at Dalat.' The thrust about the Vietnamese went home. Prak and the notables roared with indignation at such an idea. It was unanimously decided to build the sick-bay. The whole village would set to work and finish it in three days. In order to keep on the right side of the spirits, Prak added, brightening noticeably, they would inaugurate it with an un-precedented sacrifice of twenty-seven jars. 'They can't afford this kind of thing,' the administrator said, shaking his head sadly. 'It means more valuable food supplies turned into liquor.' But optimism, assisted perhaps by rice-spirit, soon returned. 'After all,' he said, 'first things first. Build up their health and numbers, and then we can start worrying about educating them out of their superstitions. The main thing is to create one model village.'

We were leaving the village when the interpreter who had been used in the palaver asked the administrator something which evidently embarrassed him. It seemed that he was inquiring for two villagers who had gone to

work on a plantation and had not returned. The administrator was afraid that they had died of malaria. Had not
the families been informed? The interpreter said, yes, but
they wanted to be quite sure, as it meant holding the
special ceremonies for those who died in a far country,
which were very expensive and took two years to complete. The administrator groaned. 'There go the quinine
and the mosquito nets. In the ordinary course of events
a death uses up the village income for a month, so
imagine what this will cost!'

But the interpreter had not finished. 'Prak has sent
five men to the plantations,' he said. The administrator
exploded, throwing up his arms in Gallic despair. 'It's
quite hopeless,' he said. 'I might as well give in ... You
see what I'm fighting against. If the planters can't get
the labour any other way, they bribe the chiefs. They
even gave one chief a jeep.' He went on to explain that
every Moï was obliged to work fifty days a year, either on
the roads or in the plantations. Once the planters got him,
he was usually tricked into signing a contract and found
himself condemned to virtual slavery, which, after the
happy-go-lucky tribal life, soon broke his heart. 'They
have to put their thumb-mark on a paper for everything
issued to them, including their tools,' the administrator
said, 'so nothing is easier than to slip in a contract worded
in any way the planter likes.'

I asked if it were not possible to investigate all cases
where men failed to return after completing their fifty
days. The administrator shook his head. 'I've gone as far
as I can go,' he said. 'I used to insist on all contracts being
signed in my presence, but the planters soon found out
that I had no legal justification. If an administrator makes
too much trouble for them they put on the pressure at
Saigon to have him removed, so the most that any of us

can do is to hamper them in small ways. There's another aspect of the situation,' he said. 'We are supposed to drill into these people how much better off they are with us than they would be with the Viet-Minh. We have to tell them that the Annamites would wipe them out if they ever came here. But what happens in practice? Why, the Viets leave them strictly alone. If they take any food from the villages, they pay for it. As for us – well, you see how it goes. The Viet-Minh can safely leave us to do their propaganda for them.'

Rangoon Express

PUNCTUALLY at 6.15 a.m., to the solemn ringing of hand-bells, the train steamed out of Mandalay station and headed for the south. Its title, the Rangoon Express, was hardly more than a rhetorical flourish, since among the trains of the world it is probably unique in never reaching its destination. It pushes on, carrying out minor repairs to the track as necessary, unless finally halted by the dynamiting of a bridge. Usually it covers in this way a distance of about 150 miles to reach Yamethin, before turning back. Thereafter follows a sixty-mile stretch along which rarely less than three major bridges are down at any given time, not to mention the absence of eleven miles of permanent way.

Here at Yamethin, then, passengers bound for Rangoon are normally dumped and left to their own ingenuity and fortitude to find their way across the sixty-mile gap to the railhead, at Pyinmana, of the southern section of the line. The last train but one had even ventured past Yamethin, only to be heavily mortared before coming to a final halt at Tatkon; but our immediate predecessor had not done nearly as well, suffering derailment, three days before, at Yeni – about ninety miles south of Mandalay.

Against this background of catastrophe, the Rangoon Express seemed invested with a certain sombre majesty, as it rattled out into the hostile immensity of the plain. Burma was littered with the vestiges of things past: the ten thousand pagodas of vanished kingdoms, and the debris of modern times; smashed stone houses with straw

183

huts built within their walls, and shattered rolling-stock, some already overgrown and some still smelling of charred wood, as we clattered slowly past. In this area, the main towns were held by Government troops, but the country districts were fought over by various insurgent groups – White Flag Communists of the Party line, and their Red Flag deviationist rivals; the P.V.O.s under their *condottieri*, the Karen Nationalists, and many dacoits. All these battle vigorously with one another, and enter into bewildering series of temporary alliances to fight the Government troops. The result is chaos.

Our train was made up of converted cattle-trucks. Benches which could be slept on at night had been fixed up along the length of each compartment. Passengers were recommended to pull the chain in case of emergency, and in the lavatory a notice invited them to depress the handle. But there was no chain and no handle. The electric light came on by twisting two wires together. Protected by the religious scruples of the passengers, giant cockroaches mooched about the floor and clouds of mosquitoes issued from the dark places under the benches. According to the hour, either one side or the other of the compartment was scorching hot from the impact of the sun's rays on the outside. This gave passengers sitting on the cooler side the opportunity to demonstrate their good breeding and acquire merit, by insisting on changing places with their fellow travellers sitting opposite.

With the exception of an elderly Buddhist monk, the other occupants of my carriage were railway repairs officials. The monk had recently completed a year of the rigorous penance known as '*tapas*', and had just been released from hospital, where he had spent six weeks recovering from the effects. Before taking the yellow robe he too had been a railwayman, and could therefore enter with vivacity into the technicalities of the others' shop-talk. He had with him a biscuit tin commemorating the coronation of King Edward VII, on which had been screwed a plaque with the inscription in English: 'God is Life, Light and Infinite Magnet.' From this box he extracted for our entertainment several pre-war copies of *News Digest*, and a collection of snapshots, some depicting railway disasters and others such objects of local veneration as the Buddha-tooth of Kandy.

Delighted to display their inside information of the dangers to which we were exposed, the railway officials kept up a running commentary on the state of the bridges we passed over, all of which had been blown up several times. It was clear that from their familiarity with these hidden structural weaknesses a kind of affection for them had been bred. With relish they disclosed the fact that the supply of new girders had run out, so that the bridges were patched up with doubtfully repaired ones. Similar shortages now compelled them to use two bolts to secure rails to sleepers instead of the regulation four. Smilingly, they sometimes claimed to feel a bridge sway under the train's weight. To illustrate his contention that a driver could easily overlook a small break in the line, a permanent-way inspector mentioned that his 'petrol special' had once successfully jumped a gap of twenty inches that no one had noticed. That reminded his friend. The other day his 'petrol special' had refused to start after he had been out to inspect a sabotaged bridge, and while he was cleaning the carburettor, a couple of White Flag Communists had come along and taken him to their H.Q. After questioning him about the defences of the local town, they expected him to walk home seven miles through the jungle, although it was after dark. Naturally he wasn't having any. He insisted on staying the night, and saw to it that they gave him breakfast in the morning. The inspector, who·spoke a brand of Asiatic-English current among minor officials, said that they were safe enough going about their work unless accompanied by soldiers. 'They observe us at our labours without hindrance. Sometimes a warning shot rings out and we get to hell. That, my dear colleagues, is the set-up. From running continuously I am rejuvenated. All appetites and sleeping much improved.'

These pleasant discussions were interrupted in the early afternoon, when a small mine was exploded in front of the engine. A rail had been torn by the explosion, and after allowing the passengers time to marvel at the nearness of their escape, the train began to back towards the station through which we had just passed. Almost immediately, a second mine exploded to the rear of the train, thus immobilizing us. The railwaymen seemed surprised at this unusual development. Retiring to the lavatory, the senior inspector reappeared dressed in his best silk *longyi*, determined, it seemed, to confront with proper dignity any emergency that might arise. The passengers accepted the situation with the infinite good humour and resignation of the Burmese. We were stranded in a dead-flat sun-wasted landscape. The paddies held a few yellow pools through which black-necked storks waded with premeditation, while buffaloes emerged, as if seen at the moment of creation, from their hidden wallows. About a mile from the line an untidy village broke into the pattern of the fields. You could just make out the point of red where a flag hung from the mogul turret of a house which had once belonged to an Indian landlord. With irrepressible satisfaction the senior inspector said that he knew for certain that there were three hundred Communists in the village. Going by past experience, he did not expect that they would attack the train, but a squad might be sent to look over the passengers. When I asked whether they would be likely to take away any European they found, the old monk said that they would not dare to do so in the face of his prohibition. He added that Buddhist monks preached and collected their rice in Communist villages without interference from Party officials. This, he believed, was due to the fact that the Buddhist priesthood had never sided with oppressors. Their complete neutrality being recognized by all sides, they were also often asked both by the Government and by the various insurgent groups to act as intermediaries.

And in fact there was no sign of life from the village. Time passed slowly and the monk entertained the company, discoursing with priestly erudition on such topics as the history of the great King Mindon's previous incarnation as a female demon. A deputy inspector of waggons, who was also a photographic enthusiast, described a camera he had seen, with which subjects, when photographed in normal attire, came out in the nude. The misfortunes of the Government were discussed with much speculation as to their cause, and there was some support for a rumour, widespread in Burma, that this was ascribable to the incompetence of the astrologer who had calculated the propitious hour and day for the declaration of Independence.

With much foresight, spare rails were carried on the train, and some hours later a 'petrol special' arrived with a breakdown gang. It also brought vendors of *samusa* (mincemeat and onion patties in puff pastry), fried chicken, and Vim-tonic – a non-alcoholic beverage in great local demand. Piously, the Buddhist monk restricted himself to rice, baked in the hollow of a yard-long cane of bamboo, subsequently sucking a couple of mepacrine tablets, under the impression that they contained vitamins valuable to his weakened state.

Quite soon the damaged rail ahead had been replaced, and we were on our way again, reaching, soon after nightfall, the town of Yamethin. Yamethin is known as the hottest town in Burma. It was waterless, but you could buy a slab of ice-cream on a stick, and the Chinese proprietor of the tea-shop made no charge for plain tea if you bought a cake. With traditional magnificence a burgher of the town had chosen to celebrate some wind-fall by offering his fellow-citizens a free theatrical show, which was being performed in the station yard. It was a well-loved piece dealing with a profligate queen of old, who had remarkably chosen to cuckold the king with a legless dwarf. The show was to last all night, and at one moment, between the squealing and the banging of the orchestra, there could be heard the thump of bombs falling in a near-by village.

It was only here and now that the real problem of the day arose. Since we were to sleep in the train, who was to occupy the upper berths, now fixed invitingly in position? Whoever did so would thus be compelled to show dis-respect to those sleeping beneath them; a situation intolerably aggravated in this case by the presence of the venerable monk who was in no state to climb to the higher position. Of such things were composed, for a Burman, the true hardships of travel in troublous lines. The perils and discomforts attendant upon the collapse of law and order were of no ultimate consequence. What was really important was the unswerving correctness of one's deportment in facing them.

Memoirs of a Massacre Town

A FEW days after I arrived in Philippeville in November 1942, I was struck by the sight of two Arabs, in morning coats, which they wore without trousers. They were loping down the main street towards the port, happily singing 'Lama el Walad Yenam' ('When the baby sleeps, I'll come for my kiss'), a current song-hit from the repertoire of the Egyptian troubadour, Abdel Wahab. These were the first Arab dock-labourers I had seen who had not been dressed in a sack in which extra holes had been cut, and it was clear that the morning coats had come from a dispensation of clothing made by the British military authorities. From that time on the sack began to go out, as the normal apparel of the working Arab, and more and more dock-workers appeared on the streets in club blazers, shooting tweeds, flannel bags, pyjamas, and various combinations of these garments. These ex-peasants worked with immense zest unloading our ships. We paid them 50 francs a day, and fed and clothed them into the bargain. The *colons* for whom they worked previously had paid 7 francs, from which 2 francs had been deducted for the ration of bread and olive oil upon which they lived. This sudden change in their fortunes filled the Arabs with jubilation, and day and night the port area resounded with the chanting of strange but ecstatic melodies. By spoiling the labour market we made deadly enemies of the *colons*.

I was present in Philippeville as a member of No. 91 Port Security Section of the Intelligence Corps, in which I was a junior N.C.O., and, having an only slightly helpful

189

smattering of Adenese Arabic, was given the task of studying and reporting upon the Arab attitude towards the Allied cause in the sub-department of which Philippeville was capital. This vague but highly educational assignment took me on motor-cycle jaunts into remote villages in the Petite Kabylie and the foothills of the Monts de Constantine, where I found the Arabs endlessly hospitable within the possibilities of their difficult circumstances, although lukewarm towards our war effort. The illiterate 99 per cent favoured Hitler because he was believed to be an orthodox Muslim, who under the name of *Haj el Jema* – the Friday Pilgrim – had made the pilgrimage to Mecca. The educated handful would have welcomed anyone prepared to rescue them from their servitude to the French. The destitution of some of these villages was the most extreme I have seen anywhere, and surpassed that of the battle areas in Tongking in the Indo-China war. Infant mortality through malaria and semi-starvation was fantastic. There were no doctors and no medicine. Women and children went completely naked in their huts. After we had been in North Africa a few weeks, the Arabs began to cheer up a little – the labouring classes seduced by the prosperity we had brought to them, and the intellectuals bemused by the hope that we might hold on to their country, or failing that, at least hand over its governance to some suitable holy madman to be produced by themselves. These people had hardly heard of communism. The leader, for example, of the nationalist movement in Philippeville, was a doctor who preached a return to the strictest standards of old-fashioned Muslim piety, with the prohibition of almost everything, including profane music, and compulsory polygamy, for the glory of the Prophet, for all males above a certain income level.

Memoirs of a Massacre Town

One of my most useful contacts among the Islamic masses was a taxi-driver called Hadef. He was a handsome, generous and irresponsible man, much given to drinking anisette in public places, partly as a political gesture against a Vichy statute not at that time repealed, which forbade the sale of alcoholic liquor to Muslims. Much of the information Hadef brought me was trivial — there were few real security problems in a base area such as Philippeville — but he was invaluable in helping to solve the mystery of the continual disappearance of stores from the base supplies depot. This depot was an irresistible magnet to a people many of whom had been slowly starving to death. With Hadef's aid I found that the goods which in one way or another were smuggled out were distributed through a receiver who happened to be one of the principal *colons*. This was a fabulous ruffian who lived in medieval style, surrounded by strong-arm men, and who, among his other feudal privileges, enjoyed, when he happened to feel like it, the droit de seigneur. We found him to be unassailable. Only the houses of Arabs could be entered without warning. This was a French citizen living in what was legally a part of metropolitan France, and we were obliged to apply for a warrant and to arrange for the presence of a gendarme before we could search his vast seigniorial house. By the time these preliminaries had been attended to our man had been tipped off. The *colon* and his gangsters stood by smiling good-naturedly while we searched for what was no longer there, although the whole house still reeked of our petrol, which had been hastily poured away down the drains.

Our port security officer, a fierce young classical scholar, since dead, knew no French, and his only non-official contact with local opinion was through the medium of a Tunisian eunuch who worked at the *mairie*, with whom

he conversed in Latin. As a result of this he was very
vulnerable to the French point of view – which was still
that of Vichy and the *colons*. The French suggested as a
cure for our problem a commando raid on the Arab
village nearest to the supplies depot. Our P.S.O. thought
this a wonderful idea; but the brigadier, when it was put
to him, was worried. The military operation finally
arranged was a compromise; a muddled and inconclusive
shambles, half-heartedly carried out by infantrymen with
normal inhibitions, in which the guilty, if any, escaped, a
few innocents were shot, and a number brought in for
interrogation. When I was called in to assist at the
questioning I risked taking Hadef along to interpret for
me. The infantry major, who had produced an Arabic-
speaking gendarme, counselled the maximum of
severity, and then made to withdraw. I told him he had
better stay; and as he was easily unnerved by a hint of
barrack-room law, he did so. The prisoners ranged from
about ten to fourteen years of age, and the interrogation
started with the gendarme trying to crush their toes by
jumping on their bare feet with his heavy boots. The
major immediately sickened, called the whole thing off,
and sent the gendarme away in disgust. He couldn't get
over the fact that these children had stood quietly to
attention while the gendarme had bullied and abused

The nineteenth century is embalmed in the ships-chandlers' shops
along the Ibizan water-front. They sell ships' stores, tortoise shells,
real Roman amphorae netted by the fishermen, false Roman
amphorae decorated with inappropriate shells, faded coral, and
small glassfuls of thin beer. The coils of rope and the pots hanging
from their walls assume under this sunshine a new solidity and a
new brilliance. Shadows loop down like black treacle and drip
from every nail-head and projection in the sun-scrubbed wood.
The ship-chandler's open door adds its breath of hemp, and tar
and canvas to the ancient aroma of this Phoenician port.

them, unwincing, their faces emptied of expression.
Hadef and I hardly had time to establish their complete
innocence before he carried them off to receive medical
attention, and no doubt conscience money. In Philippeville, it seemed that only the toughest strain of Arab had
survived.

The day before I left Philippeville, in May 1943, Hadef
arranged a farewell picnic outing with his family. He
drove out in his taxi with his wife and sister-in-law to a
safely secluded spot in the cork forest, where the girls
pulled off their black, shroud-like outer garments and
laid aside their veils. They were pretty negresses from the
deep South, nicely *kohled* and hennaed for the party, the
colour in the tattooing of their foreheads and chins freshly
renewed. Their dresses, which any palmist at Blackpool
would have envied, had been ingeniously made up from
feminine odds and ends that had come with what had
been sent to clothe the nakedness of the dock-labourers.
Both girls were probably blushing unseen under the rich
gold of their skin at this shameless exposure to a strange
male, but Hadef had insisted on the gesture. We held
hands, and danced hesitantly to Abdel Wahab on a
portable gramophone, while Hadef got sozzled on
anisette he made up on the spot from raw alcohol and a
chemical bought at the drug-store.

The coastal hamlets of the island of Formentera have no electricity,
and therefore no ice. They are accessible by road only in a cart,
and the transport by sea to the market in Ibiza of fish caught locally
is often prevented by adverse winds. When this happens, the catch is
sun-cured as shown here. Day by day, exposed on these stark, leafless
branches, its origin becomes less recognizable, and day by day the sun
transforms it more completely into a strange, surrealistic adjunct
to the landscape. The fried heads and tails of the fish are eaten
fresh by the fishermen. This, plus a few figs in summer, forms their
diet when away from home.

The Changing Sky

This was the last I ever saw of him. With the capture of Tunis, Philippeville's importance to us waned, and the base supplies depot was removed. Few ships came into port to be unloaded, but the Arab dock-labourers, having tasted of plenty, were not anxious to return to the *colons*. Some of them had managed to put by a little money, and they hung about the port disconsolately in the hope that the blessings of war might in some magic way be renewed. To the outsider it might have looked like a strike, but nothing could have been farther from the truth. The fact was that none of this collection of Simple Simons had the faintest idea of organized political action of any kind. In July, the Senegalese, who even in uniform are normally a formal and well-conducted people, broke out of their barracks, seized weapons from the armoury, which had mysteriously been left unlocked, and slaughtered every Arab they could find. These happened mostly to be the stubborn hedonists who still mooched about the port area, setting a bad example to the rest. Afterwards the bayonet-rent blazers and morning coats were carefully cleansed of blood, repaired, and passed on to close relatives, or, in extremity, sold in the market.

The Arabs who described this massacre to me were slightly surprised that all their women had been spared – a precedent which was ignored by the Foreign Legion in further operations of this kind in 1945, and again in August of 1955. Hadef, his widow told me, sorrowfully, had been chased from his taxi up to the top of the low cliff overlooking the port, and there bayoneted and thrown over the edge. The funeral of the victims had provoked a most extraordinary demonstration. Some sudden spontaneous impulse had sent all the women out into the street. In defiance of custom among the Algerian

194

Muslims they had followed the procession to the cemetery, and held up their children-in-arms to see the coffins lowered into the graves. 'No such thing had ever been seen before in our country,' Hadef's widow assured me, 'since the beginning of the world.'

Ibiza

I SPENT five consecutive summers in Spain, migrating
farther south every year before the tourist invasion
from the northern countries, which by 1954 had
provoked the building of thirty-two hotels in my favourite
Costa Brava village, with its native population of about
one thousand.

In 1955 I crossed the hundred miles of sea separating
Ibiza, the smallest and southernmost of the Balearic
Islands, from the mainland, and took a house for the
season in the coastal village of Santa Eulalia, about fifteen
miles from the island's capital, also called Ibiza. By a
stroke of luck of the kind that turns up occasionally in the
lotteries in which life involves us, this was the house I
had always been vainly looking for, a stark and splendidly
isolated villa, on the verge of ruin, with an encroaching
sea among the rocks under its windows. I paid instantly,
and without question, the extortionate price of 3000
pesetas (about £23) demanded for a season's tenancy – I
never dared admit to my Spanish friends to paying more
than half the sum – and settled down to my annual
courtship of the brilliant and infallible Spanish summer.

The Casa Ses Estaques (House of the Mooring-posts)
happened also to be the port of Santa Eulalia – or at least,
its garden was. Its original owner had been allowed to
build in this superb position among the pines on a headland commanding all the breezes, only by providing in
the rear of the premises, as a quid pro quo, several small
well-built shacks in which the fishermen stored their
tackle. This house turned its back on the basic amenities.

Ibiza

The water supply came from an underground *deposito*, normally replenished from rain-water collected on the roof, but now dry, and the alternative to the clogged and ruined installation in the lavatory was a broken marble throne among the rocks overhanging the sea.

In spite of this it offered many advantages from my point of view, not the least of these being a unique vantage-point for the study of the ways of Ibizan fishermen. These were a sober and softly-spoken breed – quite unlike the boisterous hearties of the Catalan coast – who expected the stranger to make the first move when it came to opening diplomatic relations, and only occasionally indulged in an accumulated craving for violence and noise by ritually exploding one of a store of oil drums they had recovered from the sea.

The House of the Mooring-posts had been built in the 'thirties to foster, it was said, the adventures of a gallant bachelor from the mainland, and it was full of the grandiose vestiges of a thwarted ambition. There were ten rooms, all fitted with basins and taps through which water had never run. Wires, undoubtedly intended to connect with lamps in elaborate chandeliers, curled miserably from the centre of every ceiling, although the only illumination provided was by four oil lamps of the kind carried by the Foolish Virgins in children's illustrated Bibles. Of the original furniture, stated by the fishermen to have been sumptuous, only a colossal gilt mirror remained, which must have been placed in position before the roof went on, since it would have been impossible for it to pass through the door. For the rest, there were ten simple beds, all broken in the middle, a table which could only have served for a dwarfs' tea-party, or for reclining orientals, because it was impossible for normal human beings to get their legs under it, and a country auctioneer's collection of wicker-work chairs, which sprayed the beautiful, polished-stone floor with the fine white powder of their decay whenever they were sat in. The only pictures left on the walls were seven framed engravings of early steamships, and three damp-stained lithographs of the predicaments of Don Juan. When the windows were first opened – they opened inwards – a number of nestlings which had been hatched in the space between the glass and the exterior shutters flew in and perched on the pictures. The garden was thickly coated with pine needles, and in certain lights it glistened as if gem-strewn with the fragments of the gin bottles which the fishermen claimed the last tenant – a Turkish princess – had hurled from the flat roof-top at imaginary enemies. The princess, they said, had never thought much of the place, and friction had arisen between her and them as a result of their practice of drying their nets on the front door-steps and stringing fish up to be sun-cured between convenient pine-trunks in the garden.

The Turkish princess's tenancy, which had preceded mine, with an interval of six months, had provided an episode certainly destined for incorporation in the permanent folk-lore of the island. About nine months before I arrived the princess had gone off on a jaunt to Madrid, leaving her beautiful seventeen-year-old daughter in the charge of a trusted maid. The daughter had promptly fallen in love with a young fisherman, and in keeping with the traditions of the house, which had been architecturally designed with this kind of adventure in mind, she had succeeded in receiving him in her room at night, without the maid's knowledge. Returning from Madrid to learn the worst, the mother had placed her daughter in a convent in Majorca, and given up the house. But in the course of time the girl suddenly turned up again in Santa Eulalia and went to live with the young fisher-man's parents. The civil guard were called up to intervene, but in Spain a romance is never abandoned as hopeless on the mere grounds of an extreme disparity in the social position of the parties involved, and eventually, notwithstanding the mother's wrath, the marriage took place. The couple are now in the process of living happily ever after – their first child has already arrived – on a fisherman's average income of 25 pesetas (or about 4s.) a day.

One of the pleasures of Ses Estaques was the contempla-tion of archaic modes of fishing, which were always graceful and unhurried, and not very productive. Soon after dawn every day a boat would be visible from the terrace of the house, gliding very slowly over the inert water, with an old man rowing, who stood up facing the bow. This was one of the six Pedros of the port, known as 'he of the octopuses'. At intervals he would lay down his oars, pick up a pole with a barbed iron tip, jab down into the water, and snatch out an octopus. He appeared never to miss. Pedro, a gaunt, marine version of Don Quixote, had dedicated his whole life to the pursuit of octopuses, which he sold to the other fishermen to be cut up for bait. He had developed this somewhat narrow specialization to a degree where every man who fished with a hook depended upon him, and he could see an octopus lurking where another would have seen nothing but rocks and seaweed through the wash and flicker of surface reflections. Pedro, whose daily activities were circumscribed by the light-shunning habits of his prey, also gave a spookish flavour to the early hours of the night – particularly when there was no moon – by mov-ing afreet-like about the black-silhouetted rocks with a torch with which he examined the pools and shallows.

Another picturesque adjunct to the scene was Jaume, an artist in the use of the *raï*. The raï is a circular, lead-weighted net, in use in most parts of the world, which in the Mediterranean is thrown from the shore over shoals of fish feeding in the shallows. Usually these are *saupas*, a handsome silver fish with longitudinal golden stripes, considered very inferior in flavour, but highly exciting to stalk and catch. Jaume's routine was to patrol the shore when, in periods of flat calm, certain flat-topped rocks were just covered by the high tide. Schools of saupas would visit these to graze like cattle on the weed which had recently been exposed to the air and, as there were only a few inches of water, would thrash about in a gluttonous orgy, their tails often sticking up right out of the water, and completely oblivious of Jaume's pantherish approach. Jaume had been doing this for thirty years, and, just like Pedro, he never missed. At the moment of truth his body would pivot like a discus-thrower's, the net launched on the air spreading in a perfect circle, then falling in a ring of small silver explosions, Jaume's arm still raised in an almost declamatory gesture in the second before he sprang forward to secure his catch. Sometimes he caught as many as thirty or forty beautiful fish at one throw, but they were worth very little in the market. Jaume also fished with a kind of double-headed trident with a twelve-foot haft called a *fitora*, usually at night, spearing fish by torchlight as they lay dozing in the shallows after rough weather. This kind of fishing too was unprofitable, depending, as it did, too much on time and chance, and the fishermen who went in for it were usually bachelors, without mouths at home to feed, who had an aristocratic preference for sport as opposed to profit. The great aesthetic moment of any day was when,

all too rarely, Pedro and Jaume appeared together in the
theatrical seascape laid out under our windows, Pedro
passing like an entranced gondolier while in the fore-
ground Jaume stalked, postured, and invoked Poseidon
with a matador's flourishes of his net.

These were the dedicated artists in our community.
Besides them there were others who fished with hook and
net, and thereby wrested a slightly more abundant living
from the sea within the limits imposed by their anti-
quated methods and tackle, their superstitions, their
hidebound intolerance of all innovation, and their lack of
a sound commercial outlook. Even the hooks these men
used were exact replicas of those employed by the
Romans, to be seen in the local museum, and when these
were in short supply nothing would ever persuade them
to use others of foreign origin having a slightly different
shape.

Only three of the Ses Estaques men, working as a
team, made anything like a living by Western standards.
They fished all night, putting down deep nets at a
conflux of currents off a distant cape, and at about nine
in the morning their boat would swing into sight round
the headland, its lateen sail slicing at the sky. All the
citizens of Santa Eulalia with a fancy for fish that day
would be gathered in our garden awaiting the boat's
arrival, which would be heralded by three long, mournful
blasts on a conch shell. Each day this little syndicate
landed between six and twenty kilograms of fish, about
half of which would be of the best quality – mostly red
mullet. Within a few minutes the catch would be sold,
the red mullet at the fixed price of 16 pesetas a kilogram,
while the rest, gurnets, bream, mackerel and dorados,
fetched about 10 pesetas. In summer there was never
enough fish to go round, but there was no question of

raising the price to take advantage of this situation. Ibiza may well be unique in the world in that here the laws of supply and demand are without application. Whatever the catch, the price is the same. The system by which in Barcelona or Majorca, for example, prices are advanced to as much as 60 pesetas a kilogram when hauls are scanty is considered highly immoral, although this strange island morality of Ibiza can hardly survive much longer in the face of the temptations offered by the defenceless and cash-laden foreigner.

From this it will be understood that no fisherman of Ses Estaques has ever made money to free himself – even if he wanted to – from the caprices of wind and tide. There is no question of his ever rising to the bourgeois level of a steady income from some small enterprise, nights of undisturbed sleep, and a comfortable obesity with the encroaching years. If he leaves the sea at all, he is driven from it by failure, not tempted from it by success. This is regarded as the worst of catastrophes. The life of a fisherman is a constant adventure. He realizes and admits this, and it is this element of the lottery that attaches him to his calling. In the long run he is always poor, but a tremendous catch may make him rich for a day, which gives him the taste of opulence unsoured by satiety. The existence of a peasant, with its calculation and lack-lustre security, and that of the generous, improvident fisherman, are separated by an unsoundable gulf. For an ex-fisherman to be condemned to plant, irrigate and reap, bound to the wheel of the seasons, his returns computable in advance to the peseta, is considered the most horrible of all fates.

The village of Santa Eulalia lay across the bay from Ses Estaques. It was built round a low hill which

glistened with Moorish-looking houses and was topped by
a blind-walled church, half fortress and half mosque.
The landscape was of the purest Mediterranean kind –
pines and junipers and fig trees growing out of red earth.
Looking down from the hill-top, the plain spread between
the sea and the hills was daubed and patched with henna,
iron rust and stale blood – the fields curried more darkly
where newly irrigated, the threshing-floors paler with
their encircling beehives of straw, the roads smoking with
orange dust where the farm-carts passed. From this
height the peasants' houses were white or reddish cubes
and the cover of each well was a gleaming egg-shaped
cupola, like the tomb of an unimportant saint in Islamic
lands. The course of Ibiza's only river was marked across
this plain by a curling snake of pink-flowered oleanders.
Oleanders, too, frothed at most of the well-heads. A firm
red line had been drawn enclosing the land at the sea's
edge. Here the narrow movements of the Mediterranean
tides seemed to submit the earth to a fresh oxidation each
day, and after each of the brief, frenzied storms of
midsummer, a bloody lake would spread slowly into the
blue of the sea, all along the coast. The sounds of this
sun-lacquered plain were those of the slow, dry clicking
of water-wheels turned by blindfold horses, the distant
clatter of women striking at the tree branches with long
canes to dislodge the ripe locust beans and the almonds,
the plaintive cry, '*Teu teu*' – like that of the redshank –
with which the farmers' wives enticed their chickens,
and everywhere, all round, the switched-on-and-off
electric purr of the cicadas. The whole of Santa Eulalia
was scented by great fig trees standing separated in the
red fields, each spreading a tent of perfume that came not
only from the ripe fruit, but from the dead leaves that
mouldered at their roots.

The Changing Sky

Down in the village, life moved with the placid rhythm of a digestive process. The earliest shoppers appeared in the street soon after dawn, although most shops did not close before midnight. By about 9 a.m. the first catch of fish was landed, and the fisherman who sold it arrived on the scene blowing a conch shell, a solemn, sweet and nostalgic sound, provoking a kind of hysteria among the village cats, who had grown to realize its significance. After that, nothing much happened in the lives of the non-productive members of the population until 1.30 p.m., when the day's climax was reached with the arrival of the Ibiza bus amid scenes of public emotion as travellers who had been absent for twenty-four hours or more were reunited with their families. Between three and five, most village people took a siesta. Shutters were closed, filling all the houses with a cool gloom redolent of cooking pots and dead embers. The venerable taxis, Unics, De Dions, Panhards, crowded into the few pools of shade by the plaza. The only signs of life in the streets were a few agile bantam cocks which appeared at this time, to gobble up the ants, and some elderly men of property who, preferring not to risk spoiling their night's sleep, gathered pyjama-clad on the terrace of the Royalti bar to play a card game called '*cao*'. At seven o'clock in the evening the water cart which came to replenish my drinking tank at Ses Estaques with what was guaranteed to be river water, and usually contained one or more drowned frogs, used to fill up its ex-wine-barrel at the horse-trough in the square. Then, with sprinkler fitted, it would pass up and down the only street that mattered, spraying the roseate dust. The horse's name was Astra – by which name most goats are also called in Santa Eulalia – and the driver, who was very proud and fond of it, used to urge it on with gentle, coaxing cries in what was just recognizable as Arabic which had become deformed by the passage of the centuries.

At the week-ends things brightened up. Saturday evening saw an invasion from the countryside of farm-labourers and their heavily-chaperoned girls. The farm-labourers worked cheerfully all the hours of daylight for 18 pesetas – or about 3s. – a day. On Saturday nights they paraded the principal street of Santa Eulalia, which does not possess a single neon sign, until it was time to go and dance at Ses Parres – Ibicenco for The Vineyards. Drinks at Ses Parres cost only 3 pesetas and the purchase of a round entitled the patron to watch the floor show and to dance all night. About a third of the girls still sported the local costume, which is voluminous in an early-Victorian way, a matter of many petticoats and an abundance of concealed lace, worn with a shawl like Whistler's mother, pendant ear-rings, and long-berib-boned pigtails. Many still wear the *paesa* costume because it is insisted upon by their husbands or future husbands. A friend, a prosperous small farmer, told me that of a family of eight girls, only his wife retained the paesa dress, the pigtail and the tight side curls. He had insisted on this and made it a stipulation of the marriage, as he thought it improper that another man should see his wife's legs. Women dressed in paesa style are allowed to wear 'modern' *ciudadana* clothes and rearrange their hair style if they leave the island – usually on a visit to a medical specialist in Palma.

Sunday mornings in Santa Eulalia always produced a curious spectacle. As the growth of the village away from its defensive position on the hill had left the church rather at a distance from the centre, people had taken to going to mass in the chapel of a tiny convent away among the grocers' shops and the bars in the main street. The sixty women, or thereabouts, who attended seven o'clock mass filled this building to overflowing, so that the men – who in any case were separated from them by custom – were obliged to form a devotional group on the other side of the road. Here, divided from the rest of the congregation by the flow of morning traffic, they followed the service as best they could. There were usually about twenty of them, and, as in Catalonia, I noticed that no fishermen were present. The fishermen of Ibiza are, and have probably always been, almost savagely anti-Catholic. This antagonism does not arise merely from recent conflicts over attempts to compel fishermen to attend mass or to join in religious processions, but appears to be rooted in some ancient resistance never completely overcome, to Christianity itself. It is unlucky to see a priest, or to mention the name of God unless coupled with an obscenity, and fatal, indeed, to the day's luck with the line or nets to overhear Christian prayer. One of my fisherman friends told me that his daughter, whom he had been obliged to send to the nuns to be taught her three r's, took advantage of this fear of his, to blackmail him into taking her fishing. If he refused, all she had to do was to threaten him with the Lord's Prayer. The Lord's Prayer for him was a malefic incantation of terrible power which would bring the dolphins to ruin his nets.

'And then of course,' Vicente said, 'you'll have heard of the Inquisition. They used it to try to get the better of us. All this happened somewhat before my time, fifty or sixty years ago. It was our wives they were after. Every priest's house had a hole dug in it with iron hooks on the sides and a trap door. If they took a fancy to your wife they ordered you to take her to their house for some reason or other, and you can be sure that it wasn't many minutes after you got there, before the priest had your wife, and you were down the hole.'

Ses Parres bar, dancing and cabaret, functioned on both Saturday and Sunday nights. The floor show was innocent entertainment, intended to provide something typical for foreign visitors, and usually consisted of a group of local artists performing Ibizan dances. However unexciting this might have been for the peasants in the audience it at least did nothing to dissatisfy them or endanger their cultural integrity by potentially corruptive spectacles from the outside world. In these dances of Ibiza – so unlike the bouncing jotas and sardanas of the neighbouring regions of Spain – anything that is not Moorish is pre-Moorish, or perhaps even Carthaginian, in origin. The woman twists, turns, advances, recedes, eyes cast down with resolute unconcern, body uncompromisingly stiff, feet twinkling invisibly beneath the sweeping skirt. The effect is that of an oriental doll moved by an exceptionally smooth clockwork mechanism. Her partner is more active. He postures at a distance, arms raised, hands clacking castanets, and swoops deferentially to the rhythm of flute and drum. Sometimes the rhythmic beat may be accentuated by striking a suspended sword. Occasionally the entertainers at Ses Parres are persuaded to sing those strange songs – the *caramelles* – each line of which ends in a sobbing, throaty ululation. The caramelles are properly sung before the altar on high feast days, and nobody knows anything about them, except that there is nothing to be heard like them anywhere in the world, and that their antiquity is so great that they no longer sound like music even to the most imaginative ear.

Ibiza's un-European flavour is, simply enough, the

product of the island's geographical position, of which its history has been almost the automatic consequence. It is on the nearest sea route between Spain and the two conquering North African civilizations of the past – those of Carthage and of the Moors. It was taken and colonized by Carthage only 170 years after the foundation of the mother city herself in 654 B.C. For the Moors it was the indispensable half-way port of call – in the days when a fair proportion of galleys never reached their destination – between Algiers and Valencia, the richest city of Moorish Spain. These were the two civilizing influences in the island's early history and the thousand years in between were full of the pillagings of Dark Age marauders: Vandals, Byzantines, Franks, Vikings and Normans. In 1114 Ibiza was considered by Pope Pascual II a sufficiently painful thorn in the Christian side to justify the organization of a minor crusade in which five hundred ships were necessary to carry the loot-hungry adventurers normally employed on such expeditions. But after Ibiza's final recapture from the Moors in 1235 its strategic importance was at an end. It was no more than a remote and inaccessible island,

The harbour of Ibiza is full of sailing ships, and the quayside is a permanent exhibition of their jumbled cargoes. Townspeople and peasants alike come here to watch the daily arrivals and departures of the mail steamers from Spain. At these times in the mornings and evenings the hot white sea-front comes suddenly and exuberantly to life. The citizens gather ritually under the exciting backcloth of the sea for their coffee and their 'tapas' – appetizers of calamares, octopus, prawns, liver, in narrow oval saucers. The peak of the day's excitement is reached when with three blasts of its siren a ship prepares to sail: the last-minute arrivals make their dash for the gang-plank, and the café crowds leave their tables and line the water-front, watching with nostalgia the widening spread of water between ship and shore.

with no natural wealth to attract Spanish settlers, and soon deteriorated into a hideout for corsairs, pillaged indiscriminately by Christians and Arabs. Within a few years of the recapture the population had declined to five hundred families.

Much of the island's distinctive style, and those special and subtle flavourings which differentiate it from the other Balearic islands, and also from the adjacent mainland, are likely to have been formed in the two breathing spaces of peace and plenty of antiquity. The Carthaginians taught the natives almost all they knew about agriculture, including such basic Mediterranean techniques as how to grow olives. They also instructed them in the making of garum, the most famous of Carthaginian dishes which consisted of the entrails of the tunny fish beaten up with eggs, cooked in brine and left for several months to soak in wine and oil – a modern version of which, *estofat del buche del pescado* (tunny-fish stomach stew) is still prepared. They struck enormous quantities of coins bearing the effigy of their god Eshmun, shown as a bearded, dancing dwarf, and built cave temples for the worship of Tanit, the Carthaginian Venus, who in spite of her appearance, which in her statuettes is as sensible as a Dutch barmaid's, had a sinister reputation for demanding young children as sacrifices in time of national stress.

The purest in style of Ibiza's ancient houses are without windows. Centuries ago a family will have started with a single hollow cube, and then, as its needs increased, will have added more rectangular buildings – a process apparently haphazard, but in fact governed by traditional good taste. By day the interior of the house is in perpetual cool twilight, so a kind of porch is added, where pig-killing and wedding feasts take place, and where the girls of the house carry on the complicated rigmarole of their courtships. The most important of these houses have their own defence towers, now converted to contain two or three spacious but gloomy living-rooms.

The Changing Sky

The Carthaginians were extremely systematic in the disposal of their dead, which they buried in vast necropolises, as standardized in all their details as a modern block of flats. Although most of these must have been ransacked in the past, a few still remain intact, and one or two, with their inevitable yield of ivory charms, figurines and lachrimatories, are opened every year.

During and after the Carthaginian period, the island manufactured and exported great quantities of amphorae. The Ibizan product was esteemed throughout Europe for certain magical properties attributed to the clay from which it was made, including the talismanic power of driving away snakes. Many galleys laden with them foundered in storms when outward bound along the island's excessively rocky coast, and a minor modern industry has arisen as a result of the large number of amphorae which have been salvaged intact in the fishermen's nets. These amphorae fetch between 500 and 1000 pesetas apiece in Ibiza, according to their size, shape, and the secondary interest of the marine encrustations with which they are covered. The industry consists in 'improving' genuine amphorae with interesting arrangements of shells, which are cemented in position – it took me several hours to remove those that had been stuck on a wonderful 2600-year-old pot I bought – and submerging modern amphorae in the sea until enough molluscs have attacked them to deceive the would-be buyer of a genuine antique.

The Arab contribution to the Ibizan scene is obvious and dominant. It persists in the names of all the most essential things of life – which tend to be prefixed with the Arabic definite article '*Al*'; in the cunning systems of irrigation with which the Ibizan farmer sends water coursing in geometrical patterns all over his fields; in the

semi-seclusion of the women; and above all in the architecture. An Ibizan farmhouse, which is as Moorish-
looking as its counterpart in the Atlas mountains, is in
its simplest form a hollow cube, illuminated only by its
door. With the family's growth in size and prosperity,
more cubes and rhomboid shapes are added, apparently
haphazardly, although the final grouping of stark
geometrical forms is always harmonious, and perfectly
suited to its natural setting.

In recent years poor communications and austere
standards of comfort on the island have fostered Ibiza's
individuality. An air service was inaugurated in 1958,
but when I was there the most direct route from Spain
was by a grossly overcrowded ship sailing once weekly in
winter and twice weekly in summer from Barcelona. It
required long foresight and a fair amount of luck to
obtain a passage on this; sailing times were sometimes
changed without notice, and in my experience letters
to the Compania Transmediterranea, who are the owners,
were rarely answered. One's best hope of getting to Ibiza
in the summer season was to arrive in Barcelona on the
day previous to sailing, and to be ready to queue at the
company's office soon after dawn on the following morning. The sea crossing still takes all night, and conditions
probably parallel those of a pilgrim ship plying between
Somaliland and the port of Jeddah. Decks are packed with
the recumbent but restless forms of passengers doing their
best to doze off under the harsh glare of lights installed
with the intention of reducing contacts between the
sexes to their most impersonal level. This concern for
strict morality gives the ships of the Compania Transmediterranea, as they pass in the night, an appearance of
gaiety that is deceptive.

The Changing Sky

Island transport is by buses of a design not entirely
free from the influence of the horse-drawn vehicle, taxis
which until recently were impelled by what looked like
kitchen stoves fixed to their backs, and spruce-looking
farm-carts without much springing. The choicest spots
in the island are only to be reached on foot, or with the
aid of a bicycle, which has to be carried across flowery
ravines. Once, when I was temporarily interested in
spear-fishing, I asked a Spanish friend on the mainland
where to go with a reasonable chance of seeing that
splendid Mediterranean fish, the mero, which has
practically disappeared from the coastal waters of France,
Spain and Italy. He said, 'That's easy enough. All you do
is to look out for a place without things like running
water and electric light ... a dump with rotten hotels,
where no one in his right mind wants to go.' He thought
for a moment. 'Ibiza,' he said. 'That's it. That's the place
you're looking for.'

This description was most exaggerated and unjust.
You can find a bleak, clean room in a *fonda* anywhere in
the island, and if it happens to be in Ibiza town itself,
or in San Antonio or Santa Eulalia, there may be a piped
water supply, and almost certainly a small, naked
electric bulb that will gleam fitfully through most of the
hours of darkness. What can you expect for 30 pesetas a
day, including two adequate – often classical – Mediterranean meals? Ibiza is very cheap. (I know of people
who still pay rents, fixed in the early years of last
century, of one peseta a month, for their houses.)
Resourceful explorers have found that by taking a room
only, at 5 pesetas a day, and buying their food in the
market, they can live for a third of this sum. The standard
price for drinks in back-street bars – whether beer or
brandy – is 2 pesetas, as compared to 5 pesetas in Barcelona.

Ibiza

The strong wines of Valencia and of Tarragona are sold at 6 pesetas a litre. The proper drink, though, of Ibiza, is *suisse* – pronounced as if the final 'e' were accented. This is absinth mixed with lemon juice, and costs one peseta a glass. At the *colmado* of San Carlos – a village once famous for excluding as 'foreigners' all persons not born in the village – you can see the customers on Sundays line up, a glass of suisse in hand, to receive an injection of vitamin B in the left arm, administered by the proprietress, Anita. The injection costs 5 pesetas, and is supposed to ensure success in all undertakings, especially those of the heart, during the ensuing week. These economic realities make Ibiza the paradise of those modern remittance men, the free-lance writer who sees two or three of his pieces in print a year, and the painter who sells a canvas once in a blue moon.

Every year the Spanish police decide that they must cut down on the floating population of escapists, who regard the island as a slightly more accessible Tahiti, and a purge takes place. Deportation is usually carried out on grounds of moral insufficiency. A fair amount of laxness in the private life is tolerated in Spain so long as an outward serenity of deportment is maintained. A departure from this, whether it be a matter of habitual drunkenness in public places, or brawling, or obvious sexual nonconformity, becomes officially *'un escándalo publico'*, and the perpetrator thereof receives a visit from the Commisario de Policia, who if it is a lady who is concerned will kiss her hand, before begging her to depart on the next boat. Annually, Ibiza's Bohemian plant is pruned back to the roots, and with each new season it produces a fresh crop. Most of these Gaugins are both harmless and picturesque. In 1955 the beard came in again and was adopted by all nationalities except the

Spanish. It was no longer the furious growth inherited from naval service but a sensitive and downy halo worn on, or under, the chin in true *fin de siècle* style. The female of the species looked as if she might have woven her own clothes.

A fair number of these refugees from the left-bank cellars of the northern cities drifted up the coast to Santa Eulalia. Our prize specimen, of whom we were very proud, was an English actor who had embraced a strict yoga discipline, and who regularly reached phases of reintegration in our open-air café, El Kiosko. On one such occasion he sank to his knees, eyes lifted heavenwards, in the path of a bus just about to depart for Ibiza, and remained in this position for about five minutes, while the bus awaited his pleasure with engine ticking over and a pair of civil guards sat at a near-by table eyeing him with a kind of grim connoisseurship. We also had with us for a short time, until he was removed to a madhouse, a genial American who in his less lucid moments believed himself to be Ernest Hemingway, while any evening after five it was unusual not to be accosted in one of the two popular bars by a Russian nobleman anxious to explain his solution of the problem of perpetual motion. Native – or perhaps I should say Spanish – eccentrics were comparatively rare, but they included a massive Catalan who strode through the streets perpetually cracking a stock whip, and a fair-only bullfighter who had found a summer asylum in the house of a local lady of quality and used to accompany her on long walks holding an iron bar in his extended right arm to develop the muscles employed in skewering his bulls.

These were some of the transients who brightened our lives. We also had our small colony of permanent

foreign residents who sometimes acted strangely by
Spanish standards. The only American resident, for
example, a charming lady who loved animals, built a
tower just across the water from Ses Estaques to shelter a
pony she had found with a broken leg. The tower, in
fautless local style, harmonized with the several others
that had survived in this majestic panorama from the
Middle Ages, but the quixotry of the action was complicated by the fact that it had inadvertently been built
on someone else's land. But the Spanish were as tolerant
of all such foibles as if they had been Buddhists of the
Hinayanist canon. No extravagances ever produced so
much as a raised eyebrow. If they'd had the chance to
travel, they'd probably have cut a comic spectacle in the
foreign country too. That was how the man in the street
saw it. The police sat and pondered whether or not yoga
trances in the main thoroughfare constituted a public
scandal, shrugged their shoulders and decided to refer the
matter to higher authority.

The interest I developed in Ibiza's eccentrics, both of
the present time and of the past, actually provoked me
into making a pilgrimage, to the highly inaccessible
village of San Vicente, where Raoul Villain — most
notable of them all – spent his last years.

In July 1914, Villain succeeded in concealing himself
in the French Chambre des Députés, and there shot dead
the Socialist leader Jean Jaurès, who opposed France's
entry into the First World War. This action was committed by Villain in the sincere belief that he was a
reincarnation of Joan of Arc, charged with the mission
of protecting France from the shame of a craven retreat.
He spent a few years in a lunatic asylum, after which he
was quietly released and smuggled out of the country by

his relatives, who sent him to San Vicente on the north-east corner of the island. Here he lived quietly enough until the outbreak of the Spanish Civil War in 1936, when he was killed by the anarchists.

San Vicente is about eight miles up the coast from Santa Eulalia, and as it was said to be in surroundings of extraordinary beauty, I decided one day to make a trip there. When Villain's influential kinsmen had picked out San Vicente as being, so far as Europe went, the end of the world, they were undoubtedly well-informed. The hardiest of our *taxistas* excused himself from taking me in his 1923 Chevrolet, so I hired a bicycle – as usual, devoid of brakes – which I hauled most of the way through a landscape of infernal grandeur. Peasant women robed like witches passed with a slow gliding motion over fields that were stained as if with sacrificial blood. Ancient isolated fig trees hummed and moaned mysteri-ously with invisible doves sheltering in their deep pools of foliage. The stumps of watch-towers stood up every-where half strangled with blue convolvulus, and the air was sickly with the odour of locust beans. This was a scene that had not changed since Gimnesia, the Island of the Naked, was written about in *Periplus* – except that in the matter of clothing the people had gone from one extreme to the other.

I lost my way several times and was redirected by signs and gestures by the aged women who were permitted to appear at the doors of their houses, from one of whom I received a bowl of goat's milk. San Vicente proved to be a sandy cove, deep-set among mouldering cliffs, with a derelict house, a farm, a fonda, and a shop. The beach, which was deserted, had been carefully arranged with antique wooden windlasses and a frame like a miniature gallows, from which huge, semi-transparent fillets of fish

hung drying against a violet sea. The quality and dis-
tribution of these objects in this hard, clear light, had
clothed them all in a kind of vitreous surrealism. This
may have been the chief Carthaginian port in Ibiza.
About a mile inland lies the cave temple of the goddess
Tanit, called Es Cuyerám, which is only partially excavated,
and from which in the course of amateurish investigations
great archaeological treasures have been recovered, and
most of them smuggled out of the country.

The derelict house had been built by Villain, but never
finished. The walls were painted with faded fleurs-de-lis,
and there were black holes where doors and windows had
been. The first inhabitant of San Vicente I ran into had
known the exile well, and luckily for me he spoke
Castillian Spanish. Villain, he said, had been much liked
by the village people, among whom he had developed a
kind of gentle patriarchal authority. He had been a bit
funny in the top storey, my informant said, screwing his
forefinger against his temple in a familiar Spanish
gesture – but then, clever people like that often were.
The villagers, it seemed, had shown no desire to argue
when Villain propounded his doctrine of reincarnation,
and had listened with interest and respect while he
described episodes from his previous existence, and told
them what it felt like to be burned at the stake. When
the anarchists landed there soon after the outbreak of the
Civil War in 1936, they all ran away except Villain,
who, in his grand role, and carrying the standard of Joan
of Arc, went down to the beach to meet – and perhaps
repel – the invaders. My informant's belief – which is
commonly held – was that he was on the anarchists' list
for liquidation. This strikes me as highly unlikely. The
truth of the matter probably is that they had as little
sense of humour as they had regard for human life. At

all events, Villain was shot twice and left for dead, lying on the beach. Two days later, when the villagers decided to return, he was still there, and still alive – but only just, and before a doctor could be brought, he was dead.

When you have seen enough of Ibiza's foreign birds of passage, all you have to do is to move out of one of the three centres already mentioned, where they concentrate between migrations. The interior of the island, which is 26 miles long, with an average width of about 9 miles, and has a population of 36,000, is not only unspoilt but mysterious: so much so that Don Antonio Ribas, the leading authority on everything appertaining to folk-lore in Ibiza, was unable either to confirm or to deny a rumour that a mountain hamlet exists in which women are still veiled in Moorish style.

The Ibizan peasant is the product of changeless economic factors – a fertile soil, an unvarying climate, and an inexhaustible water supply from underground sources. These benefits have produced a trance-like routine of existence, a way of life that in the absence of some social cataclysm might remain in a state of cosy ossification until doomsday. The peasant lives, on the whole, monotonously, with calculation and without surprise. He suffers from inbreeding, which produces a great deal of baldness in the women, an addiction to absinth (which in Ibiza is the real thing), and an abnormally high incidence of syphilis. Like the industrial proletarian, the Ibizan peasant carefully separates work from play, and his many fiestas and ceremonies are the sauce for the long, savourless days of hard labour. Much of the remote past is conserved in the husk of convention, and archaic usages govern his conduct in all the crucial issues of existence.

Ibiza

Of the peasant's many customs the most singular are those associated with courting, called in the Ibizan dialect *festeig*. This has no parallel elsewhere in Spain – or probably in the world – and is at least an intelligent advance on the matchmaking system employed in most oriental and semi-oriental lands. A marriageable girl's state is officially proclaimed by the act of her attending mass standing between her father and mother. Eligible young men may then present themselves formally at the girl's home and apply to her father for permission to take part in the festeig, which is staged in public. The father usually appoints an hour or more on three evenings of the week – Tuesdays, Thursdays and Saturdays – for this. Courting time begins at eight o'clock, to give the girl time to prepare herself after her day's work in the fields, and in the case of a girl who has a large number of suitors it may be continued until midnight, or even one in the morning. The highest number of suitors reported by my informant was fifteen. Three chairs are placed in the centre of the principal room, one each for the girl and her father, and a third for the suitor, and this is occupied in turn and for exactly the same number of minutes by each of the young men who have entered the amorous contest. While he puts his case the others look on critically. As soon as his time is up he is expected to get up and leave of his own accord, and if he fails in this the suitor whose turn comes next is entitled to throw small stones at him as a reminder. If this warning is ignored it is taken as a deliberate insult, and in theory at least the injured party leaves the house and waits outside for his rival, with knife drawn. The festeig – now only to be found in remote parts of the island – has in the past been responsible for numerous killings.

While docile in all other things the Ibizan is traditionally pugnacious where the heart is affected. A girl who finds herself unable to accept any of the candidates presenting themselves at her festeig, or who takes too long to make up her mind, may be publicly stoned. Peasant society – though not the Guardia Civil – approves of an admirer showing his enthusiasm for a girl by firing his pistol at a point in the ground a few inches from her toes as she leaves mass. If rejected, he sometimes, and with public toleration, gives vent to his natural frustration by firing at the ground behind the girl. In either case she loses face if she displays anything but the completest indifference. This amorous gunplay has given the police some trouble in the past. Even now a civil guard rarely passes a young peasant who is not at work when he should be, without satisfying himself that he is not concealing a weapon. The commonness of feuds in bygone days arising from breach of courting and other customs is attested by the fact that even now, no Ibizan *paes* greets another after dark: originally this was to avoid the possibility of betraying his identity to an enemy.

Such customs as these – the miming and buffoonery at the annual pig-killing, and the elaborate feasting and dancing which accompany the communal ploughing and the harvesting of various crops and, above all, marriages – are on the point of disappearance. They can no more survive improved education and 'standards of living', technical progress, and the example of how the rest of the world lives as demonstrated by the cinema, than similar customs could survive these things elsewhere. One other extraordinary custom survives, and in spite of the energetic disapproval of the Guardia Civil. This is the *encerrada* – which also continues to exist in off-the-beaten-track regions in Andalusia, and is described by Mr Gerald Brennan in his book *South from Granada*.

Ibiza

The Spaniards appear always to have felt an antipathy towards the remarriage of widows or widowers.
There is evidence to suggest that in the Bronze Age the
surviving partner was promptly killed off, since husband
and wife appear to have been buried at the same time,
squeezed into the same funeral jar. The encerrada is the
public form taken by this disapproval, which varies very
much and according to the circumstances of the case,
between the extremes of noisy but harmless peasant
horseplay and something very close to a lynching party.
The Ibicencans, who are scrupulous about the forms of
mourning, consider it particularly scandalous to remarry
within the year, the more so if either of the contracting
parties has children. The encerrada in its mildest form
consists in a party of neighbours collecting to keep the
newly-weds awake all night on the first night of the
marriage by a raucous serenade played on guitars and
accompanied by the blowing of conch shells and the
beating of tin cans. When a breach of custom has been
unusually shocking, the encerrada may be prolonged for
four or five nights and draw hundreds of participants
from other parts of the island. An atmosphere of hysteria
prevails and obscene verses are improvised and screamed
under the windows. At this point the civil guard usually
arrives, and the violence and bloodshed start. In 1950
at the village of Es Cana the police arrested the participants in an encerrada, all of whom spent fifteen days in
gaol; but the encerrada still goes on. Police permission is
actually given for an encerrada, so long as no obscene
verses are sung. When permission is refused the encerrada is still sometimes organized by the women only,
in the knowledge that they will receive milder treatment
from the civil guard, when they appear upon the scene,
than would the menfolk if they too had been involved.

The Changing Sky

The object of the encerrada, when it is seriously undertaken, is clearly to force the offenders to leave the neighbourhood, and in this it is usually successful.

On the feast of the August Virgin, which occurs on the 15th of that month, I gave a little party at Ses Estaques which in retrospect strikes me as illuminating the situation. The party was for the family of the woman who looked after the house – two daughters and a son. They had been born in the town of Ibiza, although their mother was a peasant from San José who would still intone, after a great deal of persuasion, the old warbling, elusive African melodies. In one generation the young people had moved forward a thousand years or so, even though they were still not quite modern Europeans. On this occasion they spent an hour or two happily searching for sea-snails, and prising limpets off the rocks to enrich the splendid ritual *paella* their mother would cook for their midday meal. Afterwards the boy went off to watch a football match, while the girls relaxed under the pines, half absorbed in novelettes of the kind in which servant girls marry the sons of men with race-horses and yachts. At the same time I observed the girls giving half an eye to the antics of some French women who were disporting themselves (illegally) in bikinis on the rocks near by.

This sight appeared to provoke a certain restlessness in the young women from Ibiza. It was as if they were the not wholly reluctant onlookers at the performance of some religious rite to which they felt they owed some concession of reverence, and after a while, and following a whispered conversation, both girls removed their frocks, and sat there somewhat defiantly in their petticoats.

Our garden, at the very edge of the sea, was a thoroughfare for all fiesta excursionists, and about midday a particularly imposing couple passed through with their formal escort. There were an admiral's daughter then holidaying in Santa Eulalia, her escort of two younger sisters, and a waiter from the local restaurant – a young Apollo who was not-quite hopelessly in love with her. This was an affair which, despite the obvious disparities, could have been settled in the time-honoured Ibizan way, by a formal abduction, with the girl lodged with some female person of probity until the father's consent could be obtained. Perhaps in this case a marriage by capture would be arranged, or perhaps Santa Eulalia was already too civilized. It remained to be seen.

Later that day, too, I saw the rather astonishing sight of one of our Pedros taking his wife for a pleasure trip in his boat. This, by local standards, was definitely taboo. Wives stayed at home, and women in boats were almost as unlucky as priests. But Pedro had been taking out mixed parties from the local hotel, so his wife had probably told him that if it was all right for him to take out foreign females, then he could take her too. At this time, the height of the season, Santa Eulalia was crowded with fair strangers, many of them unattached. Their admiration for the hard-muscled, sun-bronzed fishermen, who took them out for boat rides at 25 pesetas a time, was sometimes manifested indiscreetly, and a few were said to have gone so far as to make advances when the time and place was right. One of the young fellows thus favoured had only recently confided his doubts in me. Was it not a fact that foreign ladies usually suffered from syphilis?

And so this golden day passed with its contrasts and its confrontations. The French ladies came and went, happy daughters of that full turn of the wheel where sophistication joins hands with innocence, oblivious of the Bishop

of Ibiza's pastoral fulminations on the subject of decency
in dress. Pepita and Catalina got badly sunburned in
spite of the markedly olive undertone of their Mediterranean skin, and were thus chastened for their first
cautious step forward into the full enlightenment of our
times. The tide moved up a few inches and licked at the
ruins of our private sea wall. This would be the last
season that the house of Ses Estaques would embellish
this shore with its patrician decay, because the land
along the sea-front had now gone up to 40 pesetas a
square metre, so the house was to be pulled down and
replaced with the stark white cube of an hotel.

Just outside the fine ruin of the archway entrance to
what was left of the garden, a family of peasants were
gathered round their cart. They lived in a fortified farmhouse in the mountains in the centre of the island, which
sheltered several families and was in reality a hamlet in
its own right. At this time they were relaxing after a late
meal of goat's flesh and beans. One of the men had
invoked the holiday spirit by blackening his face and
dressing up like a woman, and the other, sitting apart,
was playing a wistful improvisation on his flute. The
sister had left them. She had been studying the French
women, and the Ibizan girls, and she had pinned back
her skirt from the waist so that it fell behind in a
series of dressy folds, to show an orange silk petticoat,
and was gleefully dabbling with her toes in the edge of
the tide.

The men spoke Castillian, and one of them told me
that it had taken them half the morning to get down to
Santa Eulalia, which, because of the difficulty of the
journey, they only visited once a year – on this day. But
next year, he said, things would be a lot better. The
roads were going to be made up, and the piles of flints

were already there, awaiting the steamroller. With a good surface on the roads they could cover the distance in half the time, which meant they would be able to come more often. They all agreed with me that Santa Eulalia was a very wonderful place.

Assassination in Ibiza

ANY foreigner who installs himself for the summer in Ibiza is certain sooner or later to be approached by an extraordinary dog. This will be an Ibicene hound on the look-out for temporary adoption. At first sight it may seem ludicrous to the visitor to the island that he could ever be induced to cherish such an animal. The Ibicene hound is admittedly of ancient lineage. Many local savants believe that the Phoenicians introduced the breed when they had an important settlement in Ibiza, and there is even some romantic nonsense talked about its being related to the sacred dog of the ancient Egyptians. But aesthetically it is hard to accept. There is something haphazard and unplanned about its general outlines, suggesting the result of a union between a greyhound and the most depraved-looking Indian pariah. In colour it is brown and white. Its long, pointed face ends in a pale tan muzzle, and it possesses large, pink up-pricked ears, pink toes, and amber eyes. Until one gets to know the dog better its expression, which is really mild and speculative, appears to be charged with a shifty imbecility. But above all the dog's condition is usually appalling. It will almost certainly be dreadfully emaciated, as a result of the local belief that to feed a hunting dog is to reduce its keenness. Most Ibicene hounds are kept tied up during the daytime, or at best chained to a heavy log which they drag painfully behind them. Only at night are they released, to hunt for rabbits. Despite this absence of immediate charm, the extraordinary fact is that the few dogs that make their escape and turn to beachcombing soon find someone to look after them. The secret may lie in the Ibicene hound's quiet tenacity of purpose, and the natural tact with which it finally wears away the repugnance engendered by its hideous presence. A ceremonial offering of food is all that is necessary to attach one of these wanderers to one's person and one's house. Thereafter the summer visitor never again feels himself a complete stranger. He has been formally adopted by a dog which will guard him and his possessions in the most unobtrusive way, and which will keep its distance and know its place. In fact a natural aristocrat of a dog.

This year, as usual, I passed the summer by the shores of an Ibizan bay round which five small stark Moorish-looking cottages had been put up by local enterprise for holiday occupation. By the time I arrived four of the five cottages had already been taken by miscellaneous foreign families, and each family had already acquired its dog. Within twenty-four hours I had mine too, an errant bitch known locally as Hilda, after the star in a recently shown film who had unknowingly given her name to about one-third of the female animals of Ibiza. Hilda was a normal Ibicene hound, silent and self-effacing in her disposition. Her only drawback consisted in her insistence on trotting in front of my car about twenty yards ahead – a custom carried over from the old days of the vendetta when the watch-dog had to be on the lookout for enemies lying in ambush. This reduced my speed when we made excursions together to eight miles per hour. Otherwise I was reasonably well satisfied.

The local farmer too had got himself a new dog – a six-months-old puppy – but this had turned out to be far from satisfactory. It had what was known as '*el vicio*' – that is to say it had never become resigned to its hunger – and this had caused it to devour several hens, as well as the farmer's cat, when it had been released at night. It now spent its days tied up miserably in the thin shade of a locust-bean tree fifty yards from my door. It was roped to a bough over its head in such a way that it could just manage to lie down but not walk about. For at least half the day it was in the full glare of the sun. The farmer had left a bowl for water which was dry when I inspected it, but I doubted very much that it was being fed. Its neck was raw from straining at the rope when anyone came near it. I watched it unhappily for a whole day, and when night came I took a knife, and crept out and cut it free. I was a little nervous about this interference in local affairs, and I was afraid that the dog might give me away by barking, or might even attack me as I groped towards it in the darkness. These fears turned out to be groundless. It probably took me three minutes to saw through the enormously thick, home-twisted rope. While I did so the dog licked every exposed part of my anatomy it could reach, and as soon as it was free it streaked off into the night.

Alas, I awoke next morning again to the sound of its forlorn yapping. It seemed that at dawn it had surrendered itself to its master, and was now tied up even more dreadfully than before, in a tumbril-like cart standing just by the farmhouse door. At about 6.30 a.m. a woman called Pepa, who went round the cottages doing the odd chores, came and knocked on my door. Pepa was a fisherman's daughter, now middle-aged, who worked eighteen hours a day to bring up and to pay for medical treatment for the spastic child that had been left on her door-step in the town twelve years before. She had a request to make on behalf of the farmer. Was there any chance of my making a trip shortly to Portinaix? Because if so the farmer would be glad to know if I would oblige him by taking the dog with me and abandoning it there. Portinaix was a lonely beach at the other end of the island to which I made occasional fishing trips. She added innocently that someone – certainly a foreigner – had cut the dog loose in the night, and it had slain more chickens. In that case, I suggested, what objection could there be to putting the animal out of its misery? Why not, for example, shoot it, rather than abandon it to starve?

The reply taught me how much after four summers of life in Ibiza I still had to learn about the island mentality.

'The peasants don't like to kill these dogs.' There was a hint of contempt in her voice when she spoke of the peasants.

'Not even the vicious ones?'

'No, they're too superstitious. They're afraid to kill a dog. If a peasant wants to get rid of a dog he takes it across to the other side of the island and lets it go.'

'And we get the dogs from San Miguel and Portinaix?'

'That's right. That's where Hilda came from. Mind you, if a farmer happens to be on good terms with a fisherman he usually asks him to take the dog out to one of the islands and let it go. In that way he can be sure the dog will be all right. There are plenty of rabbits on the islands.'

The fate of this dog was now beginning to assume for me a most uncomfortable importance. I fed it several times that day, but there seemed no way of defeating its chronic and ferocious hunger. It was the poorest and most repellent specimen of its breed I had seen, with the face of a monster from a bestiary, and possessed of a kind of mad vitality. In its noisy, hysterical demonstrations, too, it was most untypical of the true Ibicene. I suddenly found that I was feeling the beginnings of an attachment for this appalling dog, and the knowledge frightened me a little. A few more days' acquaintance and I knew that I should find myself asking the farmer to give it to me. And then, what was to happen when I went back to England? I was relieved of this fear by the appearance of the only other English member of the colony: a middle-aged woman. She was on the verge of tears. 'That poor, poor animal,' she wailed. 'I haven't been able to sleep for nights, for worrying about it. And of course, it's simply ruined my holiday. All I want to do now is to get away from this dreadful island, and never set foot in it again.' What was important about this visit from my point of view was that she had come to ask me to see the farmer and find out whether he would sell her the dog.

The farmer of course hadn't the slightest objection to parting with the beast. Nor did he want any money. His only stipulation was that it must be kept tied up. So the dog was removed forthwith from its tumbril and tied to a fig tree at the back of the Englishwoman's cottage. The Englishwoman put penicillin ointment on its sores and bound the loop of the rope, where it touched the dog's neck, with soft cloth. While she was tending it the dog struggled to lick her hands. It gulped down the quart of milk she gave it, and the moment it was left to itself it started its mournful barking again.

Next day Pepa brought incredible news. 'You won't believe this – the Englishwoman's going to have the dog killed!' It was the first time I had seen her shaken out of her stolid acceptance of the behaviour of foreigners in general. 'She says that the dog's hers now, so she has the right to have it killed. Please don't ask me to understand the mentality of people like that.' Pepa had shrugged off the berserk drunks, the betrousered women, the artists with their beards and sandals, the occasional nudist on the beach, and the actor who practised yoga exercises in the village square. But this was too much. To ask to be given the dog, only to have it destroyed!

But the intended mercy-killing turned out to be a harder project than the Englishwoman had expected. None of the local males could be persuaded to undertake the execution, and the village veterinary surgeon – under the pretext that he had run out of chloroform – succeeded in excusing himself too. Undismayed by this setback she took the seven o'clock bus next morning to Ibiza town, nine miles away, where she finally discovered a vet who had emancipated himself from local superstition. He promised to come out next day on his motor cycle, and said that he would arrive at about one o'clock.

Next morning a shadow had fallen upon our little colony. The atmosphere was charged with mass emotion – a kind of mob-hysteria in reverse – that made us shrink from meeting one another. The dog leaped about in the shade of the fig tree as the foreigners, French, Germans and Catalans, slunk up with their last offerings of food.

Pepa, who was to cook lunch for me that day, fussed about the kitchen doing nothing in particular, and then at midday appeared with a strained face to say that she was off home.

'Me pongo nerviosa.' ('I'm feeling upset.')

'Didn't you tell me that you killed the pigs at the matanza?' I asked her, referring to the great autumnal slaughter when every village in the island is full of the shrieking of pigs.

'That's different. Anyway, I don't kill my own pigs.'

Just as she was leaving she was treated to the spectacle of the dog being given its last meal by the Englishwoman. This contained a fair amount of meat, which Spanish fisherfolk can only afford to give to sick children. Pepa

commented on the seeming illogicality of this, in a voice
which carried at least two hundred yards.

After that began the waiting. All the foreigners had
closed the shutters of their windows facing the direction
where the dog sat under the fig tree digesting its
enormous meal, its ugly face twisted into a smirk of crazy
beatitude. The members of the farmer's family, who at
this season when the harvest was in, spent most of the
day doing odd jobs about the farmyard, had disappeared
from the scene. Even the mule-carts seemed to have
stopped coming down the road. I went into a room overlooking the sea, for no clear reason locking the door, and
tried to read, but listening all the time for the executioner's arrival. I could hear the dry clicking of the
distant water-wheels sounding as though the landscape
on which I had turned my back were full of ancient time-
pieces ticking off the seconds until one o'clock. Now I
new a little of the state of mind of prisoners confined to
their cells awaiting the obscene moment when, somewhere under the same roof, the trap door of the gallows
will be sprung. I had caught the Spanish horror of this
cool and premeditated killing, and as a foreigner, I felt
myself included in their disapproval.

The blindfolded mules turning the water-wheels
ticked off the seconds. One o'clock passed, then one-
thirty, and I was beginning to permit myself to hope that
the vet from Ibiza too might have suffered from cold feet
at the last moment. But at two o'clock death approached,
with the feeble puttering sound of a two-stroke motor
cycle bumping slowly up the terrible road. (Later I heard
that the rider had stopped at the kiosk in the village to
brace his nerves with a couple of absinths.) I went through
to the bathroom in the front of the house and looked out
through the shuttered window. The vet had leaned his

motor cycle against my wall just below, and he was unpacking the kit strapped to his carrier. The English-woman came out, and they talked in low voices. 'I shall require someone to control the animal while I administer the injection,' the vet said. 'Rest assured, there will be no struggle – no sensation of pain.' The woman said that she would hold the dog. 'It is just as well that it appears to possess an affectionate nature,' the vet said softly, filling his syringe, ' – although perhaps excessively excitable. I say this because it is not a good thing to be bitten by an animal of this kind, which is liable to carry various infections.' The woman reassured him in her halting Spanish. 'Es muy bueno. Tiene mucho cariño.' ('It has much affection.')

They went off together, walking very slowly towards the fig tree. From my angle of vision through the slats of the shutter, I could see only the lower part of their bodies for a moment as they moved away, and then I saw no more of them, but I could hear the snuffling, whining excitement of the dog and the tug of the rope as it jumped towards them, fell on its pads and jumped again. And then I heard the woman's quietly comforting voice, in English. 'Good little doggie. Good little doggie. Now keep still there's a good boy. There's a good little chap. Good little doggie.' After that, as Lorca puts it, a stinking silence settled down.

The farmer buried the unsatisfactory Ibicene hound, being paid for this service the sum of 10 pesetas – first, however, removing the rope, which was in good condition, and which he took away with him. In keeping with the discreet traditions of a people whose ancestors have suffered, on the whole silently, under many tyrannical regimes and alien people, I believe that he never commented again on this distasteful business. Pepa, who returned to duty that evening, also avoided mentioning the subject for some time. Several days later though, after a glass or two of wine, she was induced at the village stores-cum-tavern known as the *colmado* to discuss the foibles of foreigners – a subject on which she was considered by the villagers to possess expert knowledge. This time she had a new charge to add to her previous main objection about their lack of taste and common decency in matters of dress. 'They are frequently egotists,' she said. 'This applies in particular to the women, who are also spoiled. Take for example the case of the one who recently assassinated the dog. Do you really ask me to believe she did it out of love or consideration for the animal? What nonsense! She was suffering from bad nerves through having too much money and too little to do. The dog barked at night, she was distressed by the sight of it, and she could not sleep. Therefore the dog had to die. And, by the way, a woman possessing real warmth of heart will not think so much of dogs but more perhaps of certain children who go hungry. But because the children do not come to cry at her door this woman has no bad nerves for them.'

The last sentiment was applauded by several of the regulars, and then, perhaps remembering the shocking spectacle of a condemned dog eating good meat that it would never have time to digest, Pepa was struck by an idea. Perhaps, after all, it is because the foreigners never see the misery of the children. Perhaps we should tell our children to go and weep where nervous foreigners can see them.

The Bullfight Revisited

WHEN I first lived in Spain I went occasionally to a bullfight. It used up an afternoon in one of the big vociferous cities when I had nothing better to do with my time, and although I saw the leading bullfighters of the day go through their smooth, carefully-measured-out performances, I never witnessed any sight that nailed itself in my memory. The bulls came, shrewdly chosen for weight, horn-breadth and ferocity, not too much or too little, and they died in the correct manner at their appointed time, and the bullfighters, borne on the shoulders of their supporters to their waiting Cadillacs, went off with the stars of the nascent Spanish film industry. The bullfights used up some of the sad afternoons for me, but I never became a regular. I missed all the fine points, and in still shamefully enjoying seeing the man with the sword tossed, although not injured, I demonstrated a lack of natural passion for the art of tauromachy.

After that I moved to Catalonia, where the natives are seriously addicted to football but do not care for gladiatorial spectacles; so until the spring of 1957, when I found myself at a loose end on a Saturday in the southern town of Jerez do la Frontera, a period of many years had passed since I had sat on the sharp-edged *tendido* of an amphitheatre and witnessed, a little uncertain of myself, and with incomplete understanding, this ancient Mediterranean drama of men and bulls.

I went to Jerez to arrange a visit to Las Marismas, the great area of desert and marsh at the mouth of the

235

The Changing Sky

Guadalquivir, where the last of the wild camels, presumed to have been brought in from the Canary Islands, but first recorded in 1868 by a naturalist called Saunders, have only recently been captured and subdued to the plough. At Jerez it happened that the man who owned most of Las Marismas was away for two days on his country estate, so while waiting for his return I went on to Sanlúcar de Barremeda for the annual *feria* of the Divine Shepherdess. Sanlúcar is twelve miles south-west of Jerez, at the mouth of the Guadalquivir. It was the Las Vegas of Spain in the Middle Ages before the completion of the Christian reconquest, famous in particular for its homosexuals – a tradition which lingered until the Civil War, when the puritans on both sides used machine-guns to suppress entertainment by male dancers, who went in for long hair, women's clothing, and false breasts. Across the river from Sanlúcar there is nothing but desert and marshes almost all the way to the Portuguese frontier. The half-wild fighting bulls roam in the wasteland beyond the last house, and its men are fishermen and bull-herders as well as producers of splendid sherry. It is one of the many mysteries of the wine trade that an identical vine, growing in identical soil at Jerez de la Frontera, should produce a fino sherry, while at Sanlúcar it produces the austere and pungent manzanilla.

The road to Sanlúcar went through the whitish plain of the frontierland between the ancient Moorish and Christian kingdoms. A few low hillocks were capped bloodily with poppies, there was a distant sparkle of solitary adobe huts, some bulls were moving quietly in the grassy places on short, stiff legs, and storks planed majestically overhead in the clean spring sky. The peasants, holiday cigars clenched in their teeth, were coming out of their fields for the fiesta; hard, fleshless

236

men in black serge and corduroy who bestrode the rumps of their donkeys with the melancholy arrogance of riders in the Triumph of Death. The countryside smelt of the sweet rankness of cattle, and the villages of dust, saddlery and jasmine. Sometimes, as the car passed a scarlet thicket of cactus and geraniums, a nightingale scattered a few notes through the window.

Sanlúcar was a fine Andalusian town laid out in a disciplined Moorish style, white and rectangular, with high grilled windows and the cool refuge of a patio in every house. The third evening of the feria, which is spread out over four days, was flaring in its streets. There had been a horse show, and prizes for the best Andalusian costumes, and now family parties had settled round tables outside their house doors to drink sherry and dance a little in a spontaneous and desultory fashion, for their own entertainment and that of their neighbours. It was the time of the evening when handsome and impertinent gipsies had appeared on the streets with performing dogs, and a street photographer with the fine, haunted face of an El Greco saint had already taken to the use of flash bulbs. In the main square, where a great, noisy drinking party was in progress, trees shed their blossom so fast that it was falling in the sherry glasses, so that sometimes a glass of sherry was thrown out on the decorated pavement, and a gipsy's dog rushed to lick at the sweetness, and sometimes a little white blossom remained on the lip of the drinker. Down by the waterside where eight hundred years ago the first English ships arrived to buy wine from the abstemious Moors, a catch of fish had been landed and spread out with orderly pride on the sand. A hunchback chosen for his mathematical ability was Dutch-auctioning the fish at a tremendous speed, intoning the sequence of numbers so quickly that it sounded like gibberish. Girls frilled at the shoulders and flounced of skirt strolled clicking their castanets absently through the crustacean fug, and distantly the dancers clapped and stamped in all the water-front taverns.

In Andalucia a spirited impracticability is much admired, and Sanlúcar had squandered on its fiesta in true patrician style. Tens of thousands of coloured electric bulbs blinked, glared, fused, and were replaced, over its streets, and every mountebank in this corner of the ancient kingdom of El Andalus had gathered to sell plastic rubbish, penicillin-treated wrist-straps, 'novelties from Pennsylvania and Kilimanjaro', hormonized face-creams and vitamin pills. Only music and the dance were tenacious redoubts in the creeping uniformity of the modern world. The ancient orient still survived in the pentatonic shrilling of panpipes bought by hundreds of children, and although the professional dancers engaged to entertain the rich families in their private booths went in for sweaters and close-cut hair, in stylish reproof of the frills and curls of their patrons, they gyrated with snaking arms to Moorish pipe music and deep-thudding drums. The gestures of the dancers too, that trained coquettish indifference, that smile, directed not at the audience but at an inward vision, were inheritances from the palace cantatrices of Seville and Granada, not yet discarded with contempt.

The bullfight of Sanlúcar which was held at five in the afternoon of Sunday, the next day, was a *novillada*; a typical small-town affair of local boys and local bulls (which happened in this case to be formidable enough), fought in a proper ring and watched by a critical, expert, and indulgent public unable to afford stars but determined to have the real thing. Besides the formal *corrida de toros* – the bullfight seen by most foreigners – Spain offers many spectacles involving the running, the baiting, and even the ritual sacrifice, of bulls. At one end of the scale are the corridas, which are a matter of big towns, big names and big money, and at the other end are the Celto-Iberian Bronze Age ceremonies of remote villages of Castille and Aragon, sometimes involving horrific details which are properly left for description to scientific journals. In between come the *capeas* and the novilladas. The capeas are village bullfights, where the bull is rarely killed, for the village cannot afford its loss, but is played with capes by any lad who wishes to cut a public figure in a ring formed by a circle of farm-carts. The amateurs with the capes fight not for money but for the bubble reputation, sometimes receiving the bull's charge seated in a chair or in another of a dozen facetious and suicidal postures, and so many aspiring bullfighters meet their deaths in this way that the newspapers do not bother to report such incidents. The small towns possessing a real bull-ring hold novilladas in which apprentice bullfighters who are badly paid by bullfighting standards fight bulls which have not reached full maturity. In theory these should be inferior spectacles to the corrida, but often enough this is not so, owing to the dangerous determination of the young bullfighter to distinguish himself, and the fact that the bulls, although perhaps a year younger, are often larger and fiercer than those employed in the regular corrida, where they prefer the bulls not to be too large or fierce. There is less money for everyone in a novillada and therefore less temptation for behind-scenes manipulations, but on a good afternoon you can see inspired fighting, and plenty of that kind of madness sent by the gods, and most of those who meet their end in the bull-ring do so at this particular kind of fight.

The Changing Sky

Sanlúcar's novillada held the promise of unusual interest. In the home town of the breeders of the great bulls of Andalucia – which dwarf those of northern Spain and of Mexico – it would have been audacious to present any but outstanding bulls; and these, fresh from the spring pastures, would be at the top of their condition. Moreover, the first of the five superlative bulls looked for by well-informed local opinion was to be fought by a *rejoneador* – a horseman armed with a lance instead of the matador's sword, and mounted on a specially trained horse of the finest quality, and not a broken-winded picador's hack supplied by a horse-contractor. The rejoneador in action is itself a rather rare and interesting spectacle, surviving from the days of the old pre-commercial bullfight, and in this case there was an additional interest in the fact that the horseman was a local boy, who it was supposed would be out to cover himself with glory on his home territory. Finally, one of the two *novilleros* who would fight the remaining four bulls on foot was already considered an undiscovered star, equal to any of the much-advertised and top-grade matadors and certain to become one himself very shortly – if he did not push his luck too far and get himself killed in the present apprentice stage.

I spent the morning correctly, as all visitors to Sanlúcar are supposed to, tasting sherry in the different *bodegas*, and after a siesta, was driven stylishly in a victoria to the bull-ring, timing my arrival for half an hour before the fight began. The bull-ring was a small, homely structure of pink-washed brick, in the heat at the far end of the town. There was no refuge from the sun, which kept the storks, nesting on the thatched huts all round, rising stiffly to let their eggs cool off, and water-sellers with finely shaped jars were waiting at the entrances. When I arrived, a pleasant confusion was being caused by the three picadors, who were riding their horses at a creaking, shambling gallop into the crowd waiting outside, and practising bull-avoidance tactics on convenient groups of citizens. A woman protesting at being charged admission for a beautifully dressed little girl of five cried out with such passion that ripples of emotion and fury, dissociated from their origin, were stirring the fringes of the crowd a hundred yards away. Over to one side of the plaza small boys were running about under some pine trees, clapping their hands and uttering inhuman cries, in an attempt to dislodge the doves sheltering in the foliage above, and drive them over the guns of a number of Sunday sportsmen whom we could see crouching like bandits in ambush wherever they could find cover. Occasionally one of the old sporting pieces was discharged with an enormous blast, and the girls screamed prettily, and the picadors, struggling to calm their horses, swore those terrible Spanish oaths denounced ineffectively in wall posters all over the country.

In due course the promising novillero arrived, in a veteran Hispano-Suiza with lace on the seats and a tremendous ground clearance. He was in full regalia, and accompanied by three aged women in stiff black, and his manager. One of the old women was clutching what looked like a missal. The manager was a fat, gloomy and nervous-looking man, and wore a grey Sevillian hat. He and the driver lifted down the worn leather trunk containing the tackle for the fight, the swords and the capes, and the manager opened the trunk and began to forage in its contents while the others stood by, the novillero smilingly indifferent and the women with practised resignation. Something was missing from the trunk. 'I told you to count them before you put them in,' the

241

manager said fussily. 'I don't see why you couldn't have checked them from the list. It would have been just as easy.' He closed the trunk clicking his tongue, and the old woman with the religious book said, 'I made sure of the cotton. I brought it myself.' After that they went away to their special entrance. The promising novillero, who had the rather fixed serenity of expression of a blind man, and who smiled into the sky, didn't look in the least like a bullfighter (bullfighters on the whole are dark, and a trifle saturnine in a gipsy fashion); he looked perhaps more like a cheerful and promising hairdresser's assistant. Inside the bull-ring the crowd had separated into its component castes. The townsmen in stiff, dark, bourgeois fashions, with their regal wives, had massed in the best shade seats. The cattlemen, drawn together, each on his hard foot of bench, were a solemn assize of judges in grey sombreros, ready to deliver judgment on what was to come. A hilarious clique of fisherfolk in gaudy shirts and dresses kept their own slightly tipsy company. Above them all, in the gallery, a posse of civil guards under their black-winged hats, brooded down on the scene, rifles held between knees. Only the girls in their splendid Andalusian costumes were missing. It turned out that they had gone off to watch the bicycle race, which was the competing attraction of the day and something of a novelty in the bullfighting country.

Fifteen minutes after scheduled starting time, encouraged by the trumpetings of municipal band music and the exasperated slow-handclapping of the spectators, the novillada got under way. The rejoneador, Cayetano Bustillo, aged nineteen, handsome, pink-cheeked and open-faced, dressed in the Sevillian manner in short waistcoat, leather chaps and a flat-brimmed hat, made his entry on a superb horse, executing a graceful and difficult step known to the haute école as the Spanish Trot. Bustillo's mount was all fire, arched neck and flying mane, an almost mythological creature, and it would have needed only a background of fallen Grecian columns and sea, in place of the dull blood-red barrier fence and the sun curving on the wet sand, to turn this scene into a picture by Di Chirico come to life. Bustillo made a circuit of the ring, went out and returned on his working horse, a black Arab, spirited, more nervous than the first, with several small pink crescents left by old horn gashes on flanks and chest. The bugle was blown and bull number one came through the open gates of the *toril*, shattering the tensed silence of the crowd, and a kind of great contented grunt went up as they saw its size and speed. The bull came out in a quick, smooth, leg-twinkling run, at first not going dead straight but weaving a little as it looked from side to side for an enemy. Bustillo was waiting, his horse turned away, side-stepping nervously across the ring and a little to the one side; his three peons who were to work to his orders with their capes had been placed equidistant at the edge of the ring by the barrier-fence, watching the animal's movements and trying to learn quickly from what they saw. The bull appeared not to see the horse, and selecting one of the peons it went for him, tail out stiff, shoulder muscles humped and head held up until the last moment when it lowered it to hook with its horns. The peon thus chosen, Torerito de Triana by name, stood his ground instead of taking refuge behind the protective barrier, the *burladero*, which screens the entrance to the passageway, received the bull with what looked to a layman like an exceptionally smooth and well-measured pass with his cape, and turned it so sharply that the animal lost its balance and almost fell. He then proceeded to execute three more stylish and deliberate movements with the cape. The hard-faced experts all round me exchanged looks, and there was some doubtful applause from the better seating positions. The critic of *La Voz del Sur* in his somewhat sarcastic account of the fight appearing in next day's issue of the paper said: 'Four imposing passes by Torerito – who was of course quite out of order in making them, as he had appeared solely in the capacity of a peon. But then, what can you expect? The poor chap can never forget the day when he was a novillero himself.' Torerito and the other two peons were middle-aged men with worried eyes, blue chins, and fat bellies straining grotesquely in their tight ornamental breeches. You saw many of their kind sitting in the cafés of Jerez drinking coffee and shelling prawns with a quick skilful fumble of the fingers of one hand. These men had failed as bullfighters, remaining at the novillero stage through-out their long undistinguished careers. Now when their sun had set it was their task to attract and place the bull with their capes, to draw it away from a fallen bullfighter or picador, to place a pair of banderillas in the bull's neck, but not to indulge in performances competitive with that of the star of the moment.

Bustillo, who took this side-show good-humouredly enough, now called '*Huh huh!*' to attract the bull, which at last seeming to notice the horse, left the elusive Torerito and went after it with a sudden, scrambling rush. This charge Bustillo avoided by kicking his horse into an all-out gallop that took him in a flying arc across the lengthening and curving line of the bull's attack, and then when, from where I sat, it seemed certain that the bull had caught the horse, although its horn-thrust had in fact missed by inches, Bustillo leaned out of his saddle and planted a pair of banderillas in its neck.

Bustillo repeated this performance several times, using more banderillas, and then the *rejón*, which is the javelin with which the rejoneador tries – usually without success – to kill the bull. The rising tension and the suspense every time this happened was almost unbearable. Bustillo, racing away at a tangent from the bull's line of attack, his gallop slowed to the eye by the curvature of the ring, would seem to be forcing his horse into a last desperate spurt, and you saw the bull go scrambling after it over the sand as smoothly as a cat, the enormous squat bulk of head and shoulders thrust forward by the insignificant hind-quarters, short-paced legs moving twice as fast as those of the horse. After that the two racing masses would appear to fuse, the bull's head reaching up and the white crescent horns showing for an instant like a branding mark in the fluid silhouette of the horse slipping by. At this second everyone got up, moved as if by a single muscular spasm, and you found yourself on your feet with all the rest, keyed up for an intolerable sight – at the very moment when the two shapes fell apart and the tension snapped like the breaking of an electrical circuit and everyone let go his breath and sat down. Judging from his report, the *La Voz* man remained immune from nervous strain. 'As for Cayetano Bustillo,' he wrote, 'let me say at once that as a horseman he appealed to me, but as a rejoneador – no. He was content to plant his weapons where best he could in an animal that soon showed signs of tiring. And what a slovenly trick he has of throwing down the hafts of the rejóns wherever he happens to be in the ring! Has no one ever told him that the proper thing to do is to give them to the sword-handler?'

In the end Bustillo's bull, tired though it may have been, had to be killed by a novillero substituting for

Bustillo on foot. In the course of his action he gave what the critic described as several exhibitions of 'motorless flight', being caught and butted a short distance by the bull without suffering much apparent discomfort. The bull, which was too much for this novillero, died probably from fatigue and loss of blood resulting from several shallow sword-thrusts, of the kind delivered by a bull-fighter nervous of over-large horns, cutting the arteries of the neck. Bustillo was accorded the mild triumph of a tour on foot round the ring, and several hats were thrown down to him, which he collected and tossed back to their owners, showing great accuracy of aim. The bugle then blew again, the doors of the toril were thrown open, and in came the second bull.

Bull number two was prodigious. It was the largest bull I had ever seen in the ring and it brought with it a kind of hypnotic quality of cold ferocity that produced a sound like a gasp of dismay from the crowd. The three peons who were waiting for it worked in the *cuadrilla*, or troupe of the novillero Cardeño, a man in his thirties, whose face whenever I saw him was imprinted with an expression of deepest anxiety. The peon's function in this preliminary phase of the fight is to try, by the simplest possible passes, the bull's reactions to the lure of the red cape. Torerito, whose flamboyant behaviour with the first bull had caused unfavourable comment, was present again, and it was perhaps lucky for him that the bull decided on one of his colleagues, thus relieving him of the temptation to indulge in any more of the stylish bull-ring pranks of his youth. The peon chosen by bull number two, who was also a middle-aged man of some corpulence, was prudent enough to hold his cape well away from his body. The bull ripped it from his hands, turned in its own length, and went after the man who had started to run as soon as the bull passed him, and with a remarkable turn of speed for a man of his years and weight, reached the barrier fence and vaulted it perhaps a quarter of a second before the bull's horns rapped on the wood. Each peon in turn tried the bull, but taking great care to keep very close to the burladero, behind which the man skipped as soon as the bull had passed. Five minutes were spent in this way, and the bugle sounded for the entry of the picadors.

'The Luck of Spears', as this business with the picadors is picturesquely called in Spanish, is one of the three main phases in every bullfight conducted in the Spanish style in any part of the world; the other two concerning the work of the banderilleros, and of the man with the sword whether novillero or full matador. It is the part of the fight which upset most foreigners as well as many Spaniards in the past, although in the last twenty-five years the horse has been fairly effectively protected by padding, so that the spectacle so repellent to D. H. Lawrence, and in a defensive way so amusing to Hemingway, of a horse completely eviscerated trotting obediently from the ring, is no longer seen.

The purpose of the picador on his aged steed, and of the banderilleros who follow him, is to tire and damage the bull's neck muscles in such a way that without his fighting impetus being reduced he will hold his head low and thus eventually permit the swordsman, lunging forward over the lowered horns, to drive home to the bull's heart. These picadors are placed at more or less equal intervals round the ring, and each of them, if things go as they should, sustains one or more charges which he does his best to hold off by leaning with all his strength on the *pica*, jabbed into the hump of muscle at the base of the bull's neck. A metal guard a few inches from the pica's point prevents this from penetrating far and inflicting a serious injury.

In this particular case, bull number two, supplied by the Marqués de Albaserrada, when lured by the capes to the first horse, showed no inclination to attack. When finally it did, it turned off suddenly at the last moment, ripping with one horn at the horse's protective padding, in passing, and completely avoiding the pica's down-thrust. This sent up a shout of astonishment which became a continuous roar when the bull performed the same manœuvre a second and a third time. A short discussion on strategy followed between Cardeño and his men, after which the bull, enticed once again to the horse and hemmed in by the four men with capes, charged for a fourth time, this time, however, changing its previous tactics and swerving in again when it had avoided the pica, to take the horse in the rear. Horse and rider went over, carried along for a few yards by the impact and then going down stiffly together like a toppled equestrian statue. Cardeño rushing into the mêlée to draw off the bull with his cape was tossed into the air with a windmill flailing of arms and legs. He picked himself up and straightened immediately, face emptied of pain. Great decorum is maintained in the ring in moments of high drama. The bullfighters accept their wounds in silence, but the crowd screams for them. As Aeschylus witnessing a boxing match remarked to his companion, 'You see the value of training. The spectators cry out, but the man who took the blow is silent.' It was at this point the man from *La Voz* seems to have realized that he had some-thing on his hands justifying a report twice as long as the regular bullfight opening the season at Jerez was to get next day. 'This bull turned out to be an absolute Barabbas', he wrote, ' … one of the most dangerous I have seen in my life. *It gave the impression of having been fought before.'*

This sinister possibility also appeared to have suggested itself to the public, and to the unfortunate men who had to fight the bull. The first picador was carried off to the infirmary with concussion, a limp and broken figure on a board; while the others, refusing to play their part, clattered out of the ring – an almost unheard-of action – receiving, to my surprise, the public's full support. Most of the two or three thousand spectators were on their feet waving their handkerchiefs in the direction of the president's box and demanding the bull's withdrawal. The bull itself, monstrous, watchful, and terribly intact, had placed itself in front of the burladero, behind which Cardeño and his three peons had crowded wearing the kind of expression that one might expect to see on the faces of men mounting the scaffold. Occasionally one of the peons would dart out and flap a forlorn cape, and the bull would chase him back, groping after him round the corner of the burladero with its horn, without violence, like a man scooping unhopefully with blunt finger after a whelk withdrawn into the depths of its shell. The crowd was on its feet all the time producing a great inarticulate roaring of mass protest, and the bullfight had come to a standstill. A bull cannot properly be fought by a man armed only with a sword until it has been pic-ed and has pranced about a great deal, tiring itself in its efforts to free itself from the banderillas clinging to the hide of its neck. The sun-cured old herdsman at my side wanted to tell all his neighbours, some of whom were mere towns-people, just how bad this bull was. 'I knew the first moment I set eyes on him in the corral. I said someone's been having a game with that brute, and they've no right to put him in the ring with Christians ... Don't you fight him sonny,' he yelled to Cardeño. 'You're within your rights in refusing to go out there and have that devil carve you up.' That was the attitude of the crowd as a whole, and it rather surprised me. They were sympathetic to the bullfighters' predicament. They did not want the fight to go on on these terms, and when the four men edged out from behind the burladero and the bull charged them and they threw their capes in its face and ran for their lives, the girls screamed and the men cursed them angrily for the risks they were taking. The crowd hated this bull. Bullfight regulars, as well as most writers on the subject, are addicts of the pathetic fallacy. Bulls that are straightforward, predictable, and therefore easy to fight, are 'noble', 'frank', 'simple', 'brave'. They are described as 'co-operating loyally' in the neat fifteen-minute routine which is at once the purpose, climax and culmination of their existences, and they often receive an ovation – as did bull number one on this particular afternoon – from an appreciative audience as the trio of horses drag them, legs in air, from the ring. Hemingway, a good example of this kind of thinker, tells us in *Death in the Afternoon* that an exceptionally good bull keeps its mouth shut even when it is full of blood – for reasons of self-respect, we are left to suppose. No one in a Spanish audience has any affection for the one bull in a thousand that possesses that extra grain of intelligence. The ideal bull is a character like the British Grenadier, or the Chinese warrior of the last century, who is supposed to have carried a lamp when attacking at night, to give the enemy a sporting chance.

In the next day's newspaper report this bull was amazingly classified as 'tame', although it was the most aggressive animal I have ever seen in my life. When any human being appeared in the line of its vision it was on him like a famished tiger, but tameness apparently was the professional name for the un-bull-like quality of calculation which caused this bull not only to reject the cape in favour of the man but to attempt to cut off a man's flight by changing the direction of its charge. This sinister and misplaced intelligence provoked many furious reactions. I was seated in the *barrera* – the first row of seats behind the passageway. Just below me a Press photographer was working with a Leica fitted with a long-focus lens, and this man, carried away by his passion, leaned over the barrier fence and struck the bull on the snout with his valuable camera. A spectator, producing a pistol, clambered down into the passageway, where he was arrested and carried off by plain-clothes policemen and bull-ring servants. The authorities' quandary was acute, because the regulations as laid down prevented their dismissing a bull on any other grounds than its physical inability to fight in a proper manner, or the matador's failure to kill it within fifteen minutes of the time when he takes his sword and goes to face it. But physically this bull was in tremendous shape, and although half an hour had passed, the third episode of the fight, sometimes referred to in Spanish as 'the Luck of Death', had not yet begun.

The outcome of this alarming farce was inevitably an anticlimax, but it taught me something I had never understood before: that bullfighters – at least some of them – can be brave in a quite extraordinary way. Black banderillas had been sent for. They are banderillas of the ordinary kind, wrapped in black paper, and their use imposes a kind of rare public degradation on the bull like the stripping of an officer's badges of rank and decorations before his dishonourable discharge for cowardice in the face of the enemy. The peons, scampering from behind cover, managed to place two of the six banderillas, one man hurling them like enormous untidy darts into the bull's shoulders while another distracted its attention with his cape. After that, Cardeño, shrugging off the pleadings of the crowd, took the sword and muleta – the red square of cloth stretched over wooden supports that replaces the cape when the last phase of the drama begins – and walked towards the bull followed by his three obviously terrified peons. Although Cardeño had been standing in the shade for the last ten minutes, his forehead and cheeks were shining with sweat and his mouth was open like a runner's after a hard race. No one in this crowd wanted to see Cardeño killed. They wanted this unnatural monster of a bull disposed of by any means, fair or foul, but the rules of the bull-ring provided no solution for this kind of emergency. There was no recognized way out but for Cardeño to take the sword and muleta and try to stay alive for fifteen minutes, after which time the regulations permit the president to order the steers to be driven into the ring to take out a bull which cannot be killed.

Cardeño showed his bravery by actually fighting the bull. Perhaps he could not afford to damage his reputation by leaving this bull unkilled, however excusable the circumstances might have made such a course. With the unnerving shrieks of the crowd at his back he went out, sighted along the sword, lunged, and somehow escaped the thrusting horns. It was not good bullfighting. This was clear even to an outsider. Good bullfighting, as a spectacle, is a succession of sculptural groupings of man and beast, composed, held, and reformed, with the appearance almost of leisure, and contains nothing of the graceless and ungainly skirmishing that was all that the circumstances permitted Cardeño to offer. Once the sword struck on the frontal bone of the bull's skull, and another time Cardeño blunted its point on the boss of the horns. Several times it stuck an inch or two in the muscles of the bull's neck, and the bull shrugged it out, sending it flying high into the air. The thing lasted probably half an hour, and, contrary to the rules, the steers were not sent for – either because the president was determined to save Cardeño's face, even at the risk of his life, or because there were no steers ready as there should have been. In the end the too-intelligent bull keeled over, weakened by the innumerable pinpricks that it had probably hardly felt. It received the coup de grâce and was dragged away, to a general groan of execration. Cardeño, who seemed suddenly to have aged, was given a triumphant tour of the ring by an audience very pleased to see him alive.

After that the novillada of Sanlúcar went much like any other bullfight. The stylish young novillero who had arrived in the Hispano-Suiza killed his bulls, who were big, brave and stupid, in an exemplary fashion. This performance looked as good as one put on by any of the great stars of Madrid or Barcelona, and it was pretty clear that the old Hispano would soon be changed for a Cadillac. The bulls did their best for the man, allowing themselves to be deluded by cape flourishes and slow and deliberate passes of supreme elegance, and the novillero tempted fortune only once, receiving the bull over-audaciously on his knees and being vigorously tossed as it swung round on him for the second half of the pass. Miraculously all he suffered was an embarrassing two-foot rent in his trousers, and was obliged to retire, screened by capes from the public, to the passageway, for this to be sewn up, probably with the very cotton the old lady in black had remembered to bring. The crowd did not hold this against the bull, and it was accorded a rousing cheer, when five minutes later it was removed from the ring.

With this the fight ended, to the satisfaction of all but the critic of *La Voz*. The two novilleros were carried back to their hotel on the shoulders of their supporters, followed by a running crowd of several hundred enthusiasts. Just before the hotel was reached they unfortunately collided with another crowd running in the other direction who were honouring the winner of the bicycle race; but bicycle racing being an alien importation with a small following in this undisturbed corner of Spain, the bull-ring crowd soon pushed the others into side streets, smothered their opposition, and fought on to reach their objective. When I passed the bull-ring half an hour later the old Hispano-Suiza was still there. The enthusiasts had pushed it about twenty yards and it had broken their spirit, and a man with a peaked cap and withered arm stood by it waiting to collect a peseta from whoever came to drive it away. Otherwise the place was deserted, and the circling storks had come down low in the colourless evening sky.

Previously published by

ELAND BOOKS

MEMOIRS OF A
BENGAL CIVILIAN

JOHN BEAMES
The lively narrative of a Victorian district-officer

With an introduction by Philip Mason

They are as entertaining as Hickey . . . accounts like these illuminate the dark corners of history.
Times Literary Supplement

John Beames writes a spendidly virile English and he is incapable of being dull; also he never hesitates to speak his mind. It is extraordinary that these memoirs should have remained so long unpublished . . . the discovery is a real find.
John Morris, The Listener

A gem of the first water. Beames, in addition to being a first-class descriptive writer in the plain Defoesque manner, was that thing most necessary of all in an autobiographer – an original. His book is of the highest value.
The Times

ELAND BOOKS
specialise in the literature of travel.
If you wish to receive details of forthcoming publications,
please send your address to
Eland Books, 53 Eland Road, London SW11 5JX

Previously published by

ELAND BOOKS

A VISIT TO DON OTAVIO
SYBILLE BEDFORD
A Mexican Journey

I am convinced that, once this wonderful book
becomes better known, it will seem incredible that it
could ever have gone out of print.
Bruce Chatwin, Vogue

This book can be recommended as vastly enjoyable.
Here is a book radiant with comedy and colour.
Raymond Mortimer, Sunday Times

Perceptive, lively, aware of the significance of trifles,
and a fine writer. Applied to a beautiful, various, and
still inscrutable country, these talents yield a singu-
larly delightful result.
The Times

This book has that ageless quality which is what
most people mean when they describe a book as
classical. From the moment that the train leaves New
York...it is certain that this journey will be rewarding.
When one finally leaves Mrs Bedford on the point of
departure, it is with the double regret of leaving
Mexico and her company, and one cannot say more
than that.
Elizabeth Jane Howard

Malicious, friendly, entertaining and witty.
Evening Standard

This edition is not for sale in the USA

ELAND BOOKS
specialise in the literature of travel.
If you wish to receive details of forthcoming publications,
please send your address to
Eland Books, 53 Eland Road, London SW11 5JX

Previously published by

ELAND BOOKS

VIVA MEXICO!

CHARLES MACOMB FLANDRAU
A traveller's account of life in Mexico

With a new preface by Nicholas Shakespeare

His lightness of touch is deceiving, for one reads *Viva Mexico!* under the impression that one is only being amused, but comes to realise in the end that Mr Flandrau has presented a truer, more graphic and comprehensive picture of the Mexican character than could be obtained from a shelful of more serious and scientific tomes.
New York Times

The best book I have come upon which attempts the alluring but difficult task of introducing the tricks and manners of one country to the people of another.
Alexander Woollcott

The most enchanting, as well as extremely funny book on Mexico... I wish it were reprinted.
Sybille Bedford

His impressions are deep, sympathetic and judicious. In addition, he is a marvellous writer, with something of Mark Twain's high spirits and Henry James's suavity...as witty as he is observant.
Geoffrey Smith, Country Life

ELAND BOOKS
specialise in the literature of travel.
If you wish to receive details of forthcoming publications,
please send your address to
Eland Books, 53 Eland Road, London SW11 5JX

Previously published by
ELAND BOOKS

TRAVELS WITH MYSELF AND ANOTHER

MARTHA GELLHORN

Must surely be ranked as one of the funniest travel books of our time — second only to *A Short Walk in the Hindu Kush* ... It doesn't matter whether this author is experiencing marrow-freezing misadventures in war-ravaged China, or driving a Landrover through East African game-parks, or conversing with hippies in Israel, or spending a week in a Moscow Intourist Hotel. Martha Gellhorn's reactions are what count and one enjoys equally her blistering scorn of humbug, her hilarious eccentricities, her unsentimental compassion.
Dervla Murphy, Irish Times

Spun with a fine blend of irony and epigram. She is incapable of writing a dull sentence.
The Times

Miss Gellhorn has a novelist's eye, a flair for black comedy and a short fuse...there is not a boring word in her humane and often funny book.
The New York Times

Among the funniest and best written books I have ever read.
Byron Rogers, Evening Standard

ELAND BOOKS
specialise in the literature of travel.
If you wish to receive details of forthcoming publications,
please send your address to
Eland Books, 53 Eland Road, London SW11 5JX

Previously published by

ELAND BOOKS

MOROCCO
THAT WAS

WALTER HARRIS

With a new preface by Patrick Thursfield

Both moving and hilariously satirical.
Gavin Maxwell, Lords of the Atlas

Many interesting sidelights on the customs and
characters of the Moors...intimate knowledge of the
courts, its language and customs...thorough understanding of the Moorish character.
New York Times

No Englishman knows Morocco better than Mr W.
B. Harris and his new book...is most entertaining.
Spectator (1921)

The author's great love of Morocco and of the Moors
is only matched by his infectious zest for life... thanks
to his observant eye and a gift for felicitously turned
phrases, the books of Walter Harris can claim to rank
as literature.
Rom Landau, Moroccan Journal (1957)

His pages bring back the vanished days of the unfet-
tered Sultanate in all their dark splendour; a mingling
of magnificence with squalor, culture with barbarism,
refined cruelty with naive humour that reads like a
dream of the Arabian Nights.
The Times

ELAND BOOKS
specialise in the literature of travel.
If you wish to receive details of forthcoming publications,
please send your address to
Eland Books, 53 Eland Road, London SW11 5JX

Previously published by

ELAND BOOKS

FAR AWAY AND LONG AGO

W. H. HUDSON

A Childhood in Argentina

With a new preface by Nicholas Shakespeare

One cannot tell how this fellow gets his effects; he writes as the grass grows.
It is as if some very fine and gentle spirit were whispering to him the sentences he puts down on the paper. A privileged being

Joseph Conrad

Hudson's work is a vision of natural beauty and of human life as it might be, quickened and sweetened by the sun and the wind and the rain, and by fellowship with all other forms of life...a very great writer... the most valuable our age has possessed.

John Galsworthy

And there was no one – no writer – who did not acknowledge without question that this composed giant was the greatest living writer of English.
Far Away and Long Ago is the most self-revelatory of all his books.

Ford Madox Ford

Completely riveting and should be read by everyone.
Auberon Waugh

ELAND BOOKS
specialise in the literature of travel.
If you wish to receive details of forthcoming publications,
please send your address to
Eland Books, 53 Eland Road, London SW11 5JX

Previously published by

ELAND BOOKS

A DRAGON APPARENT
NORMAN LEWIS
Travels in Cambodia, Laos and Vietnam

A book which should take its place in the permanent
literature of the Far East.
Economist

One of the most absorbing travel books I have read
for a very long time...the great charm of the work is
its literary vividness. Nothing he describes is dull.
Peter Quennell, Daily Mail

One of the best post-war travel books and, in retrospect, the most heartrending.
The Observer

Apart from the *Quiet American,* which is of course a
novel, the best book on Vietnam remains *A Dragon
Apparent.*
Richard West, Spectator (1978)

One of the most elegant, witty, immensely readable,
touching and tragic books I've ever read.
Edward Blishen, Radio 4

ELAND BOOKS
specialise in the literature of travel.
If you wish to receive details of forthcoming publications,
please send your address to
Eland Books, 53 Eland Road, London SW11 5JX

Previously published by

ELAND BOOKS

GOLDEN EARTH

NORMAN LEWIS

Travels in Burma

Mr Lewis can make even a lorry interesting.
Cyril Connolly, Sunday Times

Very funny . . . a really delightful book.
Maurice Collis, Observer

Norman Lewis remains the best travel writer alive.
Auberon Waugh, Business Traveller

The reader may find enormous pleasure here without knowing the country.
Honor Tracy, New Statesman

The brilliance of the Burmese scene is paralleled by the brilliance of the prose.
Guy Ramsey, Daily Telegraph

ELAND BOOKS
specialise in the literature of travel.
If you wish to receive details of forthcoming publications,
please send your address to
Eland Books, 53 Eland Road, London SW11 5JX

NAPLES '44
NORMAN LEWIS

As unique an experience for the reader as it must have been a unique experience for the writer.
Graham Greene

Uncommonly well written, entertaining despite its depressing content, and quite remarkably evocative.
Philip Toynbee, Observer

His ten novels and five non-fiction works place him in the front rank of contemporary English writers ... here is a book of gripping fascination in its flow of bizarre anecdote and character sketch; and it is much more than that.
J. W. Lambert, Sunday Times

A wonderful book.
Richard West, Spectator

Sensitive, ironic and intelligent.
Paul Fussell, The New Republic

One goes on reading page after page as if eating cherries.
Luigi Barzini, New York Review of Books

ELAND BOOKS
specialise in the literature of travel.
If you wish to receive details of forthcoming publications,
please send your address to
Eland Books, 53 Eland Road, London SW11 5JX

Previously published by

ELAND BOOKS

A YEAR IN MARRAKESH

PETER MAYNE

A notable book, for the author is exceptional both in his literary talent and his outlook. His easy economical style seizes, with no sense of effort, the essence of people, situations and places... Mr Mayne is that rare thing, a natural writer ... no less exceptional is his humour.
Few Westerners have written about Islam with so little nonsense and such understanding.
Times Literary Supplement

He has contrived in a deceptively simple prose to disseminate in the air of an English November the spicy odours of North Africa; he has turned, for an hour, smog to shimmering sunlight. He has woven a texture of extraordinary charm.
Daily Telegraph

Mr Mayne's book gives us the 'strange elation' that good writing always creates. It is a good book, an interesting book, and one that I warmly recommend.
Harold Nicolson, Observer

ELAND BOOKS
specialise in the literature of travel.
If you wish to receive details of forthcoming publications,
please send your address to
Eland Books, 53 Eland Road, London SW11 5JX

JOURNEYS OF A
GERMAN IN ENGLAND

CARL PHILIP MORITZ

A walking-tour of England in 1782

With a new preface by Reginald Nettel

The extraordinary thing about the book is that the
writing is so fresh that you are startled when a stage-
coach appears. A young man is addressing himself
to you across two centuries. And there is a lovely
comedy underlying it.
Byron Rogers, Evening Standard

This account of his travels has a clarity and freshness
quite unsurpassed by any contemporary descriptions.
Iain Hamilton, Illustrated London News

A most amusing book...a variety of small scenes
which might come out of Hogarth...Moritz in London,
dodging the rotten oranges flung about the pit of the
Haymarket Theatre, Moritz in the pleasure gardens
of Vauxhall and Ranelagh, Moritz in Parliament or
roving the London streets is an excellent companion.
We note, with sorrow, that nearly two centuries ago,
British coffee was already appalling.
Alan Pryce-Jones, New York Herald Tribune

ELAND BOOKS
specialise in the literature of travel.
If you wish to receive details of forthcoming publications,
please send your address to
Eland Books, 53 Eland Road, London SW11 5JX

Previously published by

ELAND BOOKS

TRAVELS INTO THE INTERIOR OF AFRICA

MUNGO PARK

With a new preface by Jeremy Swift

Famous triumphs of exploration have rarely engendered outstanding books. *Travels into the Interior of
Africa*, which has remained a classic since its first
publication in 1799, is a remarkable exception.

It was a wonder that he survived so long, and a still
greater one that his diaries could have been preserved . . . what amazing reading they make today!
Roy Kerridge, Tatler

The enthusiasm and understanding which informs
Park's writing is irresistible.
Frances Dickenson, Time Out

One of the greatest and most respected explorers the
world has known, a man of infinite courage and lofty
principles, and one who dearly loved the black African.
E. W. Bovill, the Niger Explored

Told with a charm and naivety in themselves sufficient
to captivate the most fastidious reader...modesty
and truthfulness peep from every sentence...for actual
hardships undergone, for dangers faced, and difficulties overcome, together with an exhibition of virtues
which make a man great in the rude battle of life,
Mungo Park stands without a rival.
Joseph Thomson, author of Through Masailand

ELAND BOOKS
specialise in the literature of travel.
If you wish to receive details of forthcoming publications,
please send your address to
Eland Books, 53 Eland Road, London SW11 5JX